The story drips with authentic period details, dancing between whispers in a lavish ballroom, to recording cannon damage in a ship's log once the smoke of battle has settled. Livie is a powerhouse, and I absolutely love her as a character. Well written and with room for more adventures to come, let's hope Murray expands this gem of a story into a series. Recommended.

Jamie Michele for Readers' Favorite

The Pirate's Daughter is not only a wonderful romance with twists, turns, and unexpected bumps in the road to true romance, but it is also a pirate adventure with swashbuckling action and excitement. This is an excellent book for lovers of historical fiction, romance, and exciting pirate adventures. I was completely caught up in the intricacies of this story. I thoroughly enjoyed and highly recommend it.

Grant Leishman for Readers' Favorite

This fast-paced, cleverly plotted story has the tenderness you expect in a well-crafted romance and the action that underpins sea battles. It is an exciting read.

Romuald Dzemo for Readers' Favorite

Other Books by Jodie Leigh Murray:

<u>Romantic Suspense</u>
The Gangster's Daughter
The Gangster's Mistake
The Gangster's Game

<u>Historical Romance</u>
The Duke's Daughter
The Aristocrat's Wife

The Pirate's Daughter

The Pirate's Daughter

Jodie Leigh Murray

Jodie Leigh Murray Books

Book design by Jodie Leigh Murray

Published in the United States by Jodie Leigh Murray Books
Printed in the United States

Paperback ISBN: 978-1-968598-08-2
eBook ISBN: 978-1-968598-09-9

First edition: May 2026

In The Beginning . . .

Livie

January 1695

My gaze drifted up the monstrous mainmast, which towered above me, intimidating my small stature. At only four and a half feet tall, even tall for my age, the mast dwarfed me. I couldn't possibly do this. I was only eight.

"Go on." A rough hand on my shoulder shoved me closer. "Be done with it, lass, or back to your cabin you'll go."

The sunlight was strong, and the winds were gusty as I looked up at the sails lightly billowing. While at port, they weren't fully unfurled, yet they looked so daunting.

I knew my father was trying to teach me the ways of things aboard his ship, but if I'd ever been on his ship before this year, I was too young to remember. I had lived on the beach my entire life, where palm trees swayed instead of masts, and the water gently washed against sandy shores rather than slapping against the hull.

I had been on my father's ship for 103 days since a hurricane had claimed my mother's life. Islanders found me among the wreckage, my arms still wrapped around her as I struggled to free her body from beneath the tree. I often wondered if she would have survived had that tree not fallen directly through our small house near the beach. If she wouldn't have pushed me out of the way, I wouldn't be staring at the task ahead.

My father had arrived shortly after and brought me aboard his massive ship, surrounded by men who stared at me with wide, curious eyes. His crew of more than a hundred men swore an oath to keep my identity a secret. I learned later just how serious that vow was. Any man who didn't swear to it could leave, but only by death. It was a steep price to pay for a mere girl.

"Livie," my father said, his tone sharp with thinly veiled irritation. "Climb up. I want to see that there rope flapping in the wind tied quickly."

The rest of the crew, attempting to look busy with their tasks, were watching. None of them would stand up for me. I knew that now. Elias Blackwood's punishments were something to be feared, which was what made him captain of *The Executioner*. I learned quickly what a loose tongue could get me, what would happen if I looked at him the wrong way, or what would follow if I didn't show him that I could climb this mast with ease. Banishment to my room, sometimes with no supper, would be the consequence.

I took a small step, and another shove sent me flying into the mast, my hands splayed to catch my fall. Squeezing my eyes tight, I grabbed the rope netting and began to climb, quaking at the thought of falling.

"Faster," my father snapped. "We'll do this all night should we need to."

With jerky movements, I climbed faster until I reached the main yard and looked down. Looking down at those staring up at me was such a mistake. If I fell, I was certain no one would catch me, and I would die.

Disappointment in his hard blue eyes stared back at me. I'd inherited those blue eyes from him, and my golden hair was courtesy of my mother, God rest her soul. She had been beautiful, and I knew enough to remember that he loved her. I had seen it, even as young as I was.

Gritting my teeth, I clambered up until I was halfway to the main-topmast, swaying in the wind. Clutching the netting, I waited for the gust to pass, too afraid to climb down and face his wrath, and too afraid to continue.

"Livie!" he yelled, shaking the netting and forcing me to grip tighter. "Move!"

Sticking one foot after the other through the netting, I climbed as if the wind itself propelled me. He would never let me out of this chore. When he said we'd be here all night, he meant it. I didn't want to do this after dark. Finally, I reached the main-topmast and reached out, trying to pull the loose rope back in.

"Almost there," I heard from the crow's nest above me. I whipped my gaze up to see the man posted at the lookout peering down at me. "You can do it, Liv."

I *could* do it. I knew I could. Reaching out and stretching my fingers, I nearly had it. And then I slipped, my foot getting caught in the netting and my surroundings blurred as I screamed. Upside down, I hung there, disoriented from my task and unsure how to get out of this. If my foot came free, I would fall head-first to my death.

"Rand," my father called up, disappointment thick in his voice. "Help her."

"No!" The shout tore from my lips. "I don't need no help!"

I grabbed the netting below me, squeezing as hard as I could while wiggling my foot loose. If this didn't work, I would surely fall. Once my foot came free, my entire body would flip. Losing my grip on the net would ensure that I plunged to my death. I felt my foot slide free, and a scream burst from my throat as my legs went over, my hands holding so tightly to the rough netting that I could feel the burn against my palms.

Tears pricked my eyes as my small body slammed into the netting, and I heard a collective gasp from below. I would need to regain what I'd already climbed to catch that rope.

"Devil take me," I whispered, holding my body close to the netting while my heart raced in fear.

"Liv, look at me." I looked up, Rand's kind brown eyes meeting mine. "Come on now, dove. Make your papa proud."

I climbed, wanting to make him proud. I'd done everything he'd asked since I'd been aboard. It didn't seem like he would ever be pleased with me. I figured it was because I was a girl and had no place on his ship. At least, those were some of the whispers I'd heard from those who didn't think I paid attention.

But I did pay attention. Close attention. When my father made me sit and tie rope after rope until my small fingers ached, I listened to my surroundings. Or when he had me practicing defensive skills with daggers, my eyes and ears were alert. I tried to miss nothing, but I still had a lot to learn.

I climbed up and swung out, grasping the wayward rope and hauling it back to me. Quietly, I could hear Rand chuckling from the crow's nest, even though he'd ducked back in by that time. No use getting punished for a little girl, although some of them would if they could. Some of them had.

With my arm entwined in the netting to keep from falling, I tied the rope into knots with lightning speed, tugging on it to ensure it wouldn't come undone again. None of my knots came undone. Hours of practice had taught me to tie knots better and faster than any man aboard this ship.

A deep, shaky breath escaped my mouth as I began to climb back down. Fear lingered, wondering if my speed had been enough to please my father. When my bare feet finally touched the deck, I slowly turned to face him.

He leaned down, bending over to meet my gaze. "Do it again. And faster this time. Up and down, Livie. You'll do it until you no longer stop in the middle. Up and down." When he straightened, he looked at his quartermaster. "She'll continue to do it until she can do so without stopping. See to it."

"Aye, Cap'n."

The quartermaster, with his grizzled beard and wrinkled face, turned to me. "Go on, git."

I turned with the biggest breath I could muster and climbed.

The sun was setting by the time I was allowed to stop, a blaze of pink awash against the horizon. My stomach ached from hunger, my lips were dry enough to crack from thirst, and my entire body burned from the effort of going up and down so many times. I cursed my father the moment my feet touched the deck and announced that I'd completed my task as demanded. Even Rand had long since come down from his perch, replaced by Jasper.

"Go on to yer cabin now," the quartermaster said, gently pushing my shoulder toward the stairway leading below to the cabins.

Dejected, I walked with as much strength as I could muster until I reached my small cabin and flung myself onto my bed. I no longer cared about eating or my parched lips. I only wanted to lie still and not move.

"You know why I do this?"

Without moving the rest of my body, I turned my head, finding my father standing in my doorway. He was a striking man with brown hair and a full beard. His eyes could hold warmth, but they never did. Only contempt.

"Yes," I murmured, the word muffled against the bed.

He crossed his arms. "Someday you'll thank me, lass. This world isn't for the weak. You'll grow up strong, self-reliant, able to protect yourself when the day comes that I can't."

I wanted to vomit. He'd never protected me.

"Go away," I said, the words still muffled.

His deep laugh trailed behind him as he left, and my heart ached. Ached for my mother, whom I selfishly wanted to stroke my hair and tell me that everything would be fine. It ached for a father who didn't make me climb so far up a swaying mast that I thought my heart would stop from fear.

It ached for normalcy, whatever that was. I didn't know. I would never know.

Chapter One

Livie

March 1706

As the ensemble of musicians played on, women decorated in jewel-toned gowns twirled on the freshly waxed ballroom floor. Men dressed in their finest brocade jackets and satin waistcoats led the cotillion. Typically, I lingered at the edges of the room, listening to the men discuss politics and recent alliances while plotting my next move. No one, not even my uncle, suspected that a seemingly innocent woman floated among them, memorizing every detail. They saw only a gently reared young lady, mysterious in her own way. No one truly knew me.

Known to the high aristocratic society of London as the ward of Marjory Thornton, my father's sister, I was well aware that whispers followed me wherever I went. After all, such things would happen with rumors abound that my father had turned to piracy. It was true. A crown-licensed privateer during the Nine Years' War, Elias Blackwood was a wanted man by the Admiralty, operating in the Caribbean and along the African coast, wielding a letter of marque that was no longer valid.

He was wanted perhaps for questioning rather than the hangman's noose, but wanted all the same. I knew my father would never yield. He coveted riches too thoroughly. He coveted rare gems, just like my mother. The Crown would never find him. His hiding place was a mystery to all but those who sailed under his command. Even I did not know his hiding place.

Born into privilege and a noble house, my father's past respectability allowed me to move in polite circles, while my aunt presented me as a marriageable ward with merchant connections through my deceased mother. While my father sailed as a privateer under the Crown's colors, capturing foreign vessels, my mother and I had lived quietly in the Caribbean until her death when I was seven. Our lives were so quiet that society believed she had passed away recently, explaining my sudden appearance in London three years ago.

Aunt Marjory and her husband Winston knew nothing of my clandestine prowling among the sheep. Uncle Winston was an intelligent man, as most high-society men were, but even he had been deceived into believing I was a truly innocent woman. It was a lonely existence, but I did what I must.

Just days ago, while attending a musicale, I learned from a customs official's wife that her husband had been particularly generous lately, claiming it was due to river gratuities. Little did she know that I'd been eavesdropping, and I knew exactly what that meant. Someone in customs was being bribed, and undeclared cargo was arriving through Wapping, the one place in this city where I spent many evenings in disguise.

Mention was made, not by me, of course, of someone's cousin who was interested in moving West Indian goods discreetly. Her hushed response was to seek out the right merchants in Wapping. Whispers could travel on the right breeze, and I had heard her while discreetly staying close by. But that was not all. Later that evening, she mentioned the King's Arms near Wapping Old Stairs and provided a name. All of this I'd learned in an evening just by staying close enough to hear, but looking innocently as though I were hiding.

Plans were hatched, and I was eager to get to Wapping tonight after this dreadful ball, where I'd not been able to gather any other information to take with me to the docks, but the night was still young.

My eyes swept over the packed room, mindlessly gazing at the beeswax candles flickering in every chandelier and wall sconce, and at the tall windows lining the western side of the immaculate Kingsley home. All the while, I listened to men discussing Queen Anne's successor and the current conflict in the Spanish Netherlands. The increased tariffs and bans had made smugglers a fortune, which could include me if I could gain access to information that might prove of value to my father.

While I dared not risk anyone discovering the truth about me, my father's parting words when he had me sent to Aunt Marjory were to make myself useful while I was here. And I did. I had no choice. Unless I wanted to become cargo for him to offload, I needed to find a way to assist his livelihood and pave a way for my own future. Over the past few years, I had followed leads, connecting with his agents whenever I found valuable information to share, yet my father had not come to retrieve me.

Occasionally, someone would raise a hand to me in greeting, accompanied by sly smiles from the women present and openly desirous stares from the men, not all of whom were eligible bachelors. Even as the daughter of an heiress who had been the victim of a storm in the Caribbean and a former crown-licensed privateer, I learned how to perform the role of a genteel lady quickly. Since my arrival, I had honed my performance skills: a carefully placed curtsy, hollow laughter, and innocent smiles, all meticulously planned, my composure never faltering.

It was difficult when a mere rumor could reduce a genteel woman to something worse than the plague, whispered about in drawing rooms over tea. Even while shopping for the latest fashionable fabrics, women were relentless in their gossip. This was all the more reason to be exceedingly careful when under the cloak of darkness in Wapping.

The shadows of the room, where lesser noble families had gathered, silently beckoned me. My feet glided between dancers and bystanders with enough stealth to avoid slipping on the overly waxed floors.

I didn't always hide in the shadows, but this time I had a good reason. Percival Monteclaire, the Baron of Vensworth, was present. He was a polite enough gentleman haunting London, but he did not make my list of eligible suitors for whom I would consider promising the rest of my life. The last week had proven difficult, with him continuously sending me notes and cornering me at social gatherings in a weak attempt at chasing my affections. It hadn't taken me more than a few days to sense what Percival was really after: my undeclared inheritance.

My uncle was well acquainted with him, and both men attended many of the same social gatherings during our visits to London, especially in the warmer months, as both were members of Parliament. Uncle Winston was considered a high-ranking member of society, well-respected and wealthy. Percival was not quite as high-ranking with his title, but it was clear that he aimed for more. While Parliament was in session, it opened the marriage mart for overly enthusiastic mothers, serving as a means of networking and socializing for men in pursuit of political gain.

None of that was the issue at hand.

The real issue, as I settled into a shadowy corner to watch the endless blur of dancers, was that while Percival had not announced his intentions, it was blatantly clear to me that he was pursuing my hand in marriage. He had yet to ask Uncle Winston for permission, as the head of the family, but I knew it was only a matter of time. However, I had a bargaining chip: Uncle Winston would not be able to finalize negotiations without knowing my true worth, and since my mother's family was not returning his messages, my value as a potential bride remained a mystery.

Never mind that I had no intention of marrying anyone, least of all someone from this crowd. Percival was nearly the same age as my father, and he was mistaken if he thought I would be easy to pressure. Most men frequenting these circles knew me to be difficult and steered clear of courting me.

As I drifted through the mass of people, I smiled at the trio near the edge of the dance floor, sharing the shadows with me. Although I recognized many of them, I believed the older woman to be a viscountess, accompanied by her daughter, who tittered behind their fans and white-gloved hands. I mostly kept to myself, speaking only when necessary and melting into the shadows like a ghost.

When I arrived in London three years ago, at sixteen and seething with raw emotion, summer was at its peak. I remembered trembling with rage as I was dropped off at my aunt's doorstep with clear instructions from my father. I was to be made a lady, the epitome of society, just as I had been told my mother once was. My instructions differed from my aunt's. I was ordered to adapt to society and become a lady while keeping an ear to the ground for opportunities. Taxes were at their highest, and shipments overflowed with opportunities to make money, so long as a person was careful. Elias Blackwood amassed a fortune on land and sea, with a daughter doing his work dockside. And what better way to prove to him that I was worth more than being married off to gentry.

So be it, I thought. I swept into society, intent on embodying every aspect of a lady, but I drew the line at accepting a marriage proposal, especially since I had to sneak out many nights. Marriage would end my illegal activities at once.

With a gasp, I hurried toward the nearest wall and pressed myself against it as I spotted the tall figure with short, dark hair, flecked with grey at the temples, approaching. If Percival caught up with me, he would ask me to dance, and I would have no choice but to comply. A woman could only go so far, and a genteel lady could not refuse without a valid excuse. I would be hard-pressed to find any excuse at all.

The Kingsleys were known for their lavish balls, and the large ballroom, with its mythological painted ceilings and tall wall mirrors, was breathtaking. Countless flickering candles against the backdrop of those ceilings gave the impression of being watched over by the eyes of the gods.

It took considerable effort, but I managed to shimmy along the wall into the adjoining room, aided by the contemptible people I had reluctantly connected with despite my misgivings about this entire societal display. I had to have tea with the ladies, squeeze myself into a contraption that pushed my breasts nearly to my chin and restricted every breath, and worst of all, I had to keep secrets I had never wanted to keep. My entire existence felt like a farce. If anyone discovered that Uncle Winston and Aunt Marjory were harboring the daughter of a pirate, not only would every door be closed to me, but my father's sister and her family would ultimately pay the price. For now, the rumor about my father was a rumor, and nothing more. Yet.

Such was the punishment I faced for being caught in a compromising position aboard *The Executioner*. It had been my fault entirely, succumbing to the romantic notion that a man aboard my father's ship could actually love me.

The moment my feet touched the dock in the harbor, I vowed that I would someday return to the sea. Thanks to him, I had lived most of my life in his shadow. And when it mattered most, he had cast me onto land to continue my miserable, secretive existence for his sake. As far as anyone knew, Livie Blackwood had perished along with her mother in a hurricane.

I spotted my cousin threading his way through the swarm of elegantly dressed aristocrats, his eyes alight with mischief. As much as William abhorred the thought of settling down with one woman, he understood that mingling with these crowds could yield valuable insight. He was drawn to the forbidden, including me.

"Who is the gentleman wearing the eyepatch? He looks positively dastardly." William slid into line beside me, a sparkling flute of champagne in hand and the brightest twinkle in his eyes.

"I thought only pirates wore those? My, he looks dashing and mysterious with it, does he not?"

I eyed William warily, not interested in being pulled into a conversation regarding my future. "Pirates do not wear eyepatches any more or less than anyone else," I retorted.

"How would you know anyway?" he asked, a teasing smile on his lips as he angled his torso toward me as if whispering secrets.

William resembled a much younger version of my uncle, with sandy brown hair and soft brown eyes. Four years older than I and at least two feet taller, he had softened to my arrival instantly and had been badgering me ever since. While neither of us was particularly interested in marrying, he was the oldest and only son, and he had no choice but to find a suitable match.

Sliding his arm into mine, he drew me away from the shadows, and we navigated past the low murmurs of gossip behind raised fans on our way to the entrance hall. William couldn't know how many pirates I'd known, although he was aware of the possible circumstances surrounding my father's status abroad.

"Tell me, dear cousin, do you know who he might be?"

"Who?" I asked, preoccupied with keeping a steady eye on the perimeter of the room beyond the blur of dancers.

If it took me all night, I would stick to the shadows to avoid Percival. While I needed to listen to the conversations along the sidelines, I couldn't do so if he was wasting flattery on me.

"The man with the eyepatch, Livie! Are you even listening to me?" He took a sip from his glass, scanning the room from his height.

Trying not to be obvious about it, I stretched my neck to scan the ballroom. There was no sign of Percival, but I did notice the man with the eyepatch that William mentioned. On his arm was an exquisite woman with raven-black hair, laughing almost shamefully at something someone next to her must have said.

Nadine Whitley, the widow of a marquess, made her appearance at every high-society gathering she could attend. Her beauty was exceptional, and she had been quite young when her husband met with a hunting accident. Only a handful of years older than me, Nadine had her sights set on another marriage, advantageous or not.

Devil take me, the man on her arm had the aristocratic looks to fit in and was handsome, too. Although I could only see his dark hair and eyepatch from this distance, I imagined his eyes were as dark as his hair until one ominous eye turned and locked onto mine. A jolt coursed through me.

Abruptly, I stepped back and looked away. Whatever that gaze had sparked inside me made me feel vulnerable. Having never seen the man before, he had to be an acquaintance of Nadine or the Kingsleys. The sensation that swept through me was enough of a warning to keep my distance.

"Well?"

Laughter hummed in my throat. "You would know better than I, William. Have you seen him before?"

"I have."

I squeezed his arm, pulling him toward me. "And?"

"It's been several years, but I believe he's a family friend of Ms. Whitley. You would do well to introduce yourself, cousin. If anything, it may give Percival Monteclaire a well-deserved push."

"Not a push toward me."

William knew me well enough by now to notice how carefully I hid my emotions. We were both similar in that way, maintaining our composure. Always. William had inherited this trait from Aunt Marjory, and I strove to use her as a role model myself.

"No, I would never push Percival toward you, cousin. But I fear jealousy may overrule and the opposite occur." I stiffened. "Not that I would want that for you. You are hiding from him tonight, are you not?"

I snorted. Rather unladylike of me, but I didn't care.

"Always," I murmured.

William and his younger sister, Imogen, only knew what

everyone else had been told: that I was their cousin come to live with them after the untimely death of my mother. My mother had died from poor health, or so they believed.

No one suspected these were lies. True, my mother had died, but in a hurricane rather than from poor health. My father was presumed to be still alive, but an outlaw if the rumors proved true. My past, rather intriguing to understand, remained a secret.

William and I got along well. It was Imogen, two years younger than me, who, while we tolerated each other, disliked me rather vocally. I did not share the same closeness with her as I did with William, so I steered clear of her as much as possible, a near impossibility when residing in the same house and attending the same dreadful functions.

"If Percival asks you to marry him, will you accept?" William asked, his voice soft.

There was no need to ask such a ridiculous question. He already knew the answer. I sometimes thought he asked it just to ensure I hadn't changed my mind. I had always been open with William about my feelings toward the baron, as well as anyone else who came sniffing around.

"Not in this lifetime."

Even as I said it, I wondered if the baron would ever give up his pursuit of me and settle for another. He had wasted precious time trying to woo me, and it seemed suspicious why he was so eager to have my hand and no one else's. Regardless of my situation, I would always be suspicious of people. I needed to be.

"I know your mother would much rather the baron ask for Imogen's hand than mine, but in all honesty, he's too old for either of us," I said, smoothly redirecting the conversation away from myself.

I risked a glance back, seeing nothing but a swarm of rustling silk and the occasional flash of petticoats. Not wanting to take chances, I decided to move to another room, where I could at least find some peace away from the lively music, the hum of conversation, and the snapping of fans.

"Miss Thornton!" Percival called out behind us.

William chuckled, and I felt the urge to swat at him, the devil. I couldn't help but wonder if he'd drawn me out of the shadows for this very purpose. Knowing my aversion to courting, William liked to meddle where he shouldn't. He liked to be entertained, and my discomfort would be entertaining indeed.

Tall and elegantly masculine, with neatly trimmed hair just beginning to grey at his temples, the baron was a handsome man for his age. I could at least admit that. If I were forced to marry someone, I could do much worse than the baron. It was his pushiness I abhorred, along with the underlying threat that he might be using courtship to control my inheritance, even if only assumed at the moment.

"Good evening, William," Percival said, giving a brief bow to him before turning to me. "You have proven quite difficult to find this entire evening, my dear."

He reached for my hand, his long fingers and perfectly manicured nails beckoning me to give him my gloved hand. Inwardly sighing, I allowed him to take it and press his lips to my knuckles. When he straightened, keeping my hand captive, excitement danced in his eyes, sending an apprehensive chill down my back.

I resisted the urge to yank away. If we'd been aboard a ship, I would have done more than withdraw from his touch. Instead, a smile curved my lips, intentionally innocent, with a hint of flirtation. As cunning as I was, it never hurt to play the part.

"I'm as easily found as the next girl."

His fingers tightened around mine. "I daresay, the exquisite being before me is no longer just a girl," he murmured.

I gasped, outraged that he would say such an improper thing.

William stiffened beside me. "Quite bold of you to speak that aloud, Baron."

"My sincere apologies. I only meant to state the obvious. If you don't accept a marriage proposal soon, you'll be considered past a suitable age. It would break Winston's heart to have you remain in his household forever, wouldn't you think?"

I had considered that, but I would never share it with anyone, least of all with Percival. He did not need to know that I often contemplated my situation. Eventually, I would need to leave the Thornton house, and I intended to. I just wouldn't do so as a married woman.

"Is there a reason you've been trying to find me this evening, Mr. Monteclaire?"

He slowly released my hand. "Come now, Olivia. We know each other well enough. I thought we'd agreed to use our given names."

You agreed. I scowled internally without voicing it aloud. I would be in trouble if anyone heard the thoughts that sometimes ran through my mind. I abhorred the name Olivia. My name was Livie. My aunt referred to me as Olivia, and everyone had gone along with it ever since.

"It remains my fervent hope that you will come to your senses soon and accept me as a candidate for your husband." His eyebrows arched. "It would be in your best interest, after all."

A wicked retort burned on my tongue, but I swallowed the words and the lump in my throat, presenting him with another beguiling smile. Ever the dutiful lady attending these dreadful events, I inclined my head.

He wasn't terrible to be around when he refrained from making sidelined observations. I knew that if I stayed in London much longer, I would be in danger of being rumored a spinster. Something would have to give eventually, but I had good reason to believe it was only a matter of time before my father came to his senses and realized how much he would benefit from having me at his side rather than here among vipers.

A man of Percival's intelligence could actually provide me with the opportunity for delightful conversation. However, men like him would never engage in discussions about wars, politics, or the future state of our economy with me. No, he preferred to lower himself to talk about the latest fashions, idle gossip, and, even more dreadfully, me. I avoided discussing myself at all costs.

"Would you do me the honor of joining me for a dance?" he asked, offering me the crook of his arm.

"She was just saying how delightful it would be to dance," William said, a smile curving his lips as I shot him a glare.

Inclining my head in response, I slipped my arm away from William and allowed Percival to guide me through the throng of people. There were other reasons I had for not wanting to dance with Percival at balls or spend too much time in his company. If people saw us together too often, gossip would begin to circulate. Gossip traveled faster in this town than a pickpocket who had just been caught.

Chapter Two

Grayson

When I stepped into the lively ballroom, my gaze swept from one end to the other, searching for the woman whose name would be my salvation. Her name would signify the beginning of my release from the bonds of grief, and I was determined to get that release at whatever cost. She would lead me directly to the proof that I needed to redeem myself, avenge my brother, and move forward with my life. However, I was unprepared for the open stares directed at me, even with Nadine on my arm. I felt as elusive as the pirate Elias Blackwood. And a pirate he was, though no one in this crowd would openly voice what I already knew.

Before my arrival, I ensured that invitations to all high-society balls, luncheons, and gatherings would be handed to me without issue. Thanks to friends in high society, my family's reputation guaranteed that all doors were opened to me, including those I wished would remain closed.

Rumors about me, bolstered by connections in this elite society, would not shield me from the marriage-minded mothers eager to secure the highest title for their innocent young daughters. As Jeremiah Valle's eldest son, I would inherit his title upon his death, along with the family fortune, which had diminished considerably since the tragic loss of my older brother, Adam, when our ship was overtaken off the coast of Africa.

Society knew me as the surviving son of a wealthy merchant

family from the south of France, mysterious and from a nation with which England was not currently at war. My family's frequent travels to England added to our prestige. The wealth was an advantage, provided they could overlook my dastardly eyepatch and dark looks. I was well aware that the eyepatch drew stares, mostly out of curiosity, while my uncovered eye scanned the room with scrutiny, causing some to look away the moment our gazes met.

As soon as I stepped into the Kingsley home, the whispers grew lively. This rigid society, the same one in which the woman I sought concealed herself, couldn't be more predictable. I had heard a hopeful rumor during my travels that while Elias Blackwood's wife had perished in a hurricane, his daughter had survived, cloaked in secrecy ever since.

No one dared to openly speak of her circumstances, fearing the wrath of her father and knowing the genteel woman her mother was, albeit a foreigner such as myself. It had taken a considerable sum of money to get the information I had. Livie Blackwood was living in London as the ward of her aunt, Elias Blackwood's sister. I hoped to recognize her the instant I saw her. After all, the daughter of a pirate had to be unrefined, impossibly daring, and pointedly rude.

Nadine leaned closer to me, indecently so. "Would you care to ask me to dance, Grayson?"

Truth be told, I would rather not dance with the seductive widow beside me, even though we were both unattached at the moment. Her status as a widow seemed to heighten her quest for another suitable match, but her boldness often sent most young men at these functions running away rather than approaching her.

Connor, standing on the other side of me, raised an eyebrow, daring me silently to dance with her. My second cousin on my mother's side, who served as the quartermaster aboard my ship, was well aware of Nadine and her reputation, and generally kept his distance from her.

"I'd rather not," I replied.

Her lips puckered into a pout.

Nadine knew my sole purpose for being here this evening. In fact, she had been the one to inform me that the Thorntons, including Livie Blackwood, would be in attendance tonight. It was the perfect opportunity to insert myself into the path of the woman who hadn't been seen or heard from until a few years ago. No one knew where Elias Blackwood had kept his wife and daughter until whispers of her arrival told the story of her mother's passing.

Still reeling from my brother's death, I realized that getting close to his daughter was the perfect way to draw the man out and avenge Adam. I would avenge him, no matter who stood in my way.

"Have you seen Livie Blackwood this evening yet?" I asked.

She shrugged nonchalantly, as if bored with this party. "I have not, Grayson. It would be in your best interest to leave the little darling alone. Rumor has it Percival Monteclaire has been sniffing around her."

I gazed down at Nadine, her raven-black hair styled in soft curls that framed her face, topped with a wide fontange. Looking around the room, I noticed that almost every woman had one on, as was fashionable.

"Is that so?" I kept my tone low on purpose. "We'll have to see about that, shall we?"

Connor chuckled, but otherwise remained silent.

"She hasn't given her consent to anyone," Nadine continued. "As if she's better than the rest of us, while half of society sniffs after her like some forbidden delicacy."

My eyebrow arched. "Jealous, Nadine?"

The jealousy in her voice was unmistakable. I couldn't understand how she could be jealous of a woman who likely resembled her in boldness. Only the daughter of a pirate would leave a trail of eager gentlemen in her wake, and I imagined her taking insurmountable risks no matter whose roof she resided under.

"I am not jealous of some little nobody who waltzed in and stole all the attention from me," she huffed, snapping her fan open to wave at her flushed face. "As it is, rumors say her inheritance has still not been verified."

Connor stifled a chuckle.

"I did not bring you here to give me a hard time."

"If my memory serves me, I brought you, my dearest." She patted my forearm.

"This is a mistake." Connor scanned the room, his discomfort evident only to me and Nadine. "We won't find her here. Perhaps a message to her uncle requesting a meeting would be a better use of your time."

"Keep your tongue behind your teeth, Connor," I replied, my tone soft yet commanding. "I will find her tonight."

I knew Connor better than anyone else. He'd grown up alongside Adam and me, almost like a third brother, which is why I expected him to join us for the evening. His grumbles didn't surprise me, but the flowing spirits had loosened him up, as I knew they would. Despite his doubts, he believed the tales of Elias Blackwood were largely false, as were the rumors about the pirate's daughter blending into London's high society.

Connor swore that when I paid good money to a dockside worker, the man had given me false information and taken my money. While a considerable amount had been lost when Elias Blackwood ransacked our merchant ship, stealing loads of precious silk from France, I didn't care about money. Though I couldn't prove that it was Elias who had overtaken our vessel, I knew it was him. I cared about avenging Adam, and my father had given me orders to find the man responsible for murdering his one good son at any cost. Never mind that I was next in line to inherit, but I'd always been second best to Adam. If I accomplished this, my father might finally approve of me.

Being in London for the last several days had gotten me nowhere. But if Blackwood's daughter were here, she would likely lead me right to her father, who hasn't been seen in years. The period between her mother's death and the time she was brought to London left much to the imagination. Where the girl had been all this time plagued my thoughts.

I sniffed haughtily while tugging at the cuffs of my jacket, first one, then the other. The last thing I wanted was simpering young maids begging for attention, which is why I had brought Nadine with me. With her looks and clear desire for attention, I knew few would approach us.

I would manage any desperate woman seeking to bind me in the chains of matrimony. That wasn't my mission at all. My eyes locked with a woman making her way through the crowd with Percival Monteclaire, who was leading her toward the dance floor. Her cool blue gaze clashed with mine. While her light hair was fashionably styled in soft curls, she wore no fontange, a clear statement against society's standards. Momentarily stunned by her exquisite beauty from where I stood nearby, I noticed the instant she averted her eyes.

I watched her for several moments, oblivious to whatever Nadine and Connor were saying. The surrounding conversation faded as if someone had plugged my ears as my focus honed in on the woman. Moving toward the dance floor, I saw her scan the room, noting that she had marked the exits, her gaze sweeping carefully to assess her surroundings. A small handbag dangled from her petite wrist, her fingers curling ever so slightly amid her skirt. She showed no emotion on her face or in her eyes.

Though she moved with the grace of a mountain lion, the woman quietly began the next dance with her partner. The way Percival looked at her, devoured her, brought a growl to my throat. Predatory, calculating. She couldn't know that I was watching her from a distance while they danced.

Watching her, poised and purposeful in every step, nearly rooted me in place near the edge of the dance floor. There was a distinct way she drew attention, but appeared as though wishing to remain out of it. I occasionally caught a glimpse of her lips moving when Percival wasn't twirling her around or when partners hadn't shifted. Her eyes appeared detached, yet alert.

"This is the farthest thing from a mistake," I finally replied to Connor, my tone clipped.

"Is that her?" he asked, his voice low.

Nadine was bored, as I could tell from her silence. Dutifully, she hung on my arm while we stood near the dance floor, speaking with no one else besides Connor as my eyes tracked the woman in the pale blue dress.

"Doesn't look like the daughter of a pi—"

My gaze snapped to Connor, who immediately caught the warning glint in my eye. I had intentionally worn my eyepatch to fuel the rumors about me, uncomfortable as it was. True, my family was well known here, but I was also known as a man who rarely spoke unless necessary, and there was an air of mystery about me. During my visits to London, I typically concluded my business quickly, but many were aware of my illicit affairs with women. Most people assumed I was having an affair with Nadine, but that couldn't be more false.

The scar running over my left eye, courtesy of a well-aimed sword when I was only twenty and inexperienced, might frighten some. In truth, the scar wasn't out of the ordinary. I wore the patch to keep the surrounding party patrons guessing about who Captain Grayson Valle really was.

Whispers flitted around us in the ballroom, the music and laughter a welcome distraction while I studied the woman as closely as I could. Light on her feet, knew the steps of the dance quite well.

"Livie Blackwood. How do you propose to speak with her?" Nadine asked, leaning into me to keep our conversation private from intrusive ears.

"This is not the first time I have pursued a woman, and it very likely won't be the last," I replied, my tone rough.

Connor laughed, low and dangerous. Nadine, however, appeared unsettled by my response. To my knowledge, she had no romantic interest in me, nor should she. While we might have had an affair some years ago and I knew her to be a delightful distraction, I had other motives for being in this city. Despite how achingly long it had been since I'd been with a woman, I had no interest in her.

"And you are certain she's the key?" Connor snagged a fluted glass of sparkling champagne from a passing servant.

I shot Connor another warning glare, urging him to lower his tone. We had a reason to be here, but that didn't mean gossip wouldn't toss us out on our ears.

My jaw tensed. "I will not know until I speak with the lady. If she still has ties with him, it will lead us right to him. If not," I shrugged, "I'll find another way."

Tipping back his glass, Connor downed the honey-colored liquid while my gaze remained fixed on the woman.

My instincts told me she didn't particularly like this gentleman, though her mask of composure remained steadfast and controlled. If this woman wasn't a pirate's daughter, as I suspected, I wondered if she had any qualms about taking a lover. Her beauty complemented her cool elegance, stirring feelings I had lately ignored.

Exquisite in her pale blue gown with darker swirls in the fabric and a dark blue stomacher, the color only highlighted her fair skin. She carried herself with grace, a grace that could only be cultivated within the confines of this society. Ordinary yet extraordinary.

"That's her?" Connor's urgent whisper broke my focus.

"That's her," I replied, not taking my eyes off the couple.

The innocent smile on her full lips, briefly reflected in her vivid eyes, suggested someone who genuinely did not appreciate her companion's presence. She was astounding. If Miss Blackwood indeed still had ties with her father, she had single-handedly fooled everyone around her. I could only applaud her for it, even as my blood pumped with eagerness to speak with and question her.

As soon as the couple ended their lively dance, another began.

I calculated the steps in my mind and watched like a man sitting in a crow's nest aboard a ship. Everything about this woman screamed that I had made a grave mistake regarding her. What I knew and what I assumed could lead me to see her as a seemingly innocent young woman trying to thrive in society and find a suitable match. If that were the case, this man could easily be her father, given his advanced age, and what a true waste that would be. I was about to lean in to say something to Connor when a spark flared to life in her eyes. Anyone else would have missed it. Not me.

Still, I couldn't take my eyes off her. Given the chance, I would take this woman to my bed. The fire she tried to hide in her gaze sparked something deep within me, if she would only allow it. Even if she was that bastard Elias Blackwood's daughter.

Chapter Three

Livie

Each time Percival's hand rested on my waist, I resisted the urge to scowl. I never would, knowing how to play my part and Aunt Marjory was always watching. And watch me she did, her dark hair coiled atop her head, standing rigidly straight as she scrutinized my every movement. My aunt liked to ensure I stayed in line, and it was worse for me than for her daughter, though I had given her few reasons to lecture me on the behaviors expected of a lady.

As we danced, I tried to think of anything but being with Percival. I knew it could be worse. Many men had scrutinized me closely over the past few years, once Aunt Marjory was certain I'd been forged into the ideal lady, even with a questionable inheritance. If word came that I would not inherit, Uncle Winston would provide my dowry, thereby snatching away any say I would have in the matter.

Any other unmarried woman here likely had the opposite thoughts. Imogen, for instance, couldn't wait to be swept up by some eligible gentleman. Percival, recently widowed and titled, albeit not of immense wealth, had caught the attention of many ladies, both unmarried and widowed. But he did not give Imogen a second glance.

"We will be wed, Olivia," Percival began, sighing as though reluctant to have this conversation. "There is no denying how we can benefit each other. I think it is time you accept my proposal."

Blasted man, I thought. He hadn't even asked me, assuming I would accept. I never would. He would need Uncle Winston's permission if he had any chance of taking me as a wife, and he would need mine before that.

"And I have told you once before, my affairs remain unsettled. It wouldn't be prudent to promise what is not yet mine."

A knowing smile curved his lips. "Either way, I expect to announce our engagement soon. Make no mistake, Olivia, you could never bring uncertainty to my household."

He said it with such inevitability that a sinking feeling settled in my stomach. Had he spoken with Uncle Winston without my knowledge? Surely, my uncle would have pulled me aside to notify me immediately about such a possibility.

The very thought of marrying him filled me with horror, as did the thought of marrying any gentleman of this society. None of them would be of my choosing. Ever. This was not the life I wanted. Tea times, walks in the park, carriage rides, and attending parties and balls while in London, all with a deceitful smile, bored me to tears just to think about it.

My thoughts turned to the tall gentleman wearing an eyepatch. William may have seemed to remember seeing him before, but I had yet to discover exactly who he was. He stared at me from the sidelines. I could feel it even as I danced with Percival. Each time I looked, he was watching me.

I knew nothing about him. I had never seen him before, yet he was undeniably mysterious. I snapped out of my thoughts, mentally shaking myself. Marriage was not a future I envisioned, no matter who might be on the receiving end.

"You will want for nothing, my dear."

The grin that crept onto his lips, accompanied by fine wrinkles at the corners of his eyes, made my stomach drop. The thought of being tied to this man for life dampened my mood considerably. I would be stuck in this way of life, with no hope of returning to the sea. Not that there had been much hope to begin with, not since being left here.

"I promise, being married to me will have its benefits."

I scoffed.

The tempo increased, snapping me out of my stupor as we twirled and switched partners. Dancing had not been part of my repertoire growing up, and unaccustomed to this style, I swung right into the arms of another man.

I gasped.

One eye was covered by a black eyepatch, while the other was a mixture of brown tinged with green. The color of his uncovered eye was one of the most curious shades I'd ever seen, with sinister swirls that made me feel as if he could reach right into my lies and pluck out my secrets, one by one. I needed to be wary of this man.

I'd never seen a man wearing an eyepatch, and I inwardly laughed at such absurdity. Society gossip painted vivid pictures of the men who prowled the sea: eyepatches, peg legs, earrings, and tattoos. Yet, I had never encountered such a pirate during my years with my father. Most men thriving on ships and in seaports sported tattoos, but eyepatches? It was laughable.

With the deepness of his eyes, dark hair, and olive-toned skin as if he'd spent hours in the sun, I studied the man intently. Full lips framed by a light covering of the same dark hair traced the strong line of his jaw. I noticed a tiny indentation caressed the center of his chin, like a misplaced dimple. But his gaze, his attention, shook me. He seemed to see things. Things I would never reveal.

I looked back up, and his gaze danced with amusement, as though he'd caught me at something. If I'd ever seen this man before, I would have remembered.

He wore a fine brocade coat over a sapphire blue waistcoat, and his hair was fashionably long, not even tied back decently like that of any gentleman who didn't wear a powdered wig. Warmth flared to life in my cheeks as he looked down at me, as if he would devour me given the slightest chance.

Distantly, the hum of violins, flutes, and harpsichords faded away, dissolving into the air. If anyone else occupied the room, I couldn't tell. He mesmerized me. He unnerved me. If he had slid his long fingers into my hair and brought his lips to mine, I would have allowed it without protest. I mentally shook myself. This type of behavior is what got me ousted from my father's ship in the first place.

The man took a step away from me, pulling me to the side of the dance floor, his hand still resting on my arm. I glanced down at my gloved hand clutching his muscular forearm. Yanking it away as if burned, I snapped my gaze back to him just in time to catch the knowing smile curving his mouth. Regaining my composure, I straightened.

He took a slight bow.

"Grayson Valle," he murmured, snatching my hand and pressing a kiss to my knuckles, which I fervently wished were bare so I could feel his mouth on my skin.

Valle? Grayson Valle attending a ball? Another beguiling smile curved my lips. I shouldn't poke fun at such a handsome man. And devil take me, he was exceedingly handsome, even more so this close.

"Might I have the pleasure of your name?" he urged, his eyes locked with mine.

The way he said it, with his gaze probing, made it feel as though he wanted a confession. I could be laid bare before him, yet I'd never admit anything, which made me wonder who Grayson Valle really was. Like me, he was hiding something. I was sure of it.

"My dear." Percival pushed his way back to me, snatching my hand out of Grayson's grasp with a murderous look.

My chin tilted up, just a fraction, but I kept my wicked tongue to myself. Whatever it was about this man, my composure faltered. I fervently hoped no one noticed, for his eyes saw too closely. Grayson Valle saw entirely too much.

Ignoring Percival, I looked directly at Grayson and said, "Livie Blackwood."

"May I call on you tomorrow, Miss Blackwood?"

With Percival's hand on mine, I felt him tense. "That won't be necessary," he snapped.

Grayson eyed him. "I suppose I *should* ask permission from her father. May I call on your daughter tomorrow?"

Percival sputtered.

I hid my grin by looking away, but I knew Grayson had seen it. How impudent of him to say such a thing, and how positively humorous that he said it aloud. I nearly laughed, managing to smother my smile by avoiding Percival's gaze. If there had been any doubt in my mind that this man thought Percival had fathered me, it quickly vanished when I looked back into his eyes.

"How bold of you to say such a thing. I should call you out for such a slight," Percival snapped.

Grayson merely raised the eyebrow above his eyepatch.

How refreshing he is compared to the stiff men of society, I thought.

"My apologies. It appears you are old enough, wouldn't you agree?"

"I am *not* Miss Blackwood's father," Percival ground out. "I expect her to be my wife very soon."

I gasped, my gaze piercing Percival. There was no hint of humor on his face. He was entirely serious. Grayson narrowed one eye.

"Is that so?"

"I expect she will be making a decision in the very near future, in fact."

A cold wave washed over me despite the warmth in the room. The seriousness of his words filled me with an overwhelming sense of terror. His confidence in making such a bold assumption sickened me.

"Ah, there you are, Monteclaire!" I heard Uncle Winston call out.

Like magic, Percival's hand slipped away from me as quickly as it had appeared, and he stepped back with a tight smile as my uncle joined us. It felt as though a burst of fresh air had entered the room, and I could suddenly breathe again.

I might have been saved this time, but I knew without a doubt that it would be short-lived. Percival Monteclaire always got his way. In fact, I was surprised he hadn't yet succeeded in getting me to agree. Uncle Winston had to know his intent if Aunt Marjory did. With Percival's smooth praise of her over tea a few days ago, I was certain my uncle knew. Surely, my aunt and uncle shared these exciting possibilities with one another.

I desperately needed to get away from Percival, glancing around to see if I could spot William in the crowd. Surely, he would rescue me from this stress. If I mentioned that I needed air, Percival would only swoop in and occupy more of my time.

"Olivia," Uncle Winston said, inclining his head and subtly touching my elbow where the sleeve of my gown fell short of my glove. "I believe William is looking for you."

I smiled demurely, suppressing a full grin. Leave it to Uncle Winston to recognize when I needed to escape a situation. His eyes gleamed with mischief, a spark I'd never seen in Aunt Marjory's eyes. Opposites must have attracted in their case.

As soon as I turned, Uncle Winston engaged Percival in a conversation about the queen and her most loyal subjects. I felt the rumble of Grayson's deep voice resonate through me before he turned ever so slightly in my direction.

"If you don't mind, Miss Blackwood, would you be so kind as to dance with me?"

I blinked. The next dance was just beginning.

"I saw you earlier this evening with a young man. Once the dance is over, I will accompany you to your . . . ?"

Stiffening, I curled my lips at his open-ended question, which hinted at his curiosity about my relationship with William. I wouldn't be caught so easily. He offered his bent arm to me.

"I could say the same to you," I replied demurely. "You were with a woman as well. It's a very broad question to ask about one's companion. Is she your wife? No, that can't be. Otherwise, it would be considered rude to dance with me. Could she be your lover?"

I surprised myself by speaking so boldly to a complete stranger, managing to maintain my composure. His face showed no sign of shock, but his words suggested otherwise.

"My, you are quite a brazen young woman. Surely London society is not immune to such behavior."

My eyes narrowed. He would not catch me so easily, whoever he was.

Around him, I needed to be extra cautious. Something about him, beyond his probing questions. The way he looked at me as if he saw more than I let on, kept my hackles raised. I entwined my arm with his and allowed him to lead me into the throng of dancers.

The way his large hand curled around my waist nearly undid me right there. His other hand locked with mine, and he moved so swiftly that I nearly stumbled as we joined the other dancers. My waist burned where he touched me, heated even with several layers of clothing between us.

"You didn't answer my question."

"William is my cousin," I replied.

While we danced, I could feel his eyes on me. But I couldn't let it go. His questions were oddly amusing. Everyone knew who my parents were, yet none had felt the need to draw the words out of me.

"And you? With a beautiful woman on your arm, you must have plans for your future. Are you courting her?"

"No."

I cursed my slip. I should have asked it differently, leaving it open with another inviting question.

"Who was the man who rescued you from a third dance?"

"My uncle Winston," I replied cautiously.

The smoothness of his voice might have been endearing if I hadn't already sensed his interrogating questions. This man knew something about me. He had to have an agenda, or I wouldn't be facing such intimate inquiries.

"Unfortunately, my mother passed away, and Aunt Marjory thought it the perfect time to introduce me to London. William and I get along very well, but my cousin Imogen would rather I not live and breathe, at least not in her presence. And the woman you were with? You haven't explained."

"Nadine is a friend of my family. You seem well-versed in the rules of society for not having been raised here."

We moved together, but our eyes locked despite his efforts to slip beneath my façade while I thwarted him. I would not be exposed.

I sighed. "My mother's health made travel unavoidable, so I was educated privately."

"And your father?"

"My father is a privateer, although no one has heard from him in quite some time."

Lies, lies, lies, I inwardly groaned, having lost my composure in his presence. I would never admit that my mother had passed away more than ten years ago. That would have prompted more questions I didn't want to answer. I had already said quite enough.

"My sympathies about your mother. Recently?" he hedged.

"Recent enough," I replied tightly.

"No siblings to speak of?"

"None."

"Well then, it must be nice to have your cousins. How did you come to lose your mother?"

If someone wanted to discuss the latest fabric styles, recent engagement gossip, or who was hosting the next ball or dinner party, Imogen would be delighted to chat about those topics, not me. I cared little for trivial conversations, engaging only when absolutely necessary.

"I'd rather not speak of my family," I replied.

"I couldn't help but notice that you didn't look well while dancing with the Baron of Vensworth. Has something upset you? Perhaps the baron?"

Oh, if he only knew the root of my issues.

Instead, I smiled. "I can handle the Baron of Vensworth, never fear."

I didn't want to continue discussing it. My mood, which should have been exceptional, was only worsening by the moment.

"I haven't seen you before," I said innocently, attempting to change the subject.

He spun me around, his other hand sliding back to my waist. His dark eye bore into me intently as he moved closer. "I only arrived recently. London is my least favorite place. The sooner my business here concludes, the better."

"And where are you from? I haven't heard the surname Valle before."

"I hail from many places, but my family calls southern France home."

I tilted my head. "You hide your accent well."

"As I said, I come from many places. I've traveled for the last several years and picked up different languages along the way."

Impressive. The man became more interesting by the minute, but I held my tongue, keeping my own travels hidden. To him, I could be nothing more than a young woman in London during Parliament sessions before heading off with her family to their country estate. Off-limits to him.

Boring, incredibly boring.

"What are you thinking about? You seem upset about something," he whispered. "Is something, or someone, troubling you?"

I sighed. "As much as I was looking forward to a brawl in my honor, I must decline your previous invitation to call on me tomorrow."

Shocked at myself for openly admitting anything to him, I clamped my lips shut.

"Is that so?"

The depth of his voice and the displeasure behind those three words reverberated through me. Why, I couldn't quite say. The man had just met me. If anyone should be displeased, it was me.

"Yes."

"Give me a reason why."

He didn't merely ask for the truth. He demanded it. I felt compelled to provide an answer. Most were aware of my feelings for Percival and that I would never accept him as a husband.

"I do not entertain flatterers. It is not in my best interest to accept a marriage proposal at this time."

I didn't believe that for a moment, but Grayson didn't need to know about my future plans. They certainly didn't involve Percival, or any man.

He frowned. "What if I don't accept that?"

A thrilling sensation shot through me.

To mask my sudden trepidation, I laughed. "You and I have only just met. You don't need to accept it."

"It's rumored that Percival Monteclaire, the Baron of Vensworth, is after your hand in marriage."

My gaze snapped to his. "Whatever you are planning, Mr. Valle, please don't."

The sly grin that curved his mouth made my heart leap into my throat. I realized this man might be just as wicked as I was.

"I can be a friend or foe rather easily, Miss Blackwood."

How could one man look at me this way and make me reconsider all my choices up to this point in my life? Everywhere we touched, it felt like a flame set to flesh. I wondered what he meant by that. Did he mean to threaten me?

Air felt scarce. My stays seemed tighter than usual, though the dance hadn't been lively. My heartbeat was more pronounced than ever, even in the face of danger. My face flushed with warmth when he looked at me, really looked at me. What did he see?

I stumbled.

"Miss Blackwood," he murmured, taking my arm and pulling me to the side. "Do you need air?"

I shook my head. What I needed was something much stronger than air. A good measure of brandy or rum would do the trick. How Aunt Marjory would dissolve into vapors if she ever saw me drinking anything stronger than champagne.

"I just got a little dizzy, but I'm fine now."

It took skill to slide into the role of a swooning young lady. This time, however, I hadn't been playing a part. Under the scrutiny of his intense gaze, I genuinely felt dizzy. It made me question everything, and I was more terrified at the thought of spending the rest of my life in a dull and boring existence as a baroness with a man as old as Percival. Sharing his bed and bearing his children was not how I envisioned marriage as a shield for my lies. Marriage to Percival would be exactly that.

I felt my face drain of color.

"Are you certain? You look a bit green."

My eyes flashed. "Thank you for pointing that out."

The dark slash of his brow above the eyepatch rose.

What is wrong with me? I inwardly howled, though no one could hear me. Trapped in my own mind, playing a role I was destined to fulfill for the rest of my life. I nearly groaned aloud. This entire night was turning into a nightmare.

"I appreciate your concern, Mr. Valle—"

"Captain," he interjected. "Captain Valle. But you, Miss Blackwood, may call me Grayson."

I raised an eyebrow. Dressed as he was, I would never have guessed he frequented the seas. Unfortunately, this only made him more appealing.

As though he sensed my thoughts, he shook his head ever so slightly, almost escaping my notice. "I have my own ship and carry a letter of marque from my country, but I also have approval from the British Crown, as long as I do not intercept merchant ships from this country. I decide where I go, and London is the one place I avoid like the plague."

I tilted my head, nibbling on my bottom lip, daring to delve into curiosity. "That begs the question of why I've not seen you around before now. You are a privateer? Or perhaps you only target certain merchant ships?"

Short of calling him a pirate, I expected him to throw his head back with a dark laugh, but he merely smiled a knowing smile. "You would love to think that, wouldn't you, Miss Blackwood?"

I really should correct him and tell him to call me Livie. I wouldn't dare. This society, like many others, was not so forgiving. I sighed.

When the music came to an abrupt end, along with the dance, I straightened, feeling a twinge of sadness at the thought of leaving him or doing something I would regret. Despite our exchange, he intrigued me. Any man who looked as he did, with a ship of his own, made me dream of stowing away just to escape this awful place, leaving Percival Monteclaire far behind.

"Thank you for the dance, *Captain Valle*. Perhaps I shall see you again someday," I said, my words the epitome of decorum.

I turned and left his side without a backward glance. Another minute in his company, and I would start rethinking everything. This man screamed danger. I should have recognized it immediately upon meeting him. The sooner there was distance between us, the better.

Chapter Four

Livie

I would be in so much trouble if I got caught.

Well-raised young ladies had no business wandering about the docks in London at night, skirting the shadows and rubbing elbows with unsavory sorts. And rub elbows I did as I pushed through *The Captain's Quarters* tavern, though I didn't consider myself well-raised. Hell-raised, more like.

The familiar smell of spilled spirits soaking into the rough wooden tables and the pungent scent of unwashed bodies greeted me the moment I stepped through the front door, a sudden change from the brackish water of the River Thames.

I considered myself lucky not to have been raised to be well-behaved, though if Aunt Marjory knew I'd been sneaking off to Wapping in the dead of night, I could imagine her face turning a mottled shade of purple. I'd seen it before.

Though I was only seventeen at the time, I remembered returning home covered from head to toe in mud after falling from my horse, uninjured except for my pride. Of course, we'd been at the country house just north of London, and the ride home hadn't been easy, especially while drenched in cold, dripping mud. Aunt Marjory had insisted that I not appear for supper unless every single speck of dirt was removed.

My uncle tried with all his might to be stern, but I always spotted that telltale twitch at the corner of his mouth. He'd always try. I'd give him that. If Uncle Winston knew what I'd been doing down at the docks, he would be forced to be much more stern. He'd need to be, considering I was putting the family name at risk by being here.

Boisterous laughter filled the tavern, drunken guffaws echoing through the crowds of men who had come to enjoy a tankard of ale, either heading out to sea or returning to port for various reasons. At this time of night, ships were still typically either arriving or departing, which meant nothing but trouble could be had. I hadn't heard from Grayson Valle since I'd met him two nights ago, and I hadn't expected to. He'd appeared and disappeared as though I'd imagined him.

There were definitely perks to dressing like a man who frequented the docks, but being hindered by a cloak irritated me to no end. With the hood of my cloak hiding my pale hair and most of my face, I scanned the room and smiled secretly when someone laughed so heartily that he tipped back on his stool, his legs flying up and over. The serving wench stepped over him, heedless of groping hands, as she passed mugs of tepid ale to the rowdy men.

Grateful for the privileges life had afforded me, one that which many were unaware of, I watched her evade roaming hands as she navigated through the crowd. Grimacing at the crude treatment, I hurried toward an empty table near the back and sat down quickly. As I waited for my father's agent to arrive, I pressed against the wall behind me and lightly rested my hand on the dagger at my side. Each night I came here, I questioned how long I would be forced to continue sneaking out to do this. I would never admit that I enjoyed being near the ships, but the desire to find a way back into my father's good graces rankled me.

I kept my cloak on and hood up, needing to remain disguised to avoid recognition. It would be damaging to be recognized, even in Wapping. A genteel woman traveling from Mayfair to Wapping simply didn't happen, especially at this time of night.

During the warmer months, disguising myself became much more challenging due to my long hair, which was so light that it resembled the sandy beaches of Barbados, where I had been born. Privacy in a place like this tavern didn't come easily, especially on a night like tonight. Being in disguise was essential to my missions.

I tied my hair back with a black scarf, reminiscent of pirates, covering as much of it as possible. Rubbing dirt smudges on my face gave a rough look to my delicate features. Luckily, I never thought anyone caught on to the fact that I was a woman.

I knew where to find Niles. He frequented this tavern most often among Wapping, Stepney, and Southwark. If I couldn't find him, he would always find me. Soon enough, he was skirting through the tavern patrons and settled into the chair across from me, having received my message passed by my maid through her connections in lower society.

I worked diligently to gather scraps of information on who was eager to buy smuggled goods over the last three years, bringing Niles details about those individuals. This last tip had proven true, and my excitement that the opportunity had fallen into my lap only heightened my adrenaline. The night watch knew nothing of the illegal deals I helped bring to light. If they did, I would be headed directly to the gallows for smuggling, and, if they knew who I truly was, for piracy. It made it all the more dangerous.

I kept silent while Niles waved over one of the serving girls. A moment later, a tankard of ale was slammed down on the table in front of him. His nearly bald head gleamed in the flickering light of the sconces. The scar running the length of his jaw, puckered and ugly, hadn't deterred him from delving into illegal activities. Never once had he told me this was too dangerous for a woman.

"What do you have for me?" he asked, keeping his voice low enough for only me to hear.

"I've just come from *The King's Arms*," I said. "A man by the name of Mr. Griggs secures storage for goods just arriving . . . without paperwork."

Niles nodded once. "Any issues?"

I shook my head. "If the vessel rides light and anchors below the Pool, he'll have dockside workers alongside within the hour of arrival. All messages go through his son. Mention my name."

When I'd asked about the men he employed as dockside lumpers, he stiffened in offense and assured me they were trustworthy. If he didn't believe it, he would have already been brought in for questioning by the authorities.

I leaned closer, daring to ask the very question I should not. As much as my father had instilled fear in me, I still cared for him, much to my self-loathing. "And my father? Is he well?"

Niles leaned back in his chair, cupping his mug. "As well as can be expected from a man who rarely sees the light of day."

"Did he indicate if he might return for me someday?" I hedged.

He gave me that look that told me not to bother. My father would never come back for me. "At your age, you should be married, girl."

"That's not true, *Niles*."

"Your father will not come for you. It's too dangerous, and you know that." He shook his head, his expression harsh. "Shoulda thought about that before you got yerself involved with Edward Smith."

That wasn't very nice, but I had asked for trouble by bringing it up in the first place. "And if I insist that my father return for me?"

"You would put your father in danger?"

No, I would never. The outcome of asking such a thing would prove disastrous. The patrol would have him shackled and brought in for questioning immediately, though I knew there were ways he could retrieve me without positioning himself nearby.

My thoughts drifted to when I'd first arrived, picked up a distance away by another ship. Jasper Stone, another questionable privateer, who had made no secret of his admiration for me. My father had already warned him against touching me. Jasper must have heeded those warnings, for the remainder of my voyage had been uneventful.

"And Edward?" I murmured. "Has anyone seen or heard from him?"

I spoke of the man who had gotten me removed from *The Executioner*. The one man who had captured my heart like sails catching the wind. How foolish I had been to fall so headlong into love. In the end, we both lost.

My father had him beaten within an inch of his life and left him on a deserted island. I should know, I stayed at the stern, watching the island and the man lying in the sand for as long as I could. No matter what had happened, a piece of my heart still belonged to Edward. He couldn't be dead.

He scoffed with a smile. "That boy deserved what he got. You know what your father does with anyone who dares leave his crew." With his finger, he drew a line across his neck.

"He was more than a boy," I replied, my chin lifted with dignity. "Edward didn't leave his crew. He was forced to do so."

"He's dead. And after all these years, you need to come to terms with it. Rest assured, no one suspects you. No one cares. You were safe on the island with your mother up until recently. That's all anyone will ever know."

"He's still alive, Niles. I know he is."

"Don't you think Edward would have come for you, if he cared just a little?" He shook his head. "Edward is gone. Just you remember that what you bring me goes no where's else. Don't slip up."

"In the three years I've been here, I've never slipped."

He sighed. "What are your marriage prospects, if you don't mind me asking?"

"I *do* mind your asking," I replied tartly. "But at this moment, I have none other than a baron my father's age, who is only after my money. I would rather not marry this man, given his advanced age."

"Girl, perhaps you should take what you can get. Every man is after money."

Spurned, I lifted my chin. "You do realize that if I marry, this liaison will end. No man would allow his wife to gallivant down at the docks, doing what I've been doing."

The sinister smile that curved his mouth sent a chill through me. "There are ways around such things."

Eventually, my luck would run out. I knew it would. Besides, my father was a wealthy man for a pirate. How much longer would I need to continue to prove myself? And what was he doing with his wealth when he so rarely withdrew from hiding?

The sound of a tankard smashing, with shards of clay crumbling to the muddied floor, made my gaze dart toward the noise, momentarily stealing my attention from our conversation. When I snapped back to Niles, who was still hovering over his mug, he met my eyes with his calm demeanor.

A heavy-set man with a curling black mustache pushed through the crowd, followed closely by a scrawny fellow until they reached us. Instantly, I tensed. Brady Nilson and his faithful sidekick, Tommy.

Niles immediately stood to block the two unsavory-looking men from joining us. He motioned for them to step aside, away from me and our table, but not without the heavy-set man glancing at me once more. Instinctively, I pulled my hood lower to cover more of my face, but the way he looked at me sent shivers of apprehension down my spine.

Niles kept a level head while I had a tendency to chase trouble, but it wasn't trouble I sought tonight. Nevertheless, I would never admit defeat.

Dealing with men coming in from the sea was my area of expertise, having spent most of my life on the water among pirates, thieves, and cutthroats. Yet, Niles never ceased to amaze me with his calm demeanor, though there were moments when he was almost too calm.

The two men moved away, melting back into the crowd as Niles returned to the table. Instead of sitting, he leaned over and grabbed his ale.

"It's time for me to go," he said, tipping his mug back and downing the remainder of his drink. "Be safe, Livie."

After Niles and the two men left, I remained there for several more moments while I finished my ale. Time was growing late, and I needed to return soon or risk getting caught sneaking back into my bedroom.

Finally, I pushed up from the bench. The drunken behavior in the tavern escalated as I made my way toward the front door, with men bumping into me unceremoniously. I stood my ground, walking steadily through the chaos, mindful of the dagger within my reach. I had daggers tucked into my waistband and more hidden in my boots, though wearing a cloak had its drawbacks.

Halfway to the door, a fight broke out, and I heard the barkeep, Boon, bellow over the noise for the brawl to move outside. Still holding my ground, I was pushed roughly from side to side, struggling to keep my hood up and maintain my grip on my sheathed dagger. With so many people in the cramped space, I needed more room to draw my weapons, or accidentally stab someone who didn't deserve it.

Boon would be irate if any weapons were drawn inside his tavern, but sometimes it couldn't be helped. Men were men. I pressed my way through.

Niles usually kept his calm to a point, but push him too far, and he'd fight back. Sometimes, we had no choice. Business was business, and in the smuggling trade, fights happened. I'd been in my fair share of them, having learned enough during my time on *The Executioner* to know how to fight like the best.

The sound of tankards shattering nearby assaulted my ears as I pushed through the crowd. Someone stomped on my foot, and I spun around in fury, ducking just in time to avoid a punch to the face. I hurried toward the door. A punch to the face would leave a mark I couldn't explain, not to mention the pain it would cause.

In three quick steps, I stumbled out the door. I kept my dagger at my hip within my grasp, anticipating more discord beyond the tavern's entrance. In the shadows of the night, Niles was fighting two men I didn't recognize in the street. Another man nimbly exited the tavern just behind me, and the sound of the door made me spin around just in time to avoid the tip of his sword.

He used the momentum to come at me, and I barely reached for my dagger before I was shoved back against the building. The impact against my back nearly stole the breath from my lungs, and I kicked out, causing the man to stumble away from me.

I had enough time to draw two of my daggers, the feel of each in my hands welcome after so long without. My expertise in fighting would never match that of a man, especially after having little need to do so for many years. However, I knew enough to protect myself. The man grinned at me, missing several teeth. He motioned with his hand for me to come away from the building.

I would have thought this fight had nothing to do with us if not for Brady, who'd been eyeing me in the tavern, along with Tommy, who stood with swords and daggers drawn. All I could think was that whatever Niles had been dealing with did not involve me. It couldn't.

Niles danced around, wielding his sword and a dagger against foes who were equally armed. One of the men, taller than the rest, scoffed as if we were fighting a losing battle. I raised an eyebrow, though no one could see it. The man was so certain that the two of us couldn't take them all in a fight. The glint of my daggers reflected in the moonlight as I waited for the man to make a move.

"Why are you doing this?" I asked, my voice low.

"Because yer thieves," the man answered.

I laughed, shifting slightly. "We're all thieves here."

Suddenly, the man's sword came inches from my throat, and I jumped back against the building. One quick movement that I couldn't block would snuff out my life. We'd been in skirmishes before, but never against this many.

Leaning back to throw him off balance and get the tip of his weapon away from my neck, I spun around and kicked the sword out of his hand. The movement gave him momentum as he pivoted quickly.

The man proved to be a formidable opponent. Although I had received plenty of training in my life, the cloak slowed me down considerably. Eventually, the hood fell back just as he knocked the dagger from my hand and pulled me into his brutal grip.

Stunned that he had disarmed me so quickly, I straightened.

"Drop your weapons," he whispered in my ear, uncomfortably close.

I watched Niles continue to fight, even though I had been disarmed, temporarily. I refused to give up, despite the prick of the man's dagger against my throat bringing tears to my eyes. He had drawn blood, and I felt a trickle ease down the column of my neck. I wasn't ready to die yet. Better dead than married to Percival, I thought. Still, I had so much left to do before being put in the ground.

My gaze landed on Niles, now weaponless and on his knees at the end of a sword. We were in trouble this time. No one would be getting us out of this mess. Niles, about the age of my father, was still spry enough to fight back, but this time it was useless. We were outnumbered, three of them to us.

I released my daggers, the clatter of them hitting the street resounding in the quiet.

The man behind me chuckled, his sour breath wafting down to my nose and causing me to choke, pushing the blade further into my neck. Tears pricked my eyes in earnest. I could only hope that with my hair pulled back and dirt smeared on my face, he wouldn't notice I was a woman. I wasn't sure how he could miss it, given how closely he held me. It made my skin crawl.

"Don't move now, love."

He knew I was a woman after all. Perhaps he would reconsider taking my life, but I'd be damned if I allowed him to rape me. I'd cut my own throat before that happened.

"You'll fetch a pretty price," he whispered. "After you've given me whatever money you have."

The heart pounding in my chest thundered so hard I thought it might gallop right out. I closed my eyes, hoping it would be quick. Uncle Winston, I thought, I didn't mean to let you down. I couldn't claim this was for the greater good. It wasn't. I only hoped someone would get word to him, though I wasn't convinced anyone would.

No one knew me as a genteel lady down by the docks, and no one in our household knew I had snuck out. To them, I slumbered safely in my bed.

A deep voice from behind me wafted into my thundering ears. "Missing quite the merriment, aren't we?"

I clenched my hands within the folds of my cloak to hide their trembling, but when I opened my eyes, Grayson Valle slowly came into view, strolling around to the other side of us, looking as dashing as ever.

He wore no eyepatch tonight, and I noticed a thick scar running from just above his eyebrow to his high cheekbone. His eyelid bore a faint line, as if the weapon that had given him that scar had eased up just enough to avoid cutting his eye before carving into his skin again.

Seeing me in the clutches of this man, with a dagger to my throat and blood trickling from the wound, Grayson's eyes narrowed dangerously.

My God, he is imposing. I had seen men with the blackest eyes and hair the color of a raven, but Grayson was simply *dark*. His very aura was heavy with it, and the scar over his eye made him even more formidable.

Dressed like a man of the sea rather than the gentleman I had danced with, he wore a tunic and pants tucked into high boots. He was armed more heavily than any man I had ever seen: a leather jerkin strapped with weapons, more weapons secured at his waist, and a sheathed sword at his side.

He hid his identity as well as I hid mine. Just days ago, I had thought him a gentleman. He had admitted to being the captain of his own ship, though he claimed to engage in no illegal activity aboard it. Dressed this way, with this many weapons, I had to assume he was a thief like my father. Clearly, I had been misled.

Two men, both pirates, followed him out. I would know, having lived among pirates for the better part of my nineteen years. I recognized one of the men with long dark hair from the Kingsleys' ball, his eyes dancing with mischief. The man, with his arm banded around my neck and his blade still pressed against my flesh, hadn't moved. Would he? I had no way of knowing.

If we hadn't been disarmed, if they had come out moments earlier, they might have been able to assist us, and I wouldn't be in this position.

Grayson shook his head in disappointment, dark hair that had escaped his leather tie falling against his neck. I had to admit he looked fierce, not a man I would want to tangle with. But something about that dimpled chin made my heart flutter. He looked even fiercer without the eyepatch, his eyes glinting with threat.

It could be the situation, I told myself. But that didn't explain the night of the ball. What a fitful night it had been, attempting to sleep. Between the stress of the possibility of marriage and visions of the daring man I had just met, I had spent most of the night staring at the ceiling.

"This isn't your fight," the man holding me said. "Move along."

"I'm inclined to disagree. Three against two is hardly fair, regardless of any disagreement you might have with them."

Slowly, Grayson withdrew a single dagger from his belt.

Amusing that he thinks a single dagger will do anything.

He ran his finger along the blade, studying it to ensure it would suffice before flicking his wrist so quickly that I might have missed it had I not been watching. The dagger sailed through the air, aimed at me. My eyes widened slightly before it struck the man behind me.

Out of the corner of my eye, I saw it embed itself in my captor's hand, his dagger clattering to the ground as he released me. I fell to my hands and knees, glancing over to see the blade jutting out from the man's hand. Had his aim been off by just a fraction, the dagger would have hit me instead.

Pressing my hand to my neck, I pulled it away to assess the blood. My eyes widened at the crimson staining my fingers, and I looked back up to see the others engaged in a fight. My captor's injury had gone unnoticed by his friends, leveling the playing field for a much fairer fight.

The man who had held me captive cradled his hand, the dagger stuck in the center. His eyes met mine, glossy with pain, as I struggled to push myself up without success.

Grayson strode over, leaning down to yank the dagger out. The man shouted in agony, cradling his bloody hand to his chest while Grayson pressed the dagger to his neck, the man's eyes growing impossibly wide.

Men like him, who bullied others, perhaps didn't deserve mercy. I would have fought to the death rather than become a victim of rape, which only led me to believe I was more like my father than I wanted to admit. My father was without mercy.

"You will never threaten this woman again," Grayson growled. "Do you understand me?"

The man glared at me. "But she's . . . she's . . ."

Grayson increased the pressure and a drop of blood welled where flesh met steel. "Do you understand?" he repeated.

"Yes," the man moaned.

Grayson pulled the dagger away and stepped back just as the fighting ceased. I finally got to my feet, swaying for a moment until I could take in my surroundings. The men who had been fighting us scurried into the darkness. Niles lay on the dirty street, facing away from me.

I cried out, rushing toward him and pushing him over. There were no visible wounds that would have rendered him unconscious. They must have knocked him out. But why? Why the fight in the first place?

My gaze snapped up to the hand on my arm, pulling me to my feet. Once standing, Grayson tilted my chin with his long fingers to examine my wound more closely. The feel of his hands made my heart quicken. I met his gaze and realized I needed to pull my hood back up, feeling strangely confused by the intensity of his stare.

The wound throbbed, and I knew it would be a problem. Hiding the mark on my neck would be difficult, and explaining it would be even harder. The world spun around me, my heartbeat racing simply because a man was looking at me with such fervor. Between the pounding of my heart and the burning sensation from the wound, flashes of dots danced in my vision.

The dagger had cut deeper than I had anticipated, and I knew I was on the verge of fainting. I should have realized that from the amount of blood on my hand. My last thought before darkness claimed me was how I would cover this up and, if I couldn't, how I would explain it.

Chapter Five

Roaring laughter and animated conversation surrounded me in the main room of the tavern, where flickering sconces illuminated the wood-paneled walls. The spacious area was dotted with long tables and chairs, many of which were occupied. The barkeep paused in his cleaning, pressing his hands against the bar and looking up as the front door swung open. Curious, I watched the figure from where I sat at the far side of the tavern, opposite the bar, where Connor and Wiley had joined me for a drink before heading back to the ship.

As much as I enjoyed being on my ship, I occasionally liked to get away. I would take a room at *The Captain's Quarters* in Wapping. I had known the barkeep, Boon, and his wife, Matilda, for several years. Whenever I stopped in London, I rented their best room for a few nights, depending entirely on how long it took to depart and who might be warming my bed. The wind was always the deciding factor. I did not take women onto my ship for multiple reasons, the most important being that it was my domain. My space was sacred to me, as was my rest. Sleepless nights since Adam's demise plagued me, and I knew that until I avenged him, I would continue to thrive on very little sleep.

Nods were exchanged between Boon and the newcomer, who headed toward the back of the tavern to a surprisingly open table. Blonde hair peeked out from beneath the hood of her cloak, bound and covered with another layer of fabric. My eyes narrowed when she turned her face forward. I couldn't mistake her graceful stride if I tried.

"Miss Blackwood," I murmured, catching Connor's attention.

"Cap'n?" he asked. "Say something?"

"Correct me if I'm wrong, Connor, but isn't that Livie Blackwood? And do be discreet when you turn to look."

She kept her face tilted down, shadowed by her hood, but I had no doubt it was the same Livie Blackwood I'd met just two nights before. Connor took a long drink from his mug, cautiously glancing in her direction just as a bald man joined her.

My eyebrows shot up at her improper meeting. Unmarried and unchaperoned, dressed like a man and far from her home in Mayfair. I mentally ticked off the signs that this lady still had connections to her father.

"Is that her?" Wiley asked, his wild auburn hair sprouting above a red scarf tied around his forehead. As my master gunner, he took his position seriously, and he should, given our current professions. Always on guard, Wiley didn't partake in drink often. But neither he nor Connor would allow me to have drinks without them.

Connor turned back with a nod.

Delight coursed through me when she scanned the room and didn't see me or Connor. I couldn't forget the beauty from the Kingsley ball two nights ago. Her eyes had seemed to absorb every detail as they swept across the room, somehow missing me. My dark hair, height, and eyepatch tended to be memorable.

I had left off the eyepatch, reserving it for more formal gatherings and meetings, but now I wished I had kept it on to instill some fear in her. It was serious business for her to be traipsing through the worst parts of town.

Connor and Wiley swiveled inconspicuously in their chairs, curious about my fixation. Connor chuckled deeply, while Wiley whistled, which vexed me. My crew knew the mission, but Wiley didn't understand just how far I would go to get answers. Livie Blackwood held them. I knew she did. I planned to question her thoroughly before we departed from port. I just didn't know how I would accomplish it. Yet.

The tavern was becoming rowdier. I pressed myself against the wall to ensure she didn't see me while she conversed with her companion. I had seen the man during previous stays before, but I had yet to make his acquaintance.

Two men momentarily drew him away, and I noticed she watched the trio intently. The larger man often redirected his gaze back to her. Curious about this exchange, I waited patiently, even after the two men exited the tavern. Her companion drained the contents of his mug before he, too, left, leaving her behind to finish her ale. It seemed she had no desire to rush out, though I had to imagine she didn't hire a hackney to bring her here.

Seeing her here only brought more questions forth. Did Winston Thornton know where his niece was right now? And where would she have gotten the clothing of a man? Surely, Winston and Marjory Thornton ran a tighter household than to allow her such liberties.

Finishing her drink, she slid off the bench and made her way toward the front door that led out to the darkened street. Every muscle in my body clenched at the known dangers lurking between here and Mayfair. That begged the question of how many times she had been to this establishment before tonight. I had never seen her here before, though I may have missed it, not knowing what I did now. She seemed well-acquainted with Boon when she nodded in his direction, and he returned the gesture.

A fight broke out before Livie could get anywhere close to the front door, her slight stature tossed between those who sought to join the fray. I grimaced when she ducked out of the way of someone's fist, inwardly taking a heavy breath. Had she been hit by that meaty fist, she might have been knocked unconscious and trampled.

"Orders, Captain?" Wiley asked.

"Give her a moment before we follow."

Connor's dark eyebrows lifted. "You're certain?"

I nodded, wanting to put some distance between us to avoid suspicion. Livie was far too perceptive. I was fairly certain she would be heading back to Mayfair, and I intended to follow to ensure her safety.

After a few moments, I stood and wound my way out of the tavern. Boon had managed to get the fighting within under control, and patrons had returned to their drinking, some nursing bloodied noses and bruised jaws. Wiley and Connor followed behind me, stepping out into the crisp night air, only to find that the fight had resumed in the street.

From the looks of it, these men had Livie and her companion at a severe disadvantage. I sincerely disliked when that happened, as often as it did, and I wondered what Livie could possibly be doing that would warrant this many men against her and her companion.

"Missing quite the merriment, aren't we?" I said, making sure my voice thundered in the dark, narrow street.

I could see her in the clutches of the large man in front of me, recognizing the cloak she wore. She appeared to be trapped, but when I walked around to face them, my entire demeanor changed.

Clutched by him was one thing, but seeing the dagger at her throat and blood trickling down the slender column of her neck nearly undid me. Fury boiled over as my eyes narrowed at him. He would lose his life tonight if he did any lasting damage to her neck.

Her hands were clenched in the folds of her cloak, but I could see the slightest tremble. Two blades lay on the ground, both likely hers. Inwardly, I scoffed, wondering what she might have expected coming down to the bowels of the earth. Wapping was not even the worst part of this town.

Just days ago, she had worn a gown of fashionable taste with her hair neatly curled. Her eyes, once watchful and intrigued, now bore the fear of life hanging in the balance. Well, I couldn't allow that.

I shook my head in disappointment.

"This isn't your fight," the man holding her said. "Move along."

"I'm inclined to disagree. Three against two is hardly fair, regardless of any disagreement you might have with them."

When I withdrew my dagger and flung it directly at the man's hand, I knew if it wasn't quick enough, that if the man moved, it could hit Livie. My aim had always been true, years of practicing had taught me to expect the unexpected. But I was so quick, the man hadn't time to move and my dagger embedded in his hand, forcing him to release her.

It took every ounce of strength for me not to rush over to Livie when she fell to her hands and knees, seeing the blood that came away on her fingertips, while I went to retrieve my dagger from the man's hand with a warning.

"You will never threaten this woman again," I growled. "Do you understand me?"

I wanted to drive the dagger into his neck when he looked at Livie, sputtering, "But she's . . . she's . . . "

He might have finished his sentence, revealing something I could use against her, but seeing her bleed hadn't been in my plans. Her wound needed immediate attention, and that took precedence over information. I'd wait for a better time.

I pressed the blade further into his neck, feeling the give of his skin. "Do you understand?" I repeated.

"Yes," he moaned.

The rest of the men were quickly disarmed and ran for safety as I withdrew the dagger and stepped back, but not before noticing Livie finally get to her feet, though she swayed. No longer as poised as I'd seen her before, she let out a cry and hurried to the man lying in the street.

Never mind the man. I wanted to see how badly the injury to her neck was and I followed her, pulling her up by the arm. Her eyes flashed when I pushed her chin up with two fingers, studying the bloody slice low on her neck. The man had gotten her good. It would leave a pretty mark for many days to come.

Her eyes rolled back, and a moment later, her legs gave out. I swept her up into my arms just as she fainted.

Chapter Six

Grayson

"Keep that bandage where it is."

My voice cut across the room as soon as I saw Livie stirring. I had brought her to my rented room without a second thought and with little effort. Never in my life had I felt such a desire to slay every man in the street after seeing the blood running down her elegant neck.

I stood with my arms crossed, leaning against the closed door frame as I watched her push herself up to her elbows and survey her surroundings. Alarm lit her eyes when she realized where she was. As improper as it was to have a clandestine meeting so far from her home with a man and no chaperone, this situation was equally scandalous. If anyone knew where she was right now, her reputation would be irreparably damaged, and I would find myself on the way to the altar faster than I could draw my sword.

It would do her no good to deny what had brought her and her companion to the docks tonight. I had seen the men who attacked them, and they were well known for purchasing smuggled goods to evade taxation. I couldn't begin to guess why the men had attacked them unless provoked. Livie didn't seem like the type of woman to engage in a fight unnecessarily, unless I had imagined her cool demeanor in the ballroom.

Looking around the sparse room, she said nothing, likely pondering the impropriety of the situation. I didn't give a damn.

My only hope was that if word got out about this, any chance of Percival insisting on her becoming his wife would be gone. I didn't know how long it would be before the bastard asked Winston for her hand in marriage. Winston would not be able to deny him.

"I fainted," she whispered, as if not believing it, gingerly touching her neck and wincing.

"Aye, you did."

"Why am I here?" She looked around again. "Presumably in your rented room?"

"I wasn't about to leave you in the street. Matilda bandaged your neck. It might be wise for you to feign illness for the next few days to escape notice. Am I correct in assuming that no one in your uncle's household knows your current whereabouts?"

A smile threatened to break through when I saw her quietly curse. Regardless of why she had been at the docks when she should have been safe in her bed, I imagined she was eager to return home. Even so, I could not release her in her current condition. Boon's wife had been kind enough to help me stop the bleeding.

"Where is Niles?"

"The man you were with, who allowed you to nearly be skewered?"

"He did no such thing. Niles was fighting his own battle at the time." She swung her legs over the side of the bed. "If you'd been there moments before, you might have been able to help us fight, and I might not be in this situation."

The memory of catching her in my arms must have crossed her mind, for a flush rose to her cheeks. Her gaze lifted to mine as I pushed away from the door.

"Where is he?" she asked again.

"I don't know where he went. As soon as you fainted, I brought you up here and asked Matilda to help with your wound. You are my priority, not your cohort."

She stared at me, clear distrust deep in her blue eyes. I'd given her no reason to. She, on the other hand, had given me every reason to question her. "Boon?"

"Gone to bed. I've given him my word and some additional assurances that I would ensure the tavern is locked for the night. He knows I am worthy of his trust." She glanced at the window. "You seem awfully familiar with Boon and this establishment. Do you come here often, Livie Blackwood?"

Her eyes flashed like I'd hit a nerve.

"I need to go."

When she stood, it was too fast, and she swayed, falling back onto the bed with a bounce. I had to admit she looked rather fetching. I never claimed to be a saint, but I had to stop myself from attempting to woo whatever virtue she had, even with a wound.

My eyebrow arched, the scar stretching with it. "You will not leave this room without my permission."

"Am I under lock and key, then?"

"No," I said, drawing the word out. "You are staying here until I deem you well enough to travel home. You will not find a hackney to hire at this time of night, and I'll not have you walking alone. Should dawn come before I find you well enough to depart, I shall send word to Winston."

At that, she flinched. I had touched a nerve that sent her into a frantic worry. It was obvious that Livie was where she shouldn't be, likely where no one knew she was, except her friend, Niles.

"I want to see Niles."

I couldn't blame her, though it gave me a sour feeling. He was as old as Percival Monteclaire. What would she be doing with him?

"This Niles . . . " Her chin tilted toward me, as if she knew exactly what I would ask next. "Who is he to you?"

She scoffed. "A friend."

"A friend," I repeated.

"I already told you that it is not in my best interest to accept a proposal."

"Is that so?"

"That is so. Now, if you'd please, I'd like to reach home before the sun rises. I need to be back in my bed before the servants awaken."

I crossed my arms, tucking my hands. "Not with that wound."

When she rose from the bed, somewhat more steadily than before, she strode toward me with fire in her eyes. This woman had a spine of steel to take a dagger to the neck and still be up and walking about, especially one who appeared to be setting me straight.

"You do not issue orders to me," she snapped. "I'm not in your employ, and you have no relation to me. And even then, I answer to no one."

"Is that so?" I asked coolly.

Needing a drink, I moved away from her to pour myself two fingers of rum. After tossing it back and feeling the warmth travel down my insides, I poured another and offered it to her. She was so pale she seemed to need it more than I did. But she shook her head.

"Rum dulls my senses," she whispered.

"You took an incredible risk coming here tonight." My tone hardened. "I should bring you directly to Winston and explain to him that his charge has been gallivanting in the middle of the night without an escort."

She smirked. "I had an escort. Apparently, he left me when you decided to play hero and bring me to your private rooms."

I took a step toward her, bringing our faces close. "Do you often sneak away at night and delve into smuggling? You and your friends . . ."

"Niles," she interjected.

I continued to stare at her, waiting for an answer.

A sigh escaped her lips, a sound that piqued my interest. Such a breathy sigh made me wonder what she sounded like in the throes of passion.

"You need not think of me as some pitiful woman with antics, but neither will I share information about what I have been doing. There are more people at stake than just me in this."

She watched me drink down the dark liquid and set the glass down, the tip of her tongue darting out to run over her plump upper lip. I raised an eyebrow in question.

"I changed my mind," she announced. "I will take a glass."

"Is your wound bothering you?" I asked, pouring another glass.

When I handed it to her, my fingers brushed against hers, and the contact electrified me, allowing our fingers to linger together before I released it.

"No."

I chuckled low. "Liar."

She walked around the room, trying to be inconspicuous as she eyed the large four-poster bed she'd just been in. The room had ample space, with a table and two chairs, as well as a writing desk. She peeked around a screen beside the door to find a bathing tub with a table beside it before turning back to me.

"Captain Valle—"

"Grayson," I reminded her.

"Grayson, I need to get home. It's imperative that I do. I've traversed this journey many nights. You need not accompany me."

I lifted the glass to my lips, but instead of sipping, I downed the entire contents in one shot. "I insist."

Chapter Seven

Livie

I had lingered too long, I thought as I hoisted myself up the trellis leading to my window, and Grayson was entirely to blame. A man of his word, he had seen me home and then melted into the shadows.

It was nothing short of a blessing not to have to share a bedroom with Imogen, especially since Uncle Winston could afford a spacious house in Mayfair. Midsummer, we would retreat to the country house north of London, which made it difficult to get into the city for business. But I did anyway.

Grasping the windowsill with one hand, I pulled open the windowpanes with the other and pushed myself inside with the help of the trellis. It was a risky move, given the sparse bushes below, but I had never once fallen. A fall would surely wake the household.

The ledge caught my midriff, as it usually did, and the air whooshed from my lungs until I could swing my legs in, gracefully rolling in quietly. Smiling to myself, I turned and pulled the window closed. I pressed my palm to the raw skin at my neck, checking to ensure my wound hadn't begun to bleed again. No blood.

Immediately, I paused. Something was wrong. I caught the scent first, instinctively withdrawing my daggers. The room was cast in shadows, yet someone had been in my space.

The boots I wore had the softest soles for a reason. They made no noise as I stepped carefully into the room, holding a dagger in each hand, ready to strike if needed. Without a candle lit, it was hard to see, but it also made it difficult for anyone to see me.

Sneaking out at night for so many years had sharpened my senses, and the lingering scent was distinct, one that I recognized. The person had been here recently, if not still present. The slightest movement near the door ceased my footsteps. Whoever had been bold enough to enter my room had been foolish enough to remain.

"Halt," I said, keeping my voice just above a whisper. "Turn around and show yourself. No use hiding."

I knew before she turned who I had caught, before she could utter a sound.

"Sneaking out to meet a lover? What a shameful thing to do, Olivia."

Imogen stepped fully into the room, abandoning any hope of leaving undetected. I was just as caught as she was. The thought that she believed I had been out meeting a lover almost made me chuckle. Leave it to my seventeen-year-old cousin to think I'd been tumbling in the hay with a man. She was older than I had been when I got into trouble with Edward. Back then, I had known exactly what I was doing. Having been around pirates, I understood precisely what they did when in port. Edward had been man enough to know what he was getting into, but that didn't absolve me of any guilt. We had both fallen headlong into it, though my feelings for him may have clouded my judgment.

"Why are you in my room?" I asked, sliding my daggers back into their sheaths at my waist.

"Were those . . . daggers you just put away?" she whispered.

"That doesn't matter. What are you doing in my room, Immy?"

She scowled at the nickname. "Tell me where you were first."

"This is not a negotiation."

She approached me, her dark brown hair cascading in lustrous waves. With her looks, I knew she wouldn't lack marriage proposals for long. While others may not have noticed the young men watching her with keen interest at balls and social functions, I did. Several were already paying calls, much to my aunt's delight.

Though we did not get along well, I sensed a fire in her blood that longed to break free from the constraints of society's absurd rules. When Immy found love, it would unleash a storm.

God help the man who marries her.

It was curious that Percival sought me out rather than Immy. Immy had not only a solid dowry to offer a husband, but she was the daughter of a man well-respected in society. Percival could have a much better match with Immy. If he approached Uncle Winston and asked for his permission before Immy received an offer, Aunt Marjory would be insanely jealous. She had to know it was coming. Percival had all but told me at the Kingsley ball what his intentions were. I knew she wanted her daughter to receive offers before I did, which made sense. Immy was her daughter, not me.

Even in the dark, I could see the devious smile on her face. "I don't think so, Olivia."

Inwardly, I tensed. I hated that name. Aunt Marjory and Uncle Winston had taken it upon themselves to call me Olivia, as if my given name was some dastardly secret. With the exception of William, it was rare to hear anyone refer to me as Livie. It shouldn't have come to a surprise when Grayson used my given name. Immy, however, had a way of irritating me beyond reason.

"What don't you think?" I whispered, hoping she would just go away.

If she didn't keep her voice down, it was bound to awaken the household. That was trouble I didn't need. *She* was trouble I didn't need, and my mind raced to determine how to handle the situation. My wound would cause enough trouble unless I could find something to cover it properly.

Twisting the ties of her nightgown around her fingers, I ignored her fidgeting and kept my eyes locked on hers, never wavering and never backing down.

"Tell me who you were meeting," she urged.

I huffed out a laugh. As if I would admit such a thing to her, of all people. "The less you know about what I was doing out, the better."

She frowned. "Why are you dressed like that? And where did you get those weapons?"

I shrugged and brushed past her to get myself ready for bed. Just because I didn't want her to see where I hid the clothes I wore at night didn't mean I couldn't remove them in the meantime. But the wound on my neck posed a dilemma I didn't want to explain. She had so many questions that I wouldn't answer.

"Perhaps I needed to take in some fresh air."

She laughed softly. "I wouldn't tell a soul anything you divulge to me. I swear it!"

That's the first thing she'll do. I'm surprised she isn't blackmailing me. She has me right where she wants me.

Sighing, I unstrapped my belt of weapons from my waist and laid it carefully on the bed before leaning down to remove the daggers from my boots. I heard her sharp intake of breath. The strap of the belt was a little more difficult to unclasp, but once I managed it, it joined the rest of the weapons.

"Good heavens, what do you do with all those? I don't think Father even has as many in this house!"

"Going out at this time of night, I need to protect myself. Don't you think?"

Wisely, she remained silent, watching me.

Unclasping my cloak, I laid it over the chest at the foot of the bed before sitting down to remove my boots. I purposely draped my hair over my shoulder to hide my neck. It may have stopped bleeding, but I had yet to look at it in a mirror to truly see the mark. Any sharp movement would cause it to start bleeding again. It had been bad enough getting through the window without reopening the wound. I knew the gash would still be visible and likely an angry red for several days.

"Protect yourself from whom?" she finally asked. "It makes me nervous to think of who you might need to protect yourself from. Now, tell me why."

I set the boots carefully aside and stood, rising to my full height while pulling at my hair to ensure it covered my neck. She stood nearly as tall as I did, peering at me in the darkness. The ties of her nightgown had been abandoned, and she now stood with her arms crossed, demanding a reason I would never divulge.

That she hadn't noticed my neck gave me a surge of triumph.

"Whatever wickedness you think I'm up to at night, it isn't that," I scoffed. "If you want to believe that, be my guest."

Immy's eyes widened slightly, then narrowed as her lips pressed together. "With whom would you possibly be doing that? Are you meeting the baron?"

I sighed, suppressing a shudder. "What I'm doing has nothing to do with Percival or any man, for that matter."

"In the middle of the night?"

I peeled my breeches down and folded them neatly before placing them on the chest. "I suppose you haven't so much as kissed anyone," I said, trying to divert her.

Her cheeks turned pink. "Why would I do such a thing? You are nothing but trouble, Olivia, and so help me, you'd better not bring shame to this family."

With a grin and a slight turn away to ensure she wouldn't see my neck, I lifted my tunic off. She spun around, gasping in shock at my boldness. I knew that would make her avoid looking at me, thus missing my neck. Nudity had never been an issue for me. Luckily, the room was still dark enough for me to bring my hair back around to drape over my shoulder before she could turn around again. I again turned slightly away from her to ensure she couldn't see it and grabbed the nightgown I'd left on the bed.

"Have you no shame?"

I shimmied into my nightgown, still grinning. "No."

Sighing, Immy moved toward the door, resigned to the fact that I wasn't about to give in to her questioning. She turned back toward me. "I thought I heard something in your room, so I came in to see if anything had happened. I didn't think I'd find you gone!"

"Do not come into my room again."

"I won't have to. Once I tell Mother about this, you'll be under lock and key."

I strode over to her so quickly that she had no chance to escape. Almost pressing the tip of my nose to hers, I stared down at her. "Tell anyone about this, and you will regret it. I can promise you that, Imogen."

Her sharp intake of breath provided enough evidence that she believed my threat. It would serve her well to listen to me. I could make her life very, very miserable. I hoped that after seeing the number of weapons I possessed, she would.

"Call my bluff," I whispered, not moving an inch away from her. "See what happens."

"You wouldn't hurt me." Her voice wavered.

"I would have no choice. And I *will* hurt you if you speak of this to anyone."

After another moment of silence, she left.

I stared at the closed door. *I don't believe her for a second. She's up to something. But she underestimates me if she thinks she can get away with telling someone about this. I will need to take drastic measures to ensure she stays out of my business from this point on.*

At least she had left quietly. I didn't know what she thought she had heard when she wandered into my room, but I knew I needed to be very careful from now on. I could never know who was watching me.

Immy had always been the sneakier of my two cousins, and I never underestimated her. However, I also knew she shouldn't underestimate me.

Silence blanketed the house; not even the hoot of an owl broke the stillness. Convinced that Immy had returned to her own room and bed, I gathered my weapons, boots, and clothing, moving them to the farthest corner of the room. Kneeling down, I cast one last furtive glance at the door before lifting the loosened floorboards to reveal my hiding spot. Just deep enough to conceal my belongings, I tucked them inside.

Unfortunately, if someone were to discover my hiding place, I could explain away the clothing, but justifying the number of daggers would be more difficult without revealing the truth.

After replacing the floorboards, I finally slid into bed. Perhaps it was the events of the night, but it felt wonderful to finally be resting. I stretched out and rolled onto my side, yet my eyes refused to close.

I turned over and stared at the ceiling.

Chapter Eight

Livie

"Did you hear the news about Drucilla Billingsley?" William whispered, leaning over to grab a glass of wine from a passing servant. "I heard she was caught kissing the Earl of Benning's son in the garden at the Kingsley ball. Do you think she did it on purpose to secure a marriage proposal?"

Not a topic I wanted to discuss while hoping to catch more interesting society gossip. I had cheated death only two nights ago, feigning illness to prevent anyone from seeing my neck. This evening, the cut on my throat was concealed by my hair, delicately styled to cascade down the column of my neck, but the slightest movement could reveal it.

I had begged my maid for help that morning, as she had done since my arrival. Bethany was my go-between for messages, my secret ally for anything I needed, and she quickly assisted me in styling my hair perfectly for the day, from breakfast to this dinner party at Ansel and Aislie Bradford's home in Westminster. The money I slipped into Bethany's pocket assured her loyalty to me.

Now, I stood beside William in the parlor, awaiting the announcement for dinner. My gaze scanned the guests. Uncle Winston was speaking with Ansel and Percival by the large fireplace, a fire burning low within. Ansel's animated hand gestures punctuating his words, while Aunt Marjory and Immy conversed with Aislie on a small sofa. Other guests mingled in small clusters, but they held little interest for me: a banker and his wife, another member of parliament with his wife and daughter. These social gatherings were dull at best, and too small to get any intriguing information. At least I had William with me, and he was good company.

"You know as well as I do that she did it on purpose," I whispered, taking a sip of my own wine. "Drucilla has been eyeing Gregory since she came out earlier this year. No doubt they'll be married before everyone leaves town."

William murmured his agreement as I noticed the servants drifting in and out like ghosts, refreshing the wine with white-gloved service. Ansel and Aislie were not among the highest in society, but that didn't stop them from trying. Aislie had practically begged Aunt Marjory to attend her dinner party.

A brief gasp escaped my lips when I saw a servant enter the room, Grayson following behind him, his eye covered by the dreadful patch that made him look so sinister. He didn't need it to appear dangerous. I wondered if I was one of the few who had seen him without the patch.

"Captain Grayson Valle and Marchioness Nadine Whitley," the short, balding servant announced.

The banker's wife and her daughter drifted toward him quickly as Nadine nodded to the two women. Dressed entirely in black, I wondered if Grayson had chosen that color to intimidate others. It didn't seem to bother Nadine, who kept a tight hold on his arm. I stifled a laugh at the ominous look on his face, the slight crease between his brows.

"Indeed," William breathed.

"What is it?" I asked.

"He looks dangerous. And you, cousin, had him front and center at the Kingsley ball, didn't you? I heard that he danced with no one but you that evening."

That was a good way to put it, I thought. I would have offered to introduce them, but the moment Grayson's focus landed on me,

I froze. If his eyes could talk, I wondered what they would say. They darkened, if that was even possible. He looked at me as if he could see right through me.

Nadine took one look at me and whispered to him, causing his gaze to abruptly pull away from mine. Her jealousy would have made me snicker behind my fan, but I didn't care about their relationship. Or maybe I did. Just a little.

"Why is he looking at you that way?" William leaned closer to whisper.

"I couldn't say. Our conversation at the ball was limited, and I have not come into contact with him since."

Lies, lies, lies. I hated lying to William of all people, but no one could know I'd snuck out. No one could know I'd been in his bed, albeit innocently. Discreetly, I glanced at Percival. Although he was still listening to whatever Ansel was discussing, his eyes hardened at the sight of Grayson.

The urge to grab Grayson and demand to know what was happening overwhelmed me. The way the two men looked at each other screamed hatred. I imagined Grayson was accustomed to being seen as a rival in all things.

"He's looking at you as though he could eat you."

I choked on my wine, delicately covering it by clearing my throat. William never minced words with me, especially when we were out of earshot of his mother. I caught Aunt Marjory's disapproving gaze, but I couldn't help it.

William continued his gossip, leaning in even closer. "Do you think she's warming his bed?"

"Who?" I asked, louder than I'd intended.

"Grayson Valle. Do you think—"

"I heard you the first time, William Thornton."

The question made me uncomfortable. I didn't want to think about him in Nadine's bed. I didn't understand why I felt such suffocating jealousy. The man meant nothing to me, except that he had information about my activities that left me uneasy. In a single moment, he could ruin me. When Nadine's gaze traveled to me and met my stare, it wasn't filled with kindness.

Given the temperature shift in the room, it might matter. The appearance of Grayson with Nadine on his arm would spread faster than the gossip about Drucilla kissing Gregory. Whispers suggested that Nadine sought another suitable husband, although as a marchioness, she had enough wealth and reputation to sustain herself. Her husband had been wealthy enough for her to remain unattached without a care. I wondered why she would feel the need to secure another husband when it wasn't at all necessary.

I stood, earning a from from from William, who moved with me when I took a step away. "What are you doing?"

"I'm going to speak with him."

William grabbed my wrist, lightly but noticeably. "Do not dare."

My gaze swung to him. "And why should I not?"

"Gossip. Do not give them anything to take out of this room. Not with the baron here, watching your every move." I snorted in derision. "You know he's going to ask my father for your hand in marriage, Livie."

"It does not matter. My conversation with the marchioness and Mr. Valle would only be polite."

William didn't get the chance to stop me because Percival detached himself from his conversation with Uncle Winston and Ansel and strode toward us. His determined expression rooted me to the spot, making me wonder why he was suddenly so urgent to seek me out. This was not the place for me to lose my composure.

He inclined his head toward William. "Would you mind terribly if I begged a few moments of Olivia's time before dinner?"

With the manners befitting his station, William gave him a slight bow before flashing an impish smile in my direction. Watching William leave us, I could only muse to myself. *That man is more intelligent than most, and hides it even better. It will only be a matter of time before he sweeps someone off her feet. May God help the woman who does.* I smiled innocently at Percival, who drew me toward the window with a hand on my elbow.

"We will be wed, Olivia," he began, sighing as though reluctant to have this conversation. "There is no denying how we can benefit each other. I think it is time you accepted my proposal."

"I can't help but wonder why you are pressing me so much. Surely, there are other wealthier, *titled* young ladies for you to choose from."

I glanced around, noting that Grayson watched us carefully, as did Aunt Marjory.

"It's come to my attention that you've been leading a double life, *Livie.*"

I nearly broke my careful composure. Instead, I drew in the slightest, albeit shaky, breath. If I hadn't, I would have dropped my façade altogether and slapped him. Time slowed while the rest of the room continued to move.

If it could have, my heart would have stopped beating. I stared straight at him, not wanting to meet his gaze but trying to gauge how he might have learned anything different from what I allowed others to see. He dropped his hand from my arm and took a quick sip of his drink.

"There is no need to be frightened."

"This isn't fright," I scoffed, keeping my voice soft. "I would like to know how you think I am leading a double life."

He chuckled, low and dark. "I think you know the answer to that, my dear. Not only do I have proof that your father has not been on the right side of the law, but I also have it on good authority that you've been seen near Wapping. Imagine if others knew."

I saw stars, struggling to control my breathing while searching for a way to refute his claims. If what he said was true, I was not the only one in danger of being questioned but it also put Niles at risk. Anyone I'd been in contact with could be affected, not to mention my father would be pursued in earnest.

For three years, I'd been exceedingly careful to ensure no one knew I frequented the docks, engaging in activities that could lead me straight to the gallows. And then Grayson had stumbled upon me in a rare situation. It seemed strange that Percival was threatening me within days since Grayson had found me out. I never thought anyone would uncover my secrets.

"I see," I whispered. "Assuming you are correct, why would a pillar of society like you want to marry a woman who is leading a double life?"

The corner of his lips quirked up. "Quite easily. With my name, no one will ever look your way again. Of course, your evening travels will need to cease immediately. I won't have my wife risking my good name."

I let out a short laugh. "God forbid your wife put herself in danger, either."

Ignoring the jab, he continued. "The way I see it, you have two choices. You can either marry me, or I can hand you over to the authorities for acts of piracy. And Olivia, I would hate to see such a pretty neck stretch."

No gentleman would threaten such a thing. Yet he did, all to get what he wanted. Why, in all of heaven, did he want me so badly? I was beyond control, and should my secrets be discovered, chaos would be the least of his worries. If anyone suspected I was involved with my father's possible illegal dealings doors would slam shut. Elias Blackwood was one of the most sought-after pirates on the seas. It may only be for questioning, but if Percival stated true, the authorities would skip questioning and lead him straight to the gallows, as Captain William Kidd had been only five years ago.

"Imagine what a scandal like this would bring to your family," he continued, his gaze steady on me while I refused to look at him. "Perhaps Winston is involved in whatever it is you've been doing in Wapping," he added softly.

"You bloody blackguard," I breathed, keeping my voice low.

He chuckled again, moving closer. Too close.

"I won't deny what I want." He raised an eyebrow, his blue eyes gleaming with victory. "What shall it be? The gallows or a baroness?"

If my father could see me now, he would be furious at my lack of caution. Inwardly, I cursed. I *had* been careful. How did Percival discover this, and how could I have been so careless? I tried to imagine what my father would do, but I already knew the answer. He would kill him.

I lifted my chin.

"I will give you some time to think about it, but I believe I already know your answer. You don't seem the type of *lady* who would allow others to suffer on your behalf. I've invited your family to dine with me on Wednesday. We shall make the announcement then."

I wanted to rage, scream, and claw his face bloody for putting me in this position, but I could do none of that. The Livie Blackwood, who had lived amongst the most aristocratic people, would never cause a scene; however, the girl who had climbed riggings and palm trees would absolutely cause one.

"I promise, being married to me will have its benefits. So long as you curb your wild evening escapades. I must also insist on no further communication with your father."

"I don't-"

"Come now, my dear, do not think me a simple-minded man. Of course you're in contact with him. Why else would you be sneaking off to the docks?"

Numbness swept through me, a deathly feeling as though life had just ended.

"I have not heard from my father since he sent me here following my mother's death," I said between clenched teeth.

"Nevertheless, I know what the blackguard did to your

mother, and I'm not above doing what needs to be done so his daughter does not fall through my hands." He moved closer, and my hackles rose. "If I couldn't have your mother, I'll take you. I've bided my time long enough."

"My mother? You know nothing about my mother," I snapped, becoming decidedly agitated with him. Threatening me was one thing, but prying into my life was quite another.

His head tilted to the side. "Did you not know? Your mother was my betrothed before she was abducted in route and nearly sold into slavery for her purity until your father snatched her away from her captors. Regardless of whether her abductor or your father sullied her good name, the damage was already done, and the betrothal called off."

Shock stunned me, yet I kept my poise. I knew my mother had been abducted on her way to her intended husband before the ship she'd been held on was overtaken by my father. I did not know that Percival Monteclaire had been her betrothed. My father so rarely spoke of her. How would I have known such a thing?

The thought of this man becoming my husband made my skin crawl. That he had been betrothed to my mother all those years ago made the feeling so much worse. Percival had weaseled his way into Aunt Marjory's good graces, attempted to flatter me into accepting a courtship, and now shoved his ambition upon me with no choice left to make.

I huffed a laugh at the absurdity, the sound hidden behind the announcement for dinner. Offering me the crook of his arm, I glanced at it and then back up at him, astounded that he thought I would allow him to escort me into dinner after threatening me. When I looked back up, Grayson had swiftly appeared beside me, extending his arm.

"If I might escort you to dinner, Miss Blackwood?" he asked, his tone filled with intrigue and his eyes dancing as if delighting in thwarting Percival's offer.

I inclined my head toward Percival, sliding my arm within Grayson's. "You'll have your answer soon. In the meantime, I request that you give me time to think about it."

Percival looked ready to commit murder with his eyes narrowing at Grayson. "Very well. I shall escort Nadine into dinner, as you've left her unattended."

As he walked away, Grayson tightened his grip on my arm and continued slowly toward the door. "Are you well?"

"Well enough, thank you for asking."

"And what, if I may ask, answer must you give the baron?"

He already knew, not needing to ask, since I had shared enough information about the baron's pursuit. "You already know," I replied tightly. "He's giving me a few days to give him an answer, but he has officially asked for my hand in marriage."

Percival hadn't exactly framed his proposal as a question, but I kept my lips closed with that detail. No one needed to know that he had discovered my nightly activities or that he was leaving me with no choice but to accept him as my husband.

"It's not official until he asks your uncle," Grayson pointed out.

Not true, but that didn't mean this situation had lost its indignation. As much as I had known this day would come, the fact that he threatened me with what should be undercover operations infuriated me. No one should know about it. How the hell did he find out, and who else could? The only ones who could betray me were in this room or Niles. Niles would never do so without risking his own neck.

Grayson led me into the dining room, which was elegantly set for fifteen. The long table sparkled with crystal glasses, and the white dishes were impeccably arranged, each place setting perfectly coordinated. He pulled out a chair for me next to William, bless him, and once I was seated, he took the chair beside me.

Flanked by them, I now had to face Percival, who was glaring across the table. Clearly, he did not like the fact that Grayson had swooped in. Again. Inwardly, I smiled, even as William leaned over to tease me about the seating arrangement before picking up his wine.

"Did you betray my secrets?" I whispered once Grayson sat beside me.

Grayson dipped his head, his mouth so close to my ear that the warmth of his breath stirred the wisps of hair at my nape. "I did not betray you, Livie. Why? Has something happened?

Not about to admit to him the predicament I was in, I shook my head.

He kept his lips close to my ear. "I may have a solution for you, but you won't like it."

I turned my head, our gazes clashing like a force to be reckoned with. "And?"

"This is highly improper, but you could run away."

I laughed softly. If only it were that easy. Running away would only solidify my father's claims that I was nothing more than a fanciful girl throwing away my future. His angry words after finding me with Edward came rushing back as though they had been spoken only yesterday. Even if I had access to an inheritance from my mother's family, there would be nowhere I could go where I wouldn't be known.

"And here I thought you would offer me a place in your bed, at least while you're here at port. Why would you suggest such a thing?"

"That isn't such a terrible idea," he said as he shrugged, as though it suddenly seemed plausible even when it wasn't so many days ago that I had actually been in his bed. "I would rather compromise your reputation, or see you run away than find such a beautiful woman wasted on that man. Wealth be damned."

I laughed again, a tingling sensation spreading through me. Rarely did I laugh like this in public. "As much as I would love to be a damsel in distress, I can assure you I am not. I would never put my family at risk regarding my reputation. Not to mention, if

I did find myself compromised, Uncle Winston would simply insist that you marry me. As for running away, I have no means to support myself, which means an even more dire situation than becoming a mistress to such a handsome man as yourself."

His eyes darkened at my compliment. "Nevertheless, my offer stands should you need it. You need only ask."

"I appreciate that, Grayson. Truly."

My head spun from the presence of this man. He appeared so rigid at times, yet here he was, offering me solutions to my problem. Neither was viable, but he'd voiced them all the same. I couldn't help but wonder what Grayson would do with me as a mistress. I knew he had wealth, enough to keep a mistress comfortable, though living in Mayfair wouldn't be an option. That he'd even thought about preventing my acceptance to Percival made me think twice about his motives. He was a man of the sea, commanding a crew as my father did. The suggestion only made me more suspicious of him.

Chapter Nine

Grayson

The ladies remained in the dining room while the men retreated to the parlor for brandy. I wanted nothing more than to stay by Livie, feeling an inexplicable pull toward her. When I spoke to her in this setting, she gave no hint of being the daughter of a man rumored to have turned pirate. On the contrary, her composure was remarkable for someone rumored to have spent her youth amid piracy. There was not a trace of the jargon or mannerisms typically learned in the company of men.

My only indication that Livie could be more involved with her father, even when his whereabouts were in question, and aside from finding her near the ships at Wapping, was her constantly shifting eyes. She watched others closely, making quick glances to mark the exits upon entering a room.

I had yet to ask her about it, and I wouldn't unless provoked. The Baron of Vensworth was a troublesome issue that I needed to resolve. Even if she accepted his proposal, it would take weeks after the banns were posted, and I didn't have weeks. The longer I stayed in London, the more I abhorred it. As for Percival, I didn't like the man at all. I watched him study her whenever I could, his eyes possessively devouring her. Even though he was old enough to be her father, men like Percival only wanted her as a possession. It wasn't that I feared he would mistreat her; it was that he would place her under a shroud of protection that would eventually dim the light in her eyes. Even knowing her for a short time, I knew she craved adventure.

The entitled and arrogant man made me wish he were someone I could easily dispose of. Livie deserved better. She would never know a moment's peace as his wife. I could be completely wrong, but she didn't seem to like him much during the times I interrupted their conversations.

She might be able to hide it from everyone else, but she couldn't hide from me.

Her words regarding making her my mistress reduced me to thinking about her more than just the daughter of a man I considered my enemy. Thankfully, she hadn't accepted. The thought made the blood hum through my veins, but I would not take Elias Blackwood's daughter to my bed, no matter how pleasant to the eyes she was. Plenty of women with reputations that preceded them and held to much fewer standards had done well enough.

The thought did occur to me that having her as a mistress would mean keeping her close. I had yet to uncover any further information about my stolen cargo, but I knew enough to know now that Elias Blackwood had been behind the capture of our ship. I just needed proof before I could hand the information over to the authorities and permanently place the title of outlaw on him. I pushed back the memories of Adam, his blood on my hands mixed with the ocean water when I'd pulled him to shore. Nothing I could have done would have prevented his death.

"Captain Valle," Winston said, approaching me with his drink in hand. "We haven't seen you in many years. My condolences for your brother. I heard he met with a rather untimely death."

I inclined my head. Untimely death, indeed.

"I've been busy."

Busy chasing Elias Blackwood, I thought. I felt so much closer to finding where Elias might be hiding, even if it meant getting closer to his daughter. Surely she must know where to find him. I glanced at Percival, who was talking with Ansel, tempted to see if I could gather any information from Winston while Percival was otherwise occupied.

"Business been good?"

"As good as it can be. I'm not nearly as aggressive in my pursuit of Spanish vessels as others, but when the opportunity presents itself, I do enjoy a challenge." I raised my glass before taking a drink.

"Gentlemen," Percival called loudly. "May I have a moment of Captain Valle's time?"

I raised an eyebrow, curious about what he could possibly want to say. "What can I do for you, Percival?"

Winston, suddenly realizing that Percival wanted to speak to me alone, nodded and moved away to converse with Ansel. I took a long drink, eyeing Percival over the rim of my glass.

"I've noticed you lurking around Miss Blackwood."

Calmly, I set my glass down on the table and folded my arms in front of me, ready for a confrontation. If he thought he could deter me from her, he was sadly mistaken. I wouldn't give up my pursuit of information until I had it.

"Olivia is a pleasure to be around, and more beautiful than any woman I've seen among this year's eligible young ladies. Wouldn't you agree?"

His eyes hardened, and his mouth set in a grim line. "I would. Which is why you will leave Olivia alone. She will soon accept my proposal and become my wife. I won't have you sullying her reputation by lingering where you don't belong."

"Is that so?" I replied. "You don't think a woman like Olivia can think for herself? Judge when a situation might not be in her best interest?"

He chuckled, a dry laugh. "Olivia is young. She doesn't know better."

"Doesn't she? It seems to me that Olivia is an intelligent young woman, capable of recognizing when she might be led astray.

That, and you are old enough to be her father."

His lips pressed into a tight line. "Older men have married younger women. It's not for you to judge the age difference between us."

I held myself in check. "It seems to me that you are unaware of where I am from."

"I know where you are from, Captain Valle. What does that have to do with Olivia?"

"I believe you knew Daphne Lebeau. Her mother?" It gave me great pleasure to see the surprise flit across his eyes. "Daphne and my mother were friends. Very good friends."

I watched the baron closely for any sign of emotion, surprise at the very least, but I would take anything.

"Again, irrelevant. It seems only fitting that I take the young woman as my wife. As you probably know, I am widowed, and as such, I need a suitable wife to manage my home."

"And any inheritance she could bring into the marriage to refill your dwindling coffers," I said dryly. "Don't think I don't know enough people in this city to be aware that while you have your title, your fortune is rather modest. Livie as your wife would remedy that, as well as continue to provide you entrance into the most elite circles."

Percival sputtered softly, confirming all my assumptions. He didn't want Livie for anything other than her fortune and family name behind him.

"You will address her as Miss Blackwood from this moment on," he snapped. "I do not give you leave to address her with such familiarity."

I hadn't realized that the conversation in the room had come to a complete stop until I glanced at Winston and Ansel, who were staring openly. Had they been listening to this nonsense? When the men resumed their conversation, I turned back to Percival.

He was seething with fury. "Stay away from Olivia."

I leaned closer to him. "You might be somewhat compelling

here in London, but that power doesn't extend beyond this realm. I have many friends who cross the seas, as I do here. I suggest you think twice before threatening me."

"Stay away from her, Valle," he repeated. "She isn't for the likes of you."

Turning on his heel, Percival returned to Winston and Ansel, though I sensed our conversation had left him nearly ready to explode. How fortunate for him that he hadn't threatened me in Wapping. Southwark was not far from Wapping, and I had enough friends on both sides of the river to ensure his body would never be found again.

Chapter Ten

Voices from the parlor piqued my interest. Aunt Marjory was speaking to Immy in her authoritative tone, however unlucky for my cousin. We may not get along as well as William and I, but that didn't mean I wanted her to suffer under her mother's power. After my late-night conversation with Immy several evenings ago, I was acutely aware of what might be happening in our home. If William had been the one I found in my room, I knew he would never betray me as Immy would. Although Immy hadn't gone directly to Aunt Marjory after that night, it didn't mean she wouldn't. I hoped my threat had immobilized her.

Dressed in a flowery beige dress, the angry red slice on my neck was still concealed by the delicately curled hairstyle I'd been wearing for the past several days. The length of my hair barely covered it, but thankfully the throbbing had ceased, and it no longer pained me when I stretched my neck. I counted my lucky stars that the man hadn't aimed more accurately with his dagger, and that the wound was to the lower side of my neck rather than the center. Although it had faded to a blemish, it could still arouse suspicion.

Aunt Marjory was bound to comment on it if she saw any marks on my otherwise unblemished skin. I knew she would. I ran my palm along the smooth wooden railing as I descended, taking my time to reach the bottom of the staircase that split the house into two sides.

"He won't change his mind, Mother. And he shouldn't."

Immy's soft voice drifted from the parlor. I slipped down the rest of the wide staircase and walked silently toward the open doorway, stopping just beyond it. I wondered what they were discussing.

"I thought you were coming closer to receiving a proposal from Arvil Whitaker or Callum Benson? Perhaps we might need to look further into Percival Monteclaire. He's not a duke or even a viscount, but he is charming enough. There is still time for him to realize his error in choosing Olivia over you. All you need to do is show him that you are the better choice," Aunt Marjory said, her voice high and authoritative.

I pressed my lips together. I had known about her jealousy regarding my potential to marry before Immy ran deep, but her attempt to persuade my cousin to win the baron from me went too far. Not that I would mind *not* marrying him, especially since I felt compelled to under threat. Yet, I stayed to hear Immy's reply.

"Olivia deserves to be happy, Mother."

I almost snorted. Happy? Never had I heard Immy refer to my comfort, especially my happiness. Perhaps my threat to her in my room had done more good than harm. I doubted that would produce a marriage proposal from Percival. Unbeknownst to them, Percival had already proposed to me. Until I accepted, he would not issue another.

Aunt Marjory scoffed. "As do you."

"Olivia is older than me. She should marry first."

"She is not my daughter. *You* are."

My heartbeat quickened, irritation rising with it. I didn't get along with my aunt as well as I did with my uncle, and I had tried my best to stay out of her way these last few years. Even as my father's sister, my own blood, there was always something in her eyes that made me feel like I didn't belong here. I never had.

Being dropped at her doorstep, I had become a burden she hadn't expected. She didn't need to voice it, but she did her best to fold me into her family's daily life. Despite her evident jealousy and the rigidly run household, I knew she meant well. I didn't blame her for wanting more for her own daughter than for me. Being a mother couldn't be further from my future, but I understood her need to see Immy married first.

"And you would see William married before Olivia as well?" Immy asked.

"If I need to, yes. However, your brother's marital status differs from your own. My daughter should be married before my niece, and the baron has a comfortable enough life, even if he is not nearly as wealthy as we are. He's wealthy enough to keep you well off without missing what you're accustomed to."

"I think Olivia will make a lovely baroness, although he is a little old for her, don't you think?"

At the sound of a snap, I was certain Aunt Marjory had slapped Immy's hand with her fan. She would never slap her in the face. She may be stern, but she would never strike anyone. At least I did not think that of her.

"Age is merely a number. If the roles were reversed, and they may still be, you are never to think such a thing. Do you understand?"

"Of course."

"Now then. Percival has invited us to the Vensworth home for a dinner party on Wednesday, and you will be on your best behavior. You will smile at the baron, flirt with him, and make him realize that you are the better choice." Silence. "Do you hear me, Imogen?"

"I hear you," she bit out.

I stepped back and turned right into William, who grinned from ear to ear, having caught me eavesdropping on the conversation. Dressed in a pair of tan breeches and a light-colored tunic, his brown eyes danced with mischief.

"You see?" he whispered, playfulness in his deep voice. "You have been nothing short of a burden since you arrived. Now Mother is forcing Imogen to show you up at a dinner party that you will also be attending."

Though his words would otherwise have stung, he was only teasing me. My eyes narrowed. I knew there was jealousy among the women in this house toward me, but I hadn't realized until now how deeply it ran. If Aunt Marjory wanted Imogen to marry Percival so badly, why hadn't she stepped forward and said something?

Certainly, other eligible bachelors could be found. At my age, I had time to seek a suitable match. Suddenly, anger overwhelmed me, and I wanted nothing more than to flee. Although William meant well, staying near him would only lead to my lashing out. Not at him, of course, but at the women in the parlor.

"Nothing to say?" William urged.

"Jealousy runs rampant in this house," I replied. "If I ever accept Percival's marriage proposal, or any other for that matter, Immy should rejoice that I would no longer reside here. If I'm not mistaken, I think she rather enjoys having me here. Wouldn't you say, Will?"

His lips pressed together, a smile threatening to break free as he shook his head. "You and your nicknames, Liv."

I smiled. "Would you be so kind as to tell your mother and sister I went out for some air? I shall be back for tea shortly."

"You can't go out unchaperoned!" he exclaimed, snaking out a hand as if he could stop me, but I danced out of reach.

"Watch me."

Without making a show of hurrying away from the rascal, I turned toward the front door. I needed a stroll to think about my future, or lack thereof. I couldn't stay in this house any longer than necessary for two people who held such disdain for me. Yet if Immy had even a small chance at happiness, I would gladly give it to her on a silver platter, our differences aside.

I could hear William's footsteps striding away, no doubt to inform Marjory that I'd gone out without the benefit of a chaperone. *For shame*, I snickered silently. I thought he was on my side.

The servant was just pulling the door open for me, and I smiled at him in gratitude for his thoughtfulness. Seconds later, I realized he hadn't opened the door for me but for someone who had arrived, and I ran right into the man.

Grayson's strong arms closed around me, ensuring I wouldn't fall backward from colliding with his sturdy frame. Flustered, I looked up into a familiar dark eye. He'd donned his eyepatch for the occasion, and his visible eye danced as he met my gaze. With his dark brown hair pulled back and that cleft in the center of his chin, he looked formidable. My eyes widened at the realization that Grayson had come to call. I pulled away, but he kept his hands on me, as though ensuring I wouldn't run.

"My apologies, Miss Blackwood," he murmured, his low voice capable of sending waves over a still surface.

His deep voice rumbled through me, or perhaps it was his hands on me, or the way his eyes captured my gaze and refused to release me. I could stare into his eyes endlessly. They were such a mixture of darkness and light, yet so beautiful.

"What are you doing here?" I whispered, pulling away from him in desperate need to escape or be spellbound, but he held firm despite the servant waiting to shut the door.

My mind raced, wondering why Grayson was at our doorstep. His offer last night at dinner had taken me by surprise. Surely, he wasn't here to ask for my uncle's permission. Perhaps he intended to tell my uncle about my nightly activities, though he had given his word he wouldn't. I searched his face for any sign of his intentions, but none appeared.

"Your uncle is expecting me."

"Why?"

When he smiled, all of his teeth were visible and pearly white. I had known that from the few times I'd been in his company, but after seeing him at night without the eyepatch, I wondered if I was now prone to delusions. He cleaned up nicely. There was no trace of the man from the docks, who very much looked like a man of the sea. While in London, Grayson managed two different lifestyles, just as I did.

He tsked. "My business here is with your uncle. That is all you need to know, O-*livia*."

I tugged free from his grip, suddenly alarmed.

"Livie," William called from behind me. "Captain Valle! How are you today?"

When his hands finally left me, I stepped back.

"I am very well, Mr. Thornton."

"He has a meeting with your father," I said.

Stopping beside me, William extended his hand for Grayson to take. It didn't escape my notice how tightly the two men clasped their hands, eyes locked and backs straight. How positively stiff, I thought.

"What brings you by, Captain?" William asked.

I wanted to tell Grayson that he wouldn't divulge anything, as he wouldn't admit it to me, but Grayson answered before I had the chance.

"Your father and I have business to discuss." He looked pointedly at me. "As much as I would like to catch up with you, William, I do have a meeting to keep. If you would be so kind as to point me toward your father's study, I would be grateful," Grayson said, finally looking at William.

"I'll lead the way, but I must warn you that my father already has a visitor in his office."

William turned, giving me a sidelong glance as I fell into step behind him and Grayson, walking with a swish of my skirt toward the rear of the house where Uncle Winston's study was located.

Our walk toward the study only heightened my burning desire to find out what business he might have. Undoubtedly, he would be meeting with Uncle Winston in his office with the door closed. I didn't consider myself someone who listened at doors, but I would give it a try today, especially as many times as I'd interacted with Grayson. I had to know his business here.

I took a quick glance into the parlor and saw Aunt Marjory and Immy idly doing needlepoint, clearly too engrossed in their task to notice us passing by. Hopefully, neither would notice my absence. I was positive that I could not sit and do needlepoint today with my thoughts so wild.

The door to the study swung open unexpectedly, and Uncle Winston strode out, followed by Percival. The look of triumph on Percival's face confirmed the reason for his visit. While I had been upstairs in my bedroom, he had been here asking permission to take my hand in marriage. Fury, hot and uncomfortable, bubbled up inside me.

"Ah, Captain Valle," Uncle Winston said. "Please do come in. Good day, Percival, and I thank you for coming to see me today. We shall speak soon."

William and I shuffled to the side, making way for Percival to walk past. At the last moment, he turned to me and took my hand, pressing his lips to my knuckles. Once again, I resisted the urge to yank my hand away.

"Olivia, a pleasure to see you." He straightened and took a step before turning back to address Grayson, his voice just above a whisper. "You're too late, Captain Valle."

Dread filled me as Percival gave me a short bow and departed. Uncle Winston and Grayson disappeared into the office a moment later. Exchanging a glance with William, we turned and left them to their business until Uncle Winston closed the door. I paused just outside, looking down the hallway to ensure no one was coming before leaning against the door.

I had just settled against it, straining to hear anything through the thick wood, when William joined me with a mischievous smile. If Aunt Marjory came out of the parlor and caught us eavesdropping, there would be hell to pay.

William leaned close as we pressed our ears against the wood, hoping to catch whatever we could. When he whispered something, I swatted at him with my arm to keep him quiet. Clearly, he had never listened at doors before. But nor had I.

"Livie is special," I heard my uncle say.

Distinctly, as though a door didn't separate us, I heard a scoff reverberate from deep in Grayson's throat. I drew back, staring at the door with narrowed eyes. Uncle Winston would not dare tell anyone about my true circumstances. He wouldn't.

"That's what every father says when selling his daughter to the highest bidder," Grayson replied, his voice raising the hairs on my arms, echoing something I had heard before. "I find it humorous that her uncle is the one attempting to convince me of her worth."

"I'm not her father," Uncle Winston reminded him. "You requested a meeting. I hardly think you are here to discuss Livie with me."

"Actually, I am."

A gasp slipped from my lips as I glanced at William. His eyes widened at the revelation, but I pressed my finger to my lips. Why would Grayson be here discussing me? Overwhelmed by panic at the thought that Grayson might tell Uncle Winston about my actions, or worse, concoct a lie that we had been intimate as he'd suggested, I reached for the door handle. I didn't know Grayson well enough to know what he might be speaking to my uncle about, but I intended to stop it. William caught my wrist and shook his head.

"What do you think you're doing?" he whispered frantically.

To barge in and interrupt a private conversation, even one about me, would embarrass my uncle. Given the family's status in society, I couldn't do that. Uncle Winston would be humiliated. Word traveled fast.

Before I could respond, I heard Uncle Winston again. "I won't need to convince you of anything, Captain Valle. You've met my Liv, you understand."

Despite the direction the conversation was taking, my mouth twitched into a threatening smile. *My Liv.* William sighed and stepped away from the door, pursing his lips. He knew his father had a soft spot for me, though I hadn't done anything to encourage it. Living here, I knew it bothered Immy to no end that my uncle had accepted me into the household with such ease.

While they shared a special bond as father and daughter, I'd spent many hours in Uncle Winston's study playing chess while he peppered me with questions about sailing, the men on those ships, and my father. In reality, I believed my uncle doted on me to keep my father's wrath at bay.

My father could be a formidable man, and I was a ward in his sister's household. Despite whatever I might have done to be ousted from his ship, I knew my father believed that his treatment would make me stronger, just as it had when I was a young girl learning the ways of his ship and crew. But my uncle didn't know that. He would treat me how he would want his own daughter to be treated.

"I've spent enough time with *Liv* to understand," Grayson said.

"Have you now?" Uncle Winston continued. "Percival has been pursuing her hand for quite some time. If you are here to request her hand, I'm afraid you are too late."

"Do you think that's wise? Allowing a man twice her age to marry her?"

My jaw dropped. Grayson knew I would accept Percival's proposal. Why did it matter now? I'd told him as much, though he had responded as if he had more to say. While I didn't know it at the time, I had a feeling this meeting with Uncle Winston had everything to do with me and nothing to do with Percival.

Uncle Winston paused for dramatic effect before continuing. "Livie has no other prospects, Grayson. I owe it to her to find a suitable match. Percival is titled and wealthy, although I have it on good authority that Livie has not yet accepted his proposal. She would have informed me of such news, given her . . . aversion to marrying him."

I covered my mouth to stifle the cry of outrage that threatened to echo through the door. William and I exchanged wide-eyed glances. I'd already told Grayson that I couldn't run away, or even be a mistress to him. What was he doing here?

"Livie isn't easily backed into a corner. If you push her, you'll likely regret it. Percival as well. Mr. Valle, please take my advice and let things unfold naturally."

I nearly whirled away from the door. Never before had I felt such overwhelming anger during my years here. The sudden urge to throw open the door and give them both a severe tongue-lashing surged through me, but William still held onto my arm. Only he could prevent my actions, and he knew it would only give Grayson the upper hand.

"Captain, once the engagement is announced in a few days, the wedding will take place within three weeks of the banns. I can assure you, Percival is motivated to have Livie as his wife, and he will stop at nothing to make sure it happens."

I felt faint at the sudden rush of marriage, especially to Percival. I thought I would have had more time. It was too much to fathom. My life had begun to spiral out of control, and I had serious doubts about starting anew. Here, I had felt safe. Anywhere else, I felt powerless.

Chapter Eleven

Livie

"Are you unwell?" William asked, leaning in to look at me and trying to keep his voice low.

"I need to get away from here."

Before he could stop me, I grabbed a fistful of my skirt and marched away from the study toward the staircase, eager to escape before the two men emerged. The last thing I wanted was to face Grayson, who had indeed been too late to save me, if saving was what I needed.

I bounded up the staircase, not caring who might have seen me. I threw open my door and yanked at the ties of my stomacher to breathe as William entered behind me.

Niles. I needed to see Niles. I needed to get to him tonight and have him deliver a message to my father about what would unfold in a matter of weeks. A message would never reach him in time to stop this, but I had to try. I call Percival's bluff and stubbornly refuse his offer?

William waited at the door until I pushed it closed behind him. If anyone knew that I was now seriously considering running away, as Grayson suggested, he needed to know.

"What is going on, Livie? And what is on your neck?"

I laid my palm over the blemish.

William deserved to know what I had been keeping from him for the last three years, but revealing the truth, even to him, risked everything. If the rumors circulating about my father were proven true, they might not be as at risk as I was, but it would still affect them.

"Tell me what is happening. Tell me what I can do to help you."

I twisted my fingers together and pretended to study them. This conversation had come too quickly. There hadn't been enough time to think of something to tell him other than the truth.

"*Olivia*," he snapped.

I moved toward the window with a sigh, glancing at the brilliant green of the park across the way. It was still early spring, but the grass looked lush and inviting. As much as I needed fresh air, I committed to staying in my room for the time being.

"Such a lovely day," I said with a sigh.

"You are not changing the subject on me," he insisted. "What is happening? You swore you would never marry the baron, and yet it sounds like he's just asked Father for permission." Uncrossing his arms, he stepped closer, staring at my neck. "Is that a . . . cut on your neck? You must tell me."

"I'm not quite sure where to begin," I said. "If I tell you this, and you run to your father, he will be so angry with me."

His eyes widened. "What did you do?"

The truth spilled so easily from my lips, as though finally having someone to confess to have shaken everything loose. William listened patiently as I told him of my wish to control my own fate and future in this world, how I had been listening during social gatherings for any tidbit of information I could to bring to operate dockside and inform Niles, and how I had been involved in smuggling.

"Dear God, Livie, you should have told me sooner. I would have accompanied you to the docks rather than let you go alone. Is this why you've accepted the baron's proposal?"

"I haven't yet. Apparently, your father has. He must see the silver lining in the fact that once I'm the baron's wife, I should never have to worry about my father's choices coming to light.

They already suspect he's turned to pirating, and it's only a matter of time before they catch him. He'll be hanged, and me . . . I don't know what will become of me."

He smiled diabolically. "How positively exciting, cousin."

"I got this cut on my neck when I went to Wapping several nights ago. Remember when I spent two days abed, claiming illness? I . . . I got into a scuffle with some men, and Grayson Valle rescued me."

William laughed. "Please tell me that's only a tale, and that you were truly never in that much danger."

"Of course I was in danger, William! It's Wapping! But I dress accordingly. No one knows I'm a woman by the way I disguise myself. If they did, well . . . a healing cut on my neck would be the least of my worries."

"You must not go there again without me, Livie." He straightened his spine, his chivalry commendable.

"I was hoping my activities at the docks would yield enough money for me to leave this household without having to marry anyone. That is no longer true, but I fear that I cannot accept Percival's proposal."

My eyes hardened, staring deep into his to ensure he took me seriously.

"William Thornton, you mustn't tell anyone this. If I call his bluff, I may be brought in for questioning. Or . . ." I sighed, remembering Grayson's offer. "I could run away."

"Is that why Grayson is here? Is he taking you away from here?"

"I don't know why he was here, William. I would imagine he was trying to convince your father to withdraw his permission, for he's given me no hints that he wanted to court me. And I would still decline, as I have all the others over the last few years. I cannot marry anyone. Not now. This is not what I want for my future."

Turning, I gave him a tiny smile in hopes he wouldn't think my situation entirely dire, or perhaps I was trying to convince myself of it. His smile in return reassured me of his optimism, an optimism I wished I had, for I couldn't think of a single positive thing about this situation.

"You will not leave this house without an escort, Livie," he said. "I am serious."

I shook my head. "Please do not betray me, Will."

Laughing, he pulled me into an embrace. "I would never betray you. Liv."

Chapter Twelve

When everyone went to sleep that night, I had to be extra cautious slipping out to visit the docks. Part of me wondered if Percival had someone watching my window. He had warned me that my nightly activities needed to stop, just not when.

I couldn't lie still that night, anyway. My emotions swirled between fear, excitement, and anger. Suddenly, what I'd been doing for so long felt riskier than ever.

As I walked toward the docks, my heart ached at this goodbye. No longer did I have the comfort of knowing I would still be part of this, despite wanting to be done with it for so long. I found no solace in the realization that I would be trapped in this life forever. This life had never provided me with any comfort at all.

"Be a lady, do everything your husband tells you to do, never shout or speak your mind except when necessary." I snorted.

I was taking a terrible risk by coming here, not knowing if Percival had spies following me. William had tried to insist on coming, but I refused. I'd said enough by admitting to my secrets of these past years.

The familiarity of the dimly lit streets leading to the docks and the River Thames, where ships bobbed with the tides, gave me a comforting feeling that, no matter what might happen, perhaps I would return someday.

As it usually did, the closer I came to Wapping, the more at ease I felt. It was almost as though my presence responded to the place where I belonged. If I didn't intend to marry, perhaps I belonged on a ship.

As Grayson suggested, I could run away. So, I walked with my thoughts in the back of my mind, alert to my surroundings. It was still early in the evening, and the docks were alive with people. I melted into the crowd, hoping this time I wouldn't have any issues at the tavern.

Niles would be found when he wanted to, which meant I might be waiting for a while. I didn't mind, enjoying the atmosphere. The tangy smell of the river wafted through my senses, and my feet moved steadily along the street as shadows danced around me.

Every so often, a burst of laughter would threaten my focus, as men spilled in and out of taverns alongside the smell of sour ale. I picked up my pace, eager to reach *The Captain's Quarters*.

I wondered what Immy would say if she discovered me here. She would certainly be shocked and might even ask to join me. Immy had a missing passion in her life, I knew she did, but Aunt Marjory would forever be a thorn in her side. She would never allow her daughter to step outside the boundaries of propriety.

As I reached the tavern, I glanced around once more to take note of my surroundings. People dotted the streets, some looking for the type of woman who sold herself, while others walked home from an evening of dice and drinking. If Grayson hadn't left already, he might be loitering nearby. He never did say when he would be departing. It wouldn't surprise me if I saw him, hopefully knowing to stay away.

Almost to the door, I passed a group of swaggering men and looked up. My mistake was thinking Grayson might be among them. An audible gasp burst from my lips when I recognized one of the men. The next thing I knew, his hand shot out and grabbed my arm. Regardless, the hilt of my dagger hit my palm, ready to strike.

"As I live and breathe, if it isn't Livie Blackwood in the flesh."

The man pulled me closer, yanking my hood back to reveal my face while he leered. I could smell the ale on his breath and instantly recognized the jarring green of his eyes.

"Edward," I breathed, trying to pull free from his hold and create distance between us.

This had to be the worst luck, running into Edward after all these years, now of all times. I knew he hadn't died, and I'd told Niles as much. Now I knew what I had been fearing. I never thought it would be him who'd been feeding information about me to the wrong people.

"You nearly got me killed, love." He tilted his head to the side. "Do you know how agonizing it is to be beaten and left for dead in the baking sun? I barely had enough strength to move, let alone try to find a way off that blasted island."

"I nearly got you killed?" I shrieked. "Correct me if I'm wrong, Edward, but we both made choices on my father's ship. Perhaps you should have curbed your appetites."

I pushed against him, trying to dislodge his hand from my arm, only to see that smile curve his lips, reminiscent of the time when I was willingly in his arms, a naïve sixteen-year-old girl. Changing my tactic, I pulled away.

"I saved you," I snapped. "My father would have killed you and sent you free, right to the bottom of the ocean, but I convinced him to give you the slightest chance to live. Now, let me go."

He tsked, shaking his head. "I don't think I will. In fact, there are plenty of people who would love to know what Elias Blackwood and his daughter are doing these days."

I tilted my head, calling his bluff. "You wouldn't dare."

He shrugged. "But, seein' as you're here, I mights get something out'a it. Don't you think?"

No, I didn't think that would be good. What did he think he was going to do? Force me to do what we'd already done many times, not so many years ago? He knew something but didn't want to say. Why?

Without warning, though I completely expected it, he pushed me against the building until my back slammed against the hard wooden boards. I grunted, but the force hadn't dislodged my dagger sheathed in the belt at my waist. The front of my cloak bunched in his fists, and his face was alarmingly close to mine. He smiled, revealing charmingly crooked teeth. This couldn't be the same man who'd been my first love, my first everything.

"We could take up where we left off, y'know," he murmured, stepping closer and lowering his nose to brush against my jaw. "Like old times, Liv. I still remember how lively ya are. Just thinking about it, worth every lash I got."

He was drunk. I turned my head away, hoping he would think I was in distress, but he pulled me away from the wall only to throw me back against it. His eyes danced in the dim light coming from the tavern, filled with nothing but corruption and delight. The moment his tongue darted out to wet his lips, I brought my arm up and relished the sight of his green eyes widening with clarity.

A woman who could fight back was trouble. A woman with a weapon was a deadly mistake. I smirked, the blade touching that spot just beneath his chin, with enough pressure to make him tilt his face up to escape the bite of it.

"That's right," I whispered. "You haven't forgotten that my father taught me a thing or two, have you?"

I knew I should kill him, preventing any chance of him spreading rumors about what Livie Blackwood was doing down at the docks. Edward could bring me down just as well as Percival. My father was untouchable, and his place of hiding secure. I would be the one to pay the ultimate price.

A low laugh escaped him, but he remained still, hands still clutching my cloak. The men he'd been walking with were at the ready. They could prepare to help their friend all they wanted. My blade at his throat could cost him his life if they tried to intervene.

"Here is what is going to happen, Edward, *my love*," I said. "You're going to leave here with your companions, quietly, without bothering me further. You will tell no one about seeing me here."

"Or what?" he asked tightly.

"I have eyes and ears all over this town. You'll sleep with one eye open because you never know when someone who adores me will sneak in and slit your throat on my behalf. You'll keep your mouth closed about seeing me. Do you understand?"

He remained silent. Probably wise, given the situation with my dagger pressed against his flesh. Lies about having eyes and ears all over town would help if he believed them. It wasn't a lie that I would commission someone to slit his throat, though I didn't think it would come to that. As much as I didn't want to take anyone's life needlessly, my own was at stake here, and he had to know I was prepared to do what I had to.

Memories of what it had been like between us threatened to surface, but I pushed them back. It would never have worked, what we had. We were never meant to be anything more, despite the hushed promises we had once made.

"Do you understand?"

In answer, he released my cloak and held up his hands. "You may go, Livie Blackwood. Someday we will meet again. Perhaps under better circumstances. And I will not let you go so easily."

The blade lowered a fraction, enough for him to move away from me with his hands still in the air. There were too many of them against me should they decide to come at me, but I kept my dagger out and a wicked gleam in my eye.

"Edward," I called softly before he turned to leave. "I never regretted it. Only that we were caught."

I could have sworn the corner of his mouth lifted a fraction. It might have been a regret he would carry for the rest of his life, but at least he'd lived and gone free. That couldn't be said of many men my father had forced into a watery grave at the bottom of the ocean.

Only when they were all backing away and continuing on their way down the narrow street did I put my dagger away and released a heavy breath. In all the years I'd been traveling to Wapping, I'd never been recognized. Something was afoot, and I needed to speak with Niles. Now.

Chapter Thirteen

Grayson

I watched from the shadows as a group of men passed too closely to Livie while I tailed her, instantly prepared to come to her rescue again. Like clockwork, I knew she would come here after the meeting Winston had with Percival that morning.

I remained where I was, waiting to see if she needed me to swoop in and intervene after a man grabbed her and forced her against the building. If I kept rescuing her, she would resent me for it. A woman like Livie would always believe she could take care of herself. Perhaps she could, which made me stay rooted to my spot. Right now, she appeared pinned to the building, confidence in her eyes and a dagger gripped in her hand, hidden in the folds of her cloak from everyone but me.

The man seemed unaware, close enough to her to almost appear to be kissing her under the cloak of shadows, until she brought the dagger up so quickly that even I flinched. Livie possessed extraordinary talents. A woman with a foot in each world. I was fascinated.

With the dagger at his throat, she spoke to him so quietly that I couldn't hear the exchange. By the way he held up his hands and backed away slowly, I knew she had threatened him. What she had said, I couldn't guess.

The man and his friends left her, but not without her pausing to say something else to him, something that made him smile. I waited in the shadows while she put her dagger away and glanced around, disappearing into the tavern a moment later.

After a few moments, I strolled around to the back of the tavern, where the sounds of water lapping against the ships and docks were most prevalent. Most evenings, I slipped into the inn through the rear entrance, keeping my back protected.

Livie sat in her usual spot, as though Boon had reserved it especially for her, with her back against the wall and her hands curved around a mug of ale. I stepped silently toward the table, watching her glance around.

"Is anyone sitting there?" I asked.

The last thing I wanted was to startle a woman who carried so many daggers, but after witnessing what could have been another assault on her, I took my chances. When she turned toward me, her hood partially shadowing her flawless face and larger-than-life blue eyes, it momentarily stole my breath. I recovered quickly and motioned to the empty chair across from her.

The rolling of her eyes amused me.

"I didn't realize you were still at port. I would have thought your meeting with my uncle this morning would have sent you away," she muttered. "What did your meeting with him entail?"

Without invitation, I walked around the table and settled into the chair, raising a hand when the serving wench passed by. She smiled, all crooked teeth, and leaned down to display her ample bosom.

"What say ya, Captain? Fancy an ale, do ya?"

"I do, and make it quick."

When I turned back to Livie, her eyes had narrowed. I dared not display triumph. Yet.

"I tried to dissuade him from allowing you to marry that old goat. As for being here still, my ship is docked around the corner until my business here concludes."

"And your business is?"

"Not for you to concern yourself with. But I will be leaving soon, wind permitting. I told you I dislike this town." She tilted her head. "And I don't make it a point to frequent balls and dinners."

"Then why are you here, Grayson? Why have I run into you so many times?"

"I did it as a favor to Nadine. As you know, she's—"

"Widowed," she concluded.

I couldn't pinpoint what it was about Livie that made my blood pump faster and my heart thud a little harder, but her eyes conveyed emotions that her body didn't always reflect. A maddening combination of a woman with a mysterious past, danger thrumming through her veins, and the poise of a genteel lady navigating society. I wanted to know everything about the woman who had deceived so many, and so elegantly.

It was no wonder the baron wanted her so badly for himself, though I doubted he desired her for the same reasons I did. To him, she was merely a means to further his position. To me, she was at risk of becoming a dangerous liaison. Both of us intended to use her, and I wouldn't spend a second regretting it. Livie was a means to an end for me.

"If you could make this quick, I'm meeting someone," she said, pressing her back against the wall. "He doesn't like uninvited guests at our meetings."

The serving wench returned with my mug of ale, lingering for a moment while displaying her wares that I had never once partaken in. At least not with her. I nodded my gratitude and took a long drink before setting it on the table between us and leaning forward.

"Would you like to talk about Percival's meeting with your uncle this morning?"

"Should I?"

"Resigned to marry the old goat, are you?"

Her chin lifted.

"I thought so. Your uncle has given his permission, which

means you are as good as wed, is it not?" She folded her arms in front of her, jaw set. "What if I were to offer you a way out?"

"As much as I would like to, I won't kill him."

Throwing my head back, I laughed deeply. It felt like it had been too long since I'd truly laughed, and how refreshing it was. But she was dead serious with her mouth set in a grim line.

"Not kill him," I clarified. "Leave."

"Leave?"

"Leave London. With me. I told you running away was an option."

Her eyes widened, cheeks flushing. "What could you possibly mean?"

"We depart tomorrow evening. I'll bring you with me."

Suspicion clouded her eyes. "What's in it for you?"

"It's clear to me that there's more to you than meets the eye, Livie Blackwood. I don't believe for a moment you were destined for this life, especially not as the wife of a man who will never respect you."

"You did not answer my question."

I sighed. "I have yet to replace my clerk, and I highly doubt my quartermaster and lieutenant have been able to find one. You'll serve as my clerk for our journey to Antigua."

What I had told her wasn't a lie. I just omitted any mention of using her as bait to get to her father. Not a bargaining chip, but bait. I'd found nothing in this town to lead me to him, only that which confirmed he was the man responsible for attacking our ship when I'd found traces of the silk we carried with his insignia on the crates. Livie still had ties to him, which would lead him right to me.

I had gained information about a man at *The King's Arms* tavern who didn't demand paperwork for storing goods upon arrival, meaning the man employed men who quietly assisted in unloading cargo used for unlawful operations. Enough ears around town told me that Livie had worked with the man at the

The King's Arms, thus setting into motion cargo that would be split into three and disbursed. No woman in high society would know that. She didn't know what I knew, and if I could help it, she wouldn't. If I could convince her to willingly come with me, I could leave this cursed city and finally move forward in avenging my brother.

"Nothing more?" she hedged.

I smiled tightly. "Would you rather stay and become a baroness?"

"If I run away, I'll not be able to return."

"No," I said softly.

By the look in her eyes, I had my answer. Slowly, she extended her hand, though I could see the slight tremor in it. I grabbed it, holding on longer than necessary, wondering how such a delicate hand could wield a dagger against a man's neck with such ferocity.

If she knew how I was deceiving her, I had no doubt I might find myself in a similar situation if she had the chance. I would never give her one.

"Tomorrow night, Livie. You will meet me here, in the back, at the hour of ten. I would advise you not to bring more than is necessary."

She squeezed my hand, unwilling to release me yet. "I will have some of my belongings sent ahead of time, discreetly, of course. There are things I cannot leave behind."

I nodded once before releasing her hand, searching her eyes for any sign of relief. Satisfied, I turned and strode away, leaving her to whatever meeting she had scheduled. I couldn't help but wonder if my offer had altered the details of her meeting.

Chapter Fourteen

Livie

"Olivia, a word, if you please."

Uncle Winston's soft-spoken yet commanding voice echoed through the hallway as I stepped off the last step with William. We exchanged wary glances. It was early in the day for my uncle to request my presence, especially after I had just packed a small trunk for my maid to have secretly delivered to Grayson's ship.

My most personal belongings, some money, my father's signet ring that I had stolen, a map, and one dagger, I planned to bring myself when I snuck out for the last time that night. If anything were to go wrong, it would be tonight, and I had to ensure that it wouldn't.

I exchanged another glance with William before we parted ways at the sweeping staircase. Just as I stepped toward the study door, he caught my hand, nearly causing me to stumble into the banister.

"Stay strong, cousin." His lips curled slightly, as if he thought I would be in trouble for being called into his father's office.

He had no idea how strong I could be. Although several days had passed since the night I took a dagger to my throat, a red mark remained visible. If my hair didn't cover it, I would need to explain it.

I squeezed his hand once before continuing toward the study, where I found my uncle standing just outside the door. The sandy brown of his hair, lightly mixed with grey, brushed the tops of his shoulders, while the neat trim of his beard and mustache shared the same color. His eyes, the same shade as William's, held kindness.

Cocking his head to the side, he glanced at the wet hem of my dress before raising his eyes to meet mine, an eyebrow arched. I offered him a guilty smile, not quite a grin, but enough to convey I knew what Aunt Marjory would say if she saw me. William and I hadn't meant to walk on the grass during our stroll this morning.

"We have much to discuss, you and I," he said, sweeping an arm toward the study.

I held my breath as I stepped inside, exhaling in relief upon finding the room blissfully empty of my groom-to-be. While I waited for Uncle Winston to close the door, I walked toward the desk and the empty chairs.

There wouldn't be time to ponder that further as Uncle Winston stepped around the paper-littered desk between us, sinking into his worn leather chair and leaning back. His eyes lit with teasing gentleness. I bit my bottom lip and stared back at him.

"Sit down, Livie," he murmured softly.

Apprehension gripped me like an iron vise as I slowly lowered myself into the chair across from him. Uncle Winston and I had shared many deep conversations since I'd come to live with him and Aunt Marjory, most of them over a game of chess. Something in his voice seemed off.

"You are to be married," he began.

"I have not accepted yet," I interrupted, fully aware that particular ship had already sailed and would be sunk by the time everyone woke tomorrow to find me gone.

His eyebrows raised. "Percival seems to think differently. When he first told me about it, I thought he might have been mistaken. You seem rather disinclined to marry at all."

"I don't think it is in my best interest to do so. Not with my inheritance still undisclosed."

I pressed back against the chair at the glint in his eyes. A subtle warning.

Uncle Winston had no trouble putting anyone in their place, especially me. He also had no qualms about administering punishments when warranted. Aunt Marjory had the quicker temper of the two, but Uncle Winston had a level head, and he used it wisely.

"Percival has asked for my permission, Livie. It's time that you wed, and Percival would treat you kindly. I will, of course, provide your dowry, given your financial circumstances."

"So, you've given your permission?"

Suddenly, what I had planned to do that night sank to the pit of my stomach. Running was my only choice now, despite the possibility of angering my father. There might still be a chance to prove myself to him if he'd but give me the chance.

I'd be leaving without a goodbye, although I could still say goodbye to William. He would insist on accompanying me to Wapping, but I would not allow it. The thought of leaving him and Uncle Winston behind made me wrinkle my nose. Even Immy and Aunt Marjory deserved a farewell. I wrapped my arms around myself. Secrets would be revealed, long-buried secrets whispered in drawing rooms about the girl who arrived in the dead of night only to disappear in the same manner. Uncle Winston must have sensed my rising alarm, for he leaned forward and shook his head.

"These are things you should not worry about. You need not be concerned about Percival. You will not want for anything in life. He will protect you."

Protection from whom or what? More protection than Uncle Winston provided? He couldn't know that I could protect myself far better than either of them.

Without so much as a knock, the door opened, and Aunt Marjory breezed in, her dark hair tightly coiled, with wispy tendrils tinged with the beginnings of grey at her temples. She glanced at me briefly before focusing her dark eyes on my uncle.

"Will Olivia be joining us for tea?" she asked.

Despite being siblings, my father didn't have the pinched expression of his sister, as if she had swallowed a sour lemon tart. He maintained a calm demeanor, until he didn't. He tolerated no misbehavior of any kind. I had witnessed the punishment of men aboard his vessel for infractions far too many times to forget, especially what had happened to Edward when I had been equally to blame. He treated his crew like family, most of whom had been sailing with him since he became captain. But that didn't mean punishments weren't administered when warranted.

"I will send her along when I'm finished with her, my dear."

The thin line of her mouth turned downward. "I see."

When her gaze found mine, I quickly turned to look out the window, as if something important had captured my attention. I heard her quiet scoff, followed by the soft click of the door a moment later, likely having given my uncle a look that urged him to talk sense into me. For what reason this time, I had no idea.

Uncle Winston leaned back casually in his chair again as I returned my attention to him, lacking his usual smile. His eyes remained stern.

"What happened to your neck?" he asked bluntly.

As if burned, I covered the mark on my neck with my hand. Devil take me! I thought my hair would sufficiently hide it. And it would have, had I not stretched to look out the damned window.

"I've already seen it, Livie," he growled.

My eyebrows furrowed together. Nothing got past Uncle Winston. I struggled to find my words, devil take it. I needed more time to come up with an excuse.

I had to give my uncle an answer. He demanded it, and not just any excuse would suffice. I could never openly admit to him what I had been doing these past years. Not only would he put an end to it immediately, but it would also endanger those involved.

"Livie," he growled again.

"It was an accident," I replied tersely.

"How? What kind of accident?"

I had to give him something, and quickly. "I like to go down to the docks."

"*When?*"

I sighed. "At night. After everyone is asleep."

His eyes hardened. "To do what? Precisely?"

Uncle Winston was not about to let this go, judging by the tone of his voice. He only took on that tenor when he was angry, and his temper was rising the more vague I was. I wouldn't get out of this without giving him an explanation.

"Devil take me, I miss the ships, Uncle! I just go down there to watch them. I stay out of the way. Usually. Several nights ago, I got into a bit of a scuffle and got hurt. It is much better now, as you can see."

His mouth was set in a thin line, and his eyes bored into me. He was not happy with me at all. But it would have been much worse had I given him the full story. I hadn't lied.

"You've been going out unchaperoned? To Wapping? Stepney? Please, dear Lord, do not tell me you've been going as far as Southwark."

"Only Wapping."

For a moment, I thought he might burst into laughter. Instead, he slammed his palms on the desk so hard that papers scattered, rising to his full height. I had never seen him this furious, perhaps ever. I stood and stepped back.

"By God, Livie, I should banish you to your room for the rest of your time in this house. Do you realize, even for a single instant, how much danger you were in? How much danger you might have put this family in? What in the name of God were you thinking by doing such a thing? And how do you leave this house in the middle of the night undetected?"

Oh, that. "I go out my window."

"On my honor, I have never met such an unruly person as you! I promised your father that I would care for you, protect you, and ensure that you became a well-mannered young lady. I see now that we have been lax in your care!" He shook his head. "May Percival have all the luck with you!"

He plopped back down in his chair, laughter bubbling up from his throat until he was fully laughing. I kept my mouth firmly closed, unsure of what I would even say to him. Lord, if he knew the full truth, would he have locked me in my room until Percival retrieved me?

The darkening in his eyes showed that he was still angry, even though his laughter had subsided. Having been in disguise, I couldn't admit that Grayson Valle had been the one to save me.

"Is that the truth, Livie?"

"Yes," I answered.

He stared back at me, clearly not believing me. I couldn't blame him.

"Why would I lie? I go out in disguise." I deliberately omitted the fact that I was armed. There was no need for him to question my weapons or where I kept them, now safely en route to Grayson's ship.

He shook his head, disbelieving that I would do such a thing. Uncle Winston hadn't known me until three years ago. How could he have known what kind of girl he'd brought into his household? My father would never admit to having such a wild daughter, never confess that his daughter was just like him. Not when there was a possibility that I could have been turned away. Aunt Marjory and Uncle Winston were my only known relatives. There would have been nowhere else to send me.

"How long have you been doing this?"

Hiding my shallow breathing, I forced a light smile and sat back down on the edge of the chair. "Since I've been here. I've had no issues. As you can see, I'm fine, except for a small mark on my neck, Uncle."

"That," he said with heavy emphasis, "is not a small mark. No doubt Percival will want to know who is responsible."

A burdened sigh escaped his lips as he momentarily gazed out the window. I deduced whatever he was about to tell me couldn't be good. Whenever he grew pensive, I knew I wouldn't like what I was about to hear.

He turned back to me solemnly. "Your engagement will be announced tomorrow at Percival's dinner party, with the banns posted afterward. You will be married posthaste."

A dinner party that wouldn't include me, as I would be long gone.

"But-"

"No buts, Livie. 'Tis as good as done. You will be wed to Percival, and that is the end of this matter."

I jumped up from the chair, far faster than a lady should rise, striding toward the window he had so diligently gazed through while contemplating how to deliver the news. That feeling I always had proved true. I knew I wouldn't like what he was saying. I whirled around to face him, challenging.

"So, Percival is giving me absolutely no time to reconcile our joining in holy matrimony. We are to be married straight away?"

Silence.

"Uncle Winston!"

He rose again, his imposing six feet two inches doing nothing to intimidate me. Since I'd arrived on his doorstep as a sixteen-year-old girl, afraid of leaving behind a life with pirates to learn how to be a lady, he'd been patient and understanding. With the exception of William, he'd been the only other person I could truly confide in about my feelings. Immy would have gone straight to Aunt Marjory.

We'd spent hours playing chess, our heads together as we talked about the trials and tribulations of wearing a corset tighter than I would have ever liked, learning to sit straight and speak in hushed tones, and sitting for hours with a tutor learning mathematics, history, and French. Although I would never admit it to him, learning another language had come in handy with my smuggling activities. Uncle Winston and William had been the only two people, in a foreign land with people I did not know, to make me feel at ease.

"What would you have me say, Livie? I can't very well demand he court you for the next few months. The man has been waiting. Patiently, I might add."

I knew it, of course. Everything I had just done, pretending to be upset, was merely a ruse to ensure Uncle Winston thought I was truly distressed by the sudden events. If I didn't have an alternate plan of escape for this evening, I would have still acted as though the very thought of Percival as a husband bothered me. Because it did. Except I was stopping at nothing to ensure that it never happened. And at great risk that my father would be furious.

"I need to get ready for tea."

"Find your aunt. She'll need to make plans for your dress right away."

As I walked to the door, the realization struck me that the future I had envisioned had completely changed. I would no longer be walking toward Percival to vow before God, spending a torturous night in his bed, and worrying about what he might discover about the woman he married, despite him being the one to pursue me. A man like Percival demanded a pure wife.

Instead, I would be traveling with a man I barely knew, having already been in his bed under duress once. A voyage on a ship for weeks on end was an entirely different matter, one that could make men surly, especially with a woman on board. I had no idea how he or his crew would react to me.

As I slipped out of the study, I heard my aunt calling my name. I knew Uncle Winston had informed her of the upcoming wedding, but this was not how I had envisioned spending my last day in this house.

Chapter Fifteen

Grayson

"You're sure she'll show?" Connor asked.

Once again, I waited in the shadows near the docks for Livie. Livie *Blackwood*, I reminded myself. I dared not tell her what I knew about her or her connection to her father, otherwise my plans to get her aboard my ship would quickly diminish. She would never come with me if she knew what I knew.

"She'll show. Getting married to the Baron of Vensworth is the last thing Livie wants. I know that to be the truth of it."

"You mean the daughter of the man you mean to bring down."

I swiveled to glare at him. "You have a penchant for speaking things aloud that should be whispered."

He shrugged, not bothering to look guilty.

"Do not repeat that, Connor. Ever."

"What will you do with her once she's aboard? These men will get randy after only a few days at sea. If they know a woman, *Livie Blackwood*, is on board . . ."

My crew knew the mission to bring Elias Blackwood to justice. They just didn't know it had come down to this. Bringing Livie aboard might not go over well, but if they respected me at all, they would listen to reason. I only had to voice that reason if it was discovered.

"I plan to keep her below deck for as long as I can, or on the quarterdeck. As my clerk, that's where she should be stationed.

She'll also be in disguise, at least I hope she'll agree to that."

"And if they find out?"

"Then, other than putting the fear of God into them, she'll need to stay in the safety of my cabin."

Connor rocked back on his heels, chuckling. "I'm thinking she might not be as willing as you think, Gray. Do you honestly believe she'll fall freely into your bed?"

I frowned. "You're supposed to call me Captain. Make sure you remember that when we set sail. I will need all your help, and Wiley's too, to keep this crew in line. Those who've been with us for the last couple of years might be fine, but the newer ones will need a heavy hand."

"Aye," he replied just as a slim figure skirted the dark shadows of the alleyway. "She comes."

"Ready the ship," I ordered, stepping out of the shadows to meet Livie while Connor disappeared toward the gangplank.

In her dark cloak, Livie joined me in the shadows, slightly out of breath. She had a satchel with her, and I imagined she was armed to the teeth with daggers strapped everywhere possible, otherwise, she had nothing else with her.

A small trunk had arrived earlier in the day, placed in the cabin I had assigned to her. But I would do everything I could to convince her to stay in my cabin. It was the only way I could fully protect her, even knowing I might not be able to protect her from myself. For whatever ridiculous reason, since meeting her, I hadn't been able to touch any other woman.

Catching her breath, Livie stopped next to me and lowered her hood just enough to reveal her bright eyes, a myriad of emotions swirling in those blue depths that had been haunting my dreams. How she'd infiltrated my dreams with such stealth, I didn't know.

"Livie," I said, my tone huskier than I intended, "you understand that you will be boarding a ship with only men aboard, correct?"

"Yes," she replied, uncertainty lacing her voice.

I reached out, slowly wrapping my hand around her arm. "I would much prefer if you consented to stay in my cabin."

Her eyes widened with an innocence she couldn't possibly possess. "With you?"

"There are benefits to doing so. The nights are cold, Livie."

She yanked her arm away as though burned. "I know how to keep myself warm at night," she replied tightly. "This is London, you know. And having been to Antigua, I know that the chill at night is not going to last."

"You may be in danger alone in a cabin below deck."

"And I know how to handle myself."

"I can tell by the mark on your lovely neck," I snapped, instantly regretting the bite in my voice. "Very well, but you are forbidden from loitering on deck unless I allow it. You will also need to cover your hair and hide the fact that you are a woman."

The gasp that escaped her throat sent a shudder through me, breathy and sultry at the same time. "You're giving me an ultimatum? If I don't agree to share your bed, I have to disguise myself for several weeks?"

"Are you changing your mind about leaving this behind?"

"No," she snapped. "I'll take my chances dressing like a man."

I clasped my hands behind my back. "Very well. If you'll come with me, then."

Even in the dark, I could see Connor on the quarterdeck, ready to leave port as soon as I had Livie safely onboard. The winds were favorable, making our departure sooner rather than later. Paperwork had already been cleared by the customs officer. I dared not touch her when she stepped onto the gangplank, her feet sure and steady as though she'd done this thousands of times. And she likely had.

"One more thing," I said, stopping when she turned around. "Remember, I'll need you to act as my clerk. I couldn't find anyone else to fill that role."

She huffed. "Payment for passage, I suppose?"

"I'll teach you what you need to know come morning."

When she turned and continued up the gangplank, I heard her say, "I already know what is expected of me when it comes to acting as a clerk."

122

Chapter Sixteen

As I stepped up the gangplank, I was acutely aware of the absence of men on deck. Only Connor was at the helm on the quarterdeck, and a few others who were too engrossed in their tasks to notice the captain's arrival. Trepidation would ensue if they ever learned that a woman was aboard, even though I'd dressed in my usual men's clothing and had my hair bound and tied with a scarf.

It felt as if this moment had been anticipated. Expected.

I glanced back at Grayson, who was following closely behind. He urged me forward with a hand on my back, keeping it there as I stepped onto the main deck. A rush of emotions washed over me: the rustling sails lying still until we pushed off, and the gentle slaps of water against the ship's frame. Bracing my feet apart, I felt the sway of the vessel and inhaled deeply, taking in the tang and brine of the sea air. Somehow it felt different being on deck than dockside.

For three years, nothing had felt right. Now I was home. It didn't matter that the ship belonged to Grayson; this was my place. Not realizing my eyes had closed, I snapped them open at the pressure on my back. *Share his cabin, indeed.* Had that been his plan all along? To get me into his bed and ease his discomfort during the long days and nights at sea?

"This way," Grayson urged from behind me, his hand still on my back.

I know my way around a ship, I wanted to retort, but held my tongue. Percival may have discovered my dockside dealings, but I would be damned if I admitted it to anyone else. The secrets I kept from Grayson needed to remain hidden until I knew I could trust him, and even then, I should never reveal them. He seemed trustworthy enough, but I had been misled before, and that had dire consequences. It could happen again.

As he stepped beside me, the feeling of his hand on my back was oddly comforting. Everyone here was a stranger. I sensed eyes on me as we crossed the deck toward the stairway leading down.

Grayson went first, and when I looked back at the men on deck, I was surprised to see a young man behind me. His mouth was tilted in a slight smile, but he said nothing. His dark brown hair, straight and nearly to his shoulders, framed his boyish face. He didn't appear to be much younger than I was, but I knew boys, boys much younger than he, took to the sea early to earn money for their families or to escape trouble with the magistrate.

"I do hope there's a lock on my door," I announced.

At the landing outside the captain's quarters, Grayson stopped. "If not, are you willing to give up this folly and share my cabin?"

My chin lifted, pride stinging from his rebuttal. I could relent, perhaps have a more comfortable bed to slumber in, but I risked resembling one of the serving wenches at *The Captain's Quarters*, known to entertain men after serving them. Livie Blackwood was many things, but I was not a whore.

"There is a lock, Livie," he said, swinging his arm to let the young man go ahead of us. "Kit is my cabin boy and will also be serving as yours. I trust Kit completely. He will not betray you to the rest of the crew."

As Kit rounded the post and headed down the next set of stairs, weariness washed over me. I knew the crew would be sleeping in the berth, and I hoped Grayson wasn't purposely placing me in a cabin close to where they would rest.

"Livie," Grayson interrupted my thoughts. "Please follow Kit."

There was something in his voice that unsettled me. I should be hesitant after such a tumultuous few days of avoiding Percival and running into Edward, my trust wavering. After all, I barely knew Grayson Valle. However, he had come to my rescue and didn't have to offer me a way out of my situation. But he had. I had accepted his offer so quickly that I hadn't thought twice about trusting him, or what my father would do when he found out I was not where I was supposed to be.

I crossed my arms over my chest. "Am I to trust you?"

The impish smile faltered my judgment. "You did board my ship of your own accord."

Kit shifted his weight from one foot to the other, clearly agitated by our exchange. He looked so young. Innocent. What I wouldn't do to feel that way again. I sighed and bypassed Grayson to follow Kit wherever he led.

Through the dimly lit bowels of the ship, a door to a room at the stern appeared ahead of us. It seemed to be just below the captain's quarters, perhaps a place for tending to injuries. I wondered if the ship had a doctor on board. Most didn't, as many crew members had more than one job, and most injuries went neglected.

Kit opened the door, and once again, I hesitated until Grayson cupped my elbow and propelled me forward. He kept hold of me while Kit placed a lantern on the small table near the bed. It was indeed a cabin, complete with a chair positioned in the center of the room rather than near the table. The trunk I had sent ahead had been placed at the foot of the bed.

"Cap'n?" Kit asked, his voice barely deep enough to be considered manly.

"Leave us," Grayson replied, his tone brusque and rather rude.

Once Kit bolted from the room, the door clicked shut behind him with a distinct lock. Alarmed, I glanced at Grayson, only to be met with dark, serious eyes, eyes that told me this rescue mission had more to it than he had led on.

"Sit," he commanded. "And if I have to tell you again, you'll be tied to it."

I opened my mouth to retort when he pulled me closer, our noses almost touching, as he stared into my eyes. He had the most beautiful eyes. Now, however, they screamed danger.

"Have I escaped one tyrant for another?" I whispered.

"Sit down, *Livie.*"

I nearly fell into the chair, my heart racing as my suspicions proved true. There was more to Grayson's offer to take me away on his ship to escape Percival than I had believed. Devil take me, he had more motive than I thought. What those motives were, I had yet to discover.

Hovering over me, he looked more ominous than I'd ever seen him. "Despite what you think, I am not here to play games. You will remain in this cabin for the duration of our voyage until I say otherwise. It is for your protection."

"A cabin that locks from the outside? Apologies, *Captain*, if I don't trust what you say now. Tell me the true reason for your offer to take me away. It certainly wasn't for my benefit, was it?"

His jaw tensed as he straightened and turned away from me. He knew I had daggers on me and could easily disarm him, but the consequences would fall on how the crew would handle me if I harmed him. I knew how it worked.

"Let's not get ahead of ourselves." He turned, crossing one arm over his chest and cupping his elbow, his long fingers drumming against his chin. "The lock is for your protection, Livie. Although, if you have something to tell me, now is the time."

I lifted my chin defiantly. "What could I possibly have to tell you, other than that I do not trust you?"

"Nor do I trust you."

"What has changed in such a short amount of time?" I asked. "You were the one who suggested that I run away. Or share your bed."

"You brought up sharing my bed first."

"Interesting that I've done one, on the cusp of the other."

His eyebrow rose. "Do tell."

I pressed my lips together, not thinking he would capitalize on my words. "This will prove to be quite a long voyage if we are not honest with each other, Captain," I admitted softly.

He cursed colorfully. "You were not in London because your mother died. Perhaps you should start there. And tell me now why Percival, a rather prominent person in society, wanted you so badly for a wife?"

My eyes flashed. "I do not know why Percival wanted me. And if you think for a minute that someone is going to rescue me for ransom, you are sorely mistaken, *Captain*."

Did he know that I lied? I knew exactly why Percival wanted me. After he'd confessed to being betrothed to my mother. The truth made me want to vomit, and I would never admit it. Even then, just because he had been betrothed to my mother, did not give me the comfort that it was all he'd wanted me for. It had to be her fortune, one that I would not likely see.

I stood abruptly, only for him to push me back into the chair. With one hand on each of the chair's arms, his eyes blazed.

"You mean to tell me, a woman who bears the name of a man rumored to have gone rogue, with the blood of an heiress in her veins, can escape without anyone coming after her? Surely, you think better of yourself."

"Rumored," I replied. "My father is rumored to have turned to pirating."

"Oh, but you know differently, don't you? It would be wise for you to tell me what you know of him and his whereabouts."

I knew then it was only about my father. He wanted to get to my father for some reason. Greed? Revenge? I didn't care. I was so furious with my newly found situation. Regardless, I would be well away from Percival, which is what I wanted.

"Even if I knew where he was, why would I tell you?"

"Because I hold your future in the palm of my hand. Tell me, Livie."

"I will not."

His jaw clenched in frustration. So this was how it would be. He'd tricked me into boarding his ship, hoping to find my father. As for ransoming me, he couldn't be more mistaken. My father would never part with a penny for me, nor would he come out of hiding. Grayson was mistaken in thinking so. Especially when my father discovered that I was no longer in London.

"Come now, Livie. We are at an impasse." He folded his arms tightly across his chest, muscles bulging in his attempt to control his fury. "Tell me now where he is."

My mouth dropped open, and then closed immediately as he held up his finger.

"If you refuse one more time . . ."

Not about to be threatened, I pushed myself right up to him. "I shall not say another word to you. Leave me to rot in here, for all I care. I will not tell you a bloody thing about my father, his whereabouts, or anything else. You've taken enough liberties already. In fact, let me out, and I'll return home with no one the wiser."

He laughed, a deep, melodic sound that raised the hair on the back of my neck. I had made a grave mistake coming here with him, but I'd been bluffing when I'd told him to release me. I knew I would not leave only to find myself at the altar. This man was nothing more than a pirate himself, chasing after dreams of wealth and power. He would not use me to achieve them.

"We've already weighed anchor, as my quartermaster was tasked with doing as soon as I returned." He tsked, drawing back from me. "You've sailed with your father before. Surely, you can tell when a ship has left its port."

As countless curse words spun through my mind, my mouth flattened in anger. "You are nothing but a bloody blackguard. No better than Percival Monteclaire." His eyes narrowed, hostility threatening to unleash. "Take what you want and leave me."

"Is that what you want? For me to force myself on you? You are here for one reason, and one reason only, and it isn't for my pleasure. Although I could be easily persuaded if you changed your mind about sharing my quarters. You are a means to an end, and nothing more."

Bait, I thought bitterly. Grayson was using me to lure my father. He believed my father would come for me. If he thought that, he was about to be very disappointed. Elias Blackwood had turned his back on me years ago, never to send for me or promise to return. I'd been fighting an endless battle to control my future, and it still wasn't enough. I meant nothing to him, even though it stung to realize that. Fear crept in, for if my father did come for me, we should all be terrified.

Grayson strode to the door and rapped his knuckles against the wood to be let out. "I know you know where he is, and when word gets out that I have you, I won't need to know his whereabouts. He'll come straight for you. If not, you will fetch me a pretty price, regardless of how little you value yourself."

Tears stung my eyes as I stared at the door after he slammed it behind him. If fire could have engulfed the door based on my glare alone, we'd all be in danger of drowning in a sea of flames.

Chapter Seventeen

Grayson

As soon as I slammed the door shut, I pressed my back against it, blocking out the rage I'd seen in her eyes. The hurt. If it hadn't been for this mission, I would have never taken her. I would never have offered to rescue her from the man who desperately wanted to make her his wife.

Livie Blackwood might have had a decent life, perhaps even been widowed in a reasonable time with the Baron of Vensworth as her husband. But, like me, the man had motives that were not in her best interest. If anything, I'd saved her from a life trapped in endless balls and social niceties. She should be thanking me.

I had to strengthen my resolve when it came to her. Behind her rage, I saw fear. She could try to hide it from me, but I could see it in her eyes. Livie might be good at displaying a façade for others, but I was not among them. Even if she wouldn't confess, I was sure that Elias Blackwood would come for his daughter the moment he discovered I possessed her.

"Cap'n," Kit said from the shadows. "Is she . . . well?"

I had to be careful of my cabin boy's sympathy. Only a few years younger than the exquisite woman confined in the cabin below mine, Kit had a soft spot for women in distress. And Livie was far from distressed. Kit didn't know that, nor the tricks she might use to slide into his empathy.

"Kit," I said roughly, "you will not open this door for any

reason. I don't care if she's begging to be let out or threatening that she's done something amiss in the cabin. Do you understand me?"

He swallowed thickly. "Aye, sir. I won't open the door."

I crossed my arms. "She's the type of woman who will say anything to get inside your head and make you sympathize with her. She is armed, and she will hurt you. Do not trust her."

He nodded, eyes wide.

"You will send Sully down to guard this door, though I doubt she'll be able to get past the lock. But she is her father's daughter, and a monster's spawn will stop at nothing to escape."

Forewarning the young boy with vivid images of the woman behind the door would ensure he did not think to help her. Livie would undoubtedly try to get out by any means possible. I berated myself for not taking her weapons, although she could have reached for one of the many daggers she carried, and yet she hadn't. She must have sailed with her father for a time, and in doing so, I imagined she'd learned a thing or two.

As I climbed the stairs, I tried to shake the thoughts of how fierce she was. Despite my threats and getting as close to her as possible, she kept her composure and didn't relent, clearly not how I imagined his daughter would be.

Connor stood on the quarterdeck, one hand on the wheel while he spoke enthusiastically with Wiley. As soon as I stepped up, they ceased their conversation and looked at me with questions. Connor was likely briefing Wiley about our guest, as had been my plan since I'd latched onto her dealings in Wapping. The darling niece of Winston and Marjory Thornton had used society as a ruse for her black market dealings, dealings that put her in contact with her father from the moment she'd arrived. It had all clicked into place so easily.

Livie hadn't known what I knew: that she'd been passing information to her father about smuggling opportunities, but I'd heard enough. Enough to set my plan in motion. And here we were, sailing along the River Thames on our way out to the vast ocean. I'd dispatched a few messages before leaving. Soon enough, Elias would come out of hiding to retrieve his daughter. It was a day I'd been waiting for a long time.

"I didn't hear any hysterics," Connor said.

I shook my head. "Cool and collected, like the epitome of a perfect lady. But defiant and fierce is what she is." Connor's eyebrow rose, but I continued. "And she refuses to admit that she knows her father's whereabouts. Perhaps time locked in the cabin will loosen her tongue."

"What's your next move?" Wiley asked, bouncing off the railing to approach us.

"You dispatched the messages for me?" I asked. Wiley nodded. "We sail south toward Antigua, unload cargo, then move toward Puerto Rico, as I indicated in my message to Elias. He'll come for her."

"And if he doesn't?" Connor studied his knuckles, long since healed from our fight in London.

"He will. She's his only daughter, and he's not about to let her become a fallen woman like her mother."

Wiley's eyebrows shot up. "Her mother died."

"Yes, she did," Connor said. "But she died when Livie was seven, in a hurricane that swept through Barbados. Livie was found among the wreckage. It was kept a secret until Livie came to London a few years ago under the falsehood that her mother had recently succumbed to health-related issues. Apparently, no one thought to question the validity of her arrival."

I stepped back, impressed with the amount of information that Connor had uncovered during our time here. While I'd been busy proving that Elias had been behind the attack on our ship and stealing our cargo, Connor had been at work collecting information on Livie. More so than I had originally thought.

"You didn't think to tell me this when you discovered it?"

Connor smiled. "I'm telling you now, am I not?"

Bastard, I thought, looking at Wiley, and continued the tale. "Daphne Blackwood was nothing but a pawn, abducted on her way to her betrothed. The man she was betrothed to is none other than Percival Monteclaire, the Baron of Vensworth. After Daphne was abducted, she is said to have been ruined, and Percival moved on to marry another woman with far fewer prospects for wealth. Truth be told, Daphne, as the sole heiress, had inherited a fortune. No doubt that was what Percival was after when he'd all but begged Livie to become his wife."

"How did Daphne meet Elias?" Wiley asked.

"She was part of the prize that Elias won after he battled the ship, but ultimately, no one quite knows the history between Daphne and Elias. Without her, we wouldn't have the spawn in the locked cabin below."

Even as I said it, part of me wondered if Livie was truly the evil offspring of her father I thought her to be. She had proven me wrong in London, but she had secrets. This led me to believe there was much more to her than met the eye.

"Grayson . . . " Connor said. "Livie doesn't strike me as the kind of woman raised by pirates. Not the woman I saw at that ball. Are you so certain she's similar to her father?"

My gaze snapped to him, unwilling to admit to anyone that I might feel differently now. "I know she is. You saw her that night in Wapping. No gently reared woman would be dressed as a man in a drinking establishment. But that is beside the point. The point is, she knows where the bastard is."

"It won't matter if having her here with us draws him out, will it?" Wiley asked.

"No," I replied. "Having her admit where he is will only solidify my shot at getting to him. Having him arrested and hanged for piracy is the goal, but if he comes for her, I'll take him myself."

"A pirate's daughter will only give you trouble in the future," Connor warned. "You're going to have to strengthen your resolve or fall to her wiles."

"Is that so?" I asked, folding my arms across my chest. "You don't think I can resist her . . . charm?"

He grinned. "I wouldn't. She is a sight to behold, devil's daughter or not."

Wiley nodded in agreement, more enthusiastically than I wanted to see. "What will you do with her after you've dealt with Elias?"

"Release her. She hates me now, and she'll hate me more after Elias comes for her."

Chapter Eighteen

I paced. I slept. I watched the water outside my small window ebb and flow around the ship as we cut through the waves. How I longed to be on deck, feeling the wind against my face and through my hair. If I closed my eyes, I could imagine holding onto the rope and leaning over the side to capture the full force of the wind. Sea spray and all, I'd missed it.

Cooped up in this tiny room only fueled my madness. Grayson had wealth, unless he had made bad investments. What would he need to ransom me for, if not for that? I had had no contact with my mother's family, and the last I heard from Uncle Winston was that they had not answered his letters regarding the validity of my inheritance, assuming I had one. Once my mother had been abducted, it might have nullified her status as heiress. Daphne Lebeau had been an only child, but the inheritance could have gone to another relative unless the family recognized me as her daughter.

"Hello?" I called through the door for the twentieth time since being shoved in here last night. "I know you can hear me. I need to relieve myself."

"There's a bucket," came a voice.

My gaze fell to the bucket in the corner of the room, and I wrinkled my nose in disgust. Apparently, living among the wealthiest in London had spoiled me. Oh, how I'd missed those comforts already. By now, my letters to William and Uncle Winston had been found. I wondered if they would miss me, or if they were upset that I hadn't said goodbye in person. I would miss them terribly, knowing that I would not be able to return to London.

"Could I at least have some clothes? Something to eat? Anything!"

"The captain will bring you some food soon."

I placed my hands on my hips, a delighted smile curving my lips. If the captain himself brought me food, we could continue our discussion. We were at sea, having cleared the channel by now. I wondered how he imagined I would escape. Surely he could let me out of this room.

This hadn't been what I expected, especially since I had left my fancy dresses and hair accessories behind. If Grayson hadn't stationed someone outside the door, I could have used a hairpin to unlock it. Even if I could get it open, I doubted he would leave someone outside who could be easily overpowered by a woman. A woman with weapons could do wonders as long as she knew how to wield them. And I certainly did.

I knew better than to try my feminine wiles; he would be expecting that. Quite honestly, I wasn't sure whether I should downplay my strength or confront him directly. Whatever his reason for abducting me, if I could even call it that since I had come willingly, it was utterly ridiculous.

The only one who might consider rescuing me was Percival, in his quest to have me so badly, and he likely didn't even know I had disappeared yet. He would know soon enough, as I would be absent from his dinner party this evening when he planned to announce our engagement. I couldn't help but smile at my machinations and what they would cause Percival. No matter what had transpired to get me on board this vessel, part of me sighed in relief that I would not be stuck in such a union with him. To think, he had been betrothed to my mother and thought he would take me as a wife since he hadn't been able to take her.

I had told the truth when I told Grayson that I did not know my father's whereabouts. Only those sworn to absolute secrecy, who would die defending my father, knew where he might be in hiding. It wouldn't matter if Grayson chose not to believe me, would it? Only my pride was at stake for being tricked, for whatever reason he wanted me. If I admitted it, gave him a false location, perhaps he would release me from captivity. But would he trust a pirate's daughter?

Boredom had settled in. There was nothing to do but sleep and pace the small room. I withdrew my father's signet ring, holding it for a time before putting it away and deciding to make use of the basin of water left for washing. Used to at least being able to freshen myself with water and rags, I knew a full bath while at sea would be unlikely, so I had to wipe the grime from the docks off my body.

At the knock on my door, my head snapped up. Left with nothing but the basin of tepid water and no linen to wash with, I had no choice but to tear a strip from my own shirt to clean myself.

"May I enter?"

I heard Grayson's voice through the thick wood, surprised that he'd asked rather than barging in. It was his ship, after all, and I was his captive. He could do whatever he pleased.

"No," I replied, biting back the bitterness in my voice that I hated, despite trying to convince myself he deserved it. "You may not enter."

After a lengthy pause, I thought we were done. That he had left, determined to return when I would be more amenable to conversation. I couldn't have been more wrong when the sound of the lock disengaging signaled the door opening.

My breeches lay on the bed, my foot propped up next to them as I ran the wet cloth up my bare leg. As undignified as my position was, he had left me no other choice in this tiny room.

Anyone he stationed outside refused to speak with me.

"I said not to enter!" I dropped my foot down, standing tall despite my tunic hanging off my shoulder and nearly baring one breast, the hem barely reaching mid-thigh.

Rather than widening in shock, Grayson's eyes darkened before leisurely traveling from my bare feet to my thighs and up, glancing at my shoulder before meeting my gaze. The tip of his tongue brushed against his upper lip, his eyes traveling back down.

Heat coursed through me at his clear admiration of my body, but I wasn't about to be a victim of unwanted intentions, as much as I told myself the thought had appeal. I pushed against his impressively muscular chest until he stumbled back against the door.

"What are you doing?" he asked, his voice husky.

Certain he wouldn't stride back into the cabin, I stepped away. "What does it look like I'm doing?" I shot back. "I'm taking a bath with what little water is in the basin. Did you expect me to cry? Beg to be let out of my prison?"

His eyes widened slightly, a smooth smile tilting his full lips. "You could have much better accommodations. If you would just be honest with me—"

"Provide me with better accommodations?" I scoffed. "Perhaps your bed? I'd rather rot in the bowels of this ship than do that."

My heart fluttered at the sight of his smile widening. "Both can be arranged if you desire. It might be in your best interest to speak with me."

"I have nothing to say to you. You seem to expect my father to come for me. I assure you, he will not."

"Why?"

He had to ask me that? As though my past could be easily unraveled. Where would I even begin? I could admit to him what had transpired on *The Executioner* right before my father dumped me off with my aunt and uncle. Grayson would only see it as a weakness, like my father had: a woman applying her charms on an unsuspecting man. If only that were the case. Seducing a man was completely beyond my knowledge. Oh, and how I'd let that happen, my heart still bruised from the memories of Edward.

The issue remained. I had left London, and once my father learned of it, he would be furious with me. He may not have sent along any messages of pride at my work down at the docks and on the sidelines of social gatherings, feeding any intel I could, but he would still be angry that I was no longer stationed there.

"Get dressed," he said gruffly. "I'll return when you're ready to enlighten me."

The floor creaked as he stalked away, the heels of his boots thundering until he climbed the stairs and disappeared. Trembling with fury, I slammed the door shut and snatched my breeches up from the bed.

"Ready to enlighten me," I muttered, stabbing one leg into the breeches before the other. "I'll rot in this prison before I enlighten anyone."

Yanking the sleeve of the tunic back up, I tied the front tightly to keep it from slipping off my shoulder again. I grabbed the corset and cinched it around my waist, pulling the laces tightly until I could barely breathe. The top of the tunic still bared most of my shoulders, but it did not matter since he would not likely let me out of the cabin.

"The nerve of the man," I continued ranting, ignoring the fluttering in my stomach. His gaze had unnerved me.

If he truly wanted me, if he saw me as a woman rather than bait, I might be flattered. But the look in his eyes had to be nothing more than a response to being at sea with nothing but the company of men. I had traveled with them long enough to know they had . . . yearnings.

I scoffed. Grayson Valle wanted me like he wanted a drink, to slake his thirst and be done. But if, I dared to think, he truly felt something stirring . . . Jabbing my foot into a boot, I shook my head.

"No, I won't think of it. Nothing good can come from this farce."

Once I had the other boot on, I resumed my pacing, having no idea when Grayson would return. After a while, I stopped and looked toward the door. He had stomped away while I still had it open.

The door remained unlocked.

Chapter Nineteen

Grayson

Kit attempted to interrupt my furious stride toward my cabin, irritation boiling within me due to the woman in the cabin below. How could one woman be so exquisite, yet provoke such rage? Livie Blackwood had the mentality of a woman scorned, combined with the face and body of a seductive siren.

If she had called my bluff in that moment, I might have shown her exactly what it meant to share my bed. I suppressed a shudder as I entered my cabin, slamming the door behind me. Dear God, those lips begged to be plundered. That perfectly bare shoulder, delicately rounded and covered with pale skin that seemed impossibly soft. And her legs, long and shapely, cloaked in that same creamy skin, invited fantasies of my lips traveling up. Up. Up.

"Cap'n," Kit's voice came from the other side of the door several moments later.

Rubbing my hands over my face, I growled, "What is it?"

"The woman. She . . . she . . ."

"Spit it out, Kit."

"She's out on the main deck."

Bloody hell, I thought, spinning around and flinging open the door. She must have escaped while I stood here imagining her beneath me, and I had only myself to blame. I strode past a bewildered Kit, who hurried to keep up.

Sure enough, with her golden hair bound and covered rather than blowing in the wind, Livie strode across the main deck, creating quite a stir among my men. To others, she was just another part of the crew, a newcomer among those who had sailed with me over the past few years. Not a genteel lady in a dress, but a siren in breeches and a tunic covered by a corset. At least she had donned a cloak. I desperately wanted to believe that none of them recognized her, that none of them knew a woman walked among them. I was tempted to rub my eyes, questioning whether what I saw was real.

Her swift strides toward the bow were no match for mine. I closed the distance in mere moments, catching her swinging wrist before she sensed my presence. The gasp that escaped her lips would have been delightful, were it not for the scathing look in her blue eyes.

My grip on her wrist felt like it was burning my skin, but I held firm despite her pull. "Going somewhere?"

She took a step away from me but couldn't flee until I finally released her. Once she was no longer in my hold, she folded her arms over her chest and met my gaze with defiance. "I merely meant to take some air. Perhaps watch the water from the bow of the ship." Her lips curved into a beguiling smile. "Did you think I would jump overboard? Try to swim for . . . ? Well, I suppose France might be the closest since we've cleared the channel."

My eyes narrowed. Livie would be defiant to the end, and I couldn't help but admire it. I didn't like it, nor did I want to like her. This could be her façade, a charade she played in London to pull the wool over everyone's eyes. Yet, I had a feeling this was the real Livie Blackwood.

I sighed. I needed the truth. If she knew where her father was, it would only ensure that I trapped him. I would much rather know where he was hiding than have the man meet me on the open sea, though I would take either option.

Despite what she wanted me to believe, I knew he would come

for her. What father wouldn't come for his daughter, especially if he thought she might be in peril? No, Elias Blackwood would come for her if he knew she was the gem standing before me now. He'd make certain of it. And I would be ready.

"Well?" she asked. "Come to escort me back to my prison? Perhaps empty the water basin so there's no chance of walking in on me half-dressed again?"

My jaw tightened. Did she truly not realize how lovely she was?

"Tell me where he is, and I'll allow you more liberties. Within reason."

With her chin boldly lifted, her eyes continued to challenge me. My blood raced, eager to hear it from her lips. If she gave in now, I'd have no reason to keep her confined in the cabin below mine.

"Even if I knew, I wouldn't tell you," she whispered, her eyes blazing with unsaid emotion. "You could have been honest with me, and yet you tricked me into coming with you. Why?"

"Forgive me, but were you not looking for a way out of marrying Percival? I did you nothing short of a favor, bringing you here. And yet, you prance around on deck as though you own it."

"I would have found another way," she quipped. "It would be kind of you to tell me why I'm being held captive. Why do you need my father's whereabouts so badly? Are you working for the Crown?"

I clenched my teeth, my jaw working. None of her questions would be answered until I got mine. "You are not my captive. You boarded willingly, did you not?"

Her eyes burned with hatred.

"If I recall, you agreed to be my clerk while aboard."

"Clerks are not locked within their cabins, *Captain*."

I raised my eyebrows at her gall to speak to me that way. The last I knew, I captained this ship, and if any of my men heard her speak to me like that, I could have a mutiny on my hands.

"Livie," I took a step toward her, my voice low and warning, "you will not undermine me on my ship. Do you understand me?"

Her chin lifted. "What are you going to do? Tie me to the mast and have me flogged? I'm certain that would be a vision your men would never forget."

Fury surged within me. I grabbed her arm, hauling her up to me, my anger giving way to pleasure when her eyes widened with fear. She would do well to fear me here. The same man who sailed this ship and led these men was not the same man she met in a ballroom in London. She would find that out soon.

"You will return to your cabin immediately and remain there until I fetch you myself. If you come out, I'll tie you to my bed instead of the mast. And it won't be a flogging you'll receive. Do you understand me?"

At her wide blue eyes and nod, I released her.

Chapter Twenty

Livie

Despite favorable winds prior to the fourth day of our voyage, we were delayed off the Downs by the Royal Navy. Grayson forbade anyone from going ashore, which led to grumbling among the crew. In the meantime, the men were ordered to inspect the powder and conduct drills.

Grayson purposely positioned me by the charts, knowing it would keep me under his control. When naval officers boarded to inspect our cargo, I kept my head down to avoid recognition. By the time we were cleared to sail, the weather had turned, causing further delays and making the men even surlier.

I spent most of my time in my cabin, unwilling to trade barbs with Grayson or find myself tied to his bed. He had Sully fix the door to lock from the inside rather than the outside, which made me feel more secure. Of course, I still had my daggers. Grayson must trust me a little, as he hadn't taken them from me.

By the fifth day, I could no longer remain in my cabin. As brutal as the weather had been, I needed air on my face and the familiar chant of the waves. The rough waters created a symphony of sounds against the ship, and I wasn't disappointed when the light of day touched my face moments later. My stride took me across the main deck toward a spot near the railing where I could be alone with my thoughts.

Tilting my face to the angry spray of the sea, I relished the sensation. I remembered the first time I stepped foot on my father's ship, how frightened I had been, staring up at the enormous vessel from the skiff that picked me up on shore. My father, already an imposing figure, watched me from the quarterdeck, arms crossed and legs braced apart.

Visits from him during my childhood had been infrequent, as he was at sea for months on end with a letter of marque from the Crown, until he began to keep his loot for himself, which led to the validity of his marque failing. Many privateers did so, but only recently had it been questioned, landing him a reputation as a possible outlaw to the Crown.

I learned early in life to listen whenever I could. After a time, I wanted to learn everything and miss nothing. My parents couldn't bear to be parted, but the water was too rough to raise a child.

I let out a short laugh. In the end, that was what had happened to me. My father raised me on his ship, forcing me to learn everything a man needed to do to pull his weight. Acting as a clerk for Grayson would never be an issue. I had been educated whenever we went to port, albeit under careful disguise, and what I hadn't learned at sea, I picked up when sent ashore. Inspecting powder? I could do that. Treating wounds? I had no issues there. Tying knots? There was no one better.

The wind pounded against me, whipping my cloak into a frenzy and pushing against my face. I felt the burn of the unseasonably cool air and welcomed it. Reaching up, I untied my scarf and quickly released the pins, letting my hair fly free. I shook it out, feeling it lash against my face. This was freedom. No matter what happened, I never wanted to return to the life of a lady again. It didn't matter if anyone knew a woman was aboard this vessel. I was doomed.

A moment later, I felt a hand on my biceps as Grayson whipped me around to face him. His lips formed a thin line, his jaw clenched, and his eyes burned with rage. My hair swirled around us, but I refused to cower. In fact, I smiled. I beamed, even as tears threatened to spill. Devil take me, I was home!

Grayson was momentarily speechless, observing the happiness radiating from me. To be myself for once, though it may not have been the smartest thing to do. When I saw the men behind him, they looked as if they had just conquered the biggest prize ship.

I cursed under my breath, glancing from one man to another. Greed. Desire. Pity. A mixture of emotions stared back at me. I couldn't go back to being a faceless addition to the crew. There was no doubt in my mind that the crew knew of Grayson's plans, but I wondered if anyone had realized that a woman was aboard. Not just any woman: Elias Blackwood's daughter.

My eyes widened as I stumbled back, grasping the fact that I was severely outnumbered. I would be fighting for my life, lucky to escape this confrontation. There were too many men aboard.

"Now you see?" Grayson asked. "There will be no stopping them."

"I . . ."

A young girl of only seven sprang to mind, fear creeping into my body and threatening to set me trembling. I assessed each man, discerning who might try to force their way into my cabin, who would exploit me, and who showed me compassion. Did they know whose daughter I was? Or did they only see me as a woman Grayson had brought on board? Soon the whispers began.

"Hold!" Grayson shouted, using the rigging to climb up to the railing and survey the crew. "Hear me now and hear me well. All of you know the mission. I'll not fall victim to piracy again, and the man responsible will be brought to justice. Livie Blackwood is my prisoner. Under my protection. Should any of you harm her or touch a single hair on her head, you will face the worst punishment possible."

More murmurs swept across the deck. Connor stood at the helm, arms crossed, a fleeting smile on his face. Of all the men present, I assumed he knew Grayson best. Another man with wild auburn hair and a red scarf leaned against the railing next to Connor, legs crossed at the ankles as though he had no care in the world. No one, not even Connor, would be safe from Grayson's vengeance if they laid a hand on me. My father had done the same with his men when I boarded, just a child, and he doled out extreme punishments for the slightest provocation.

"Is that understood?"

I heard whispers of agreement, barely audible.

"Is that understood?" he repeated with more vigor.

"Aye, Captain," came the response from every man he looked at. I took a step sideways, only for Grayson to leap down and seize my arm. My eyes widened as I fought to suppress the fear that surged within me. Like my father, he was both ruthless and cold.

"We'll finish this below," he said tersely. "I must remind you once again that you will not set foot on this deck without me. Understood?"

I allowed him to pull me across the deck, prioritizing my safety above all else. I'd be damned if I let him protect me against any of his men. I had my own weapons, and I would use them.

"You needn't drag me," I protested.

"On the contrary, you *are* my prisoner to do with as I please. Forgive me if I'd rather not let you fall into the wrong hands."

I scoffed as we neared the stairs. "I've already fallen into the wrong hands. Forgive me if I care little who gains what from this. None of you will gain anything. I told you the truth when I said he would not come for me."

And I prayed fervently that my father would not come.

In the dimly lit corridor, he paused mid-stride and swung around to face me. "Just because you think that doesn't make it true. You are worth more money as a slave than anything else. And these men are greedy. But they know my mission. I will not fail."

"Your mission? You think my father captured your vessel and stole your cargo?" I asked, offering no resistance as he pulled me into his quarters.

I understood he felt I'd be safer in his quarters than my own cabin. But he was sadly mistaken. I'd face greater danger from him here than there. He had to know what threatened to break free between us. I'd seen the way he looked at me sometimes.

Was I mistaken, and did he want me only as bait? Or did he desire me?

"And me? That is why you want me to reveal his whereabouts?"

He shut the door behind us, releasing my arm only when he was certain I wouldn't bolt. To be truthful, I had nowhere to go. I could return to my cabin and lock the door, but Grayson was strong enough to kick it down if he wanted to.

"It would be much better if I caught him by surprise, yes, but either way, he will come for you, Livie. My crew is faithful to me, but that is not to say one of them has their own agenda where you are concerned."

I smirked at him, feeling a pleasant thrill at the way his eyes darkened. "Why did you tell your men I'm under your protection?"

"Do spare me your appreciation. I did so only as a strategy. I won't have you falling into the wrong hands before I achieve my goal. No one," he leaned in closer, the musky smell of him mingling with the tang of the sea invading my senses, "no one will keep me from my objective. If I have to keep you in here to protect my investment, I will."

His fingers tucked under my chin, tilting my face up to ensure our gazes connected.

"They are watching you, Livie," he breathed. "Stay invisible."

Chapter Twenty One

I tossed and turned all night in my narrow bed, the conversation with Grayson earlier that day leaving me confused. Who could possibly be seeking me out, and why was being Elias Blackwood's daughter so unsafe? As a woman, I felt I had little worth according to most men I knew. If I were Percival's wife, I'd be a pawn in politics, managing his household and upholding our social standing. It would be *his* home I kept, not mine. I would bear *his* children, along with his name. My contributions would go unacknowledged.

Had Grayson really captured me? Or perhaps he had rescued me. Given the chance, I would never return to London, to that life I secretly abhorred. Never. Damn the consequences, whatever they may be. By now, Percival might have revealed my secret dockside activities, making me as wanted as my father.

The confines of the small cabin were causing me to perspire, unable to sleep and soon struggling to breathe. We were nowhere near the Caribbean yet, and the heat would soon become unbearable. Now was the time to breathe in the clear, crisp, slightly chilled air.

Grayson's words haunted me as I slowly eased open the door to find the corridor vacant, vigilant in anyone who might be watching, waiting. Slipping out, the floorboards creaked beneath me. If anyone caught me, I would fight them with the daggers strapped to my waist. I'd forgone my cloak, needing the cool air on my skin.

The moment I saw the twinkling stars in the vast sky overhead, I took a deep breath of fresh air. Expecting some crew hands to be on deck, someone at the helm and those on lookout, I had still fully dressed before leaving the confines of my prison. Lock on the inside or not, it was still a prison.

Other than the steady swish of water slapping against the hull of the ship, the night held a certain quiet, much like secrets do. Beneath it all, however, was nothing but turbulence. Like a whisper, I moved toward the railing, tilting my face to the breeze as I had done earlier. I hadn't had enough time before to really enjoy it. To sit in the sun with the wind upon my face, I could lose myself in nostalgia.

It took only a moment for me to realize I was not alone on deck. As soon as I closed my eyes, hooking my arms over the railing and leaning just enough to feel the sea spray on my face, I heard heavy breathing.

Curious, I looked up at the quarterdeck to see Connor sitting with his feet propped up on the wheel, his eyes closed. A quiet laugh escaped me. The sound came from the other side of the ship. Before I could talk myself out of it, I moved toward the sound.

Movement behind the stacked crates and the giant mainmast slowed my steps, and I risked a glance back to ensure Connor still slumbered at his post. Still, I palmed the dagger in my right hand to be certain.

A quiet laugh caught in my throat as I pressed up against the mast, peering around at whoever might be over there, doing only God knew what with that heavy breathing. There were no other women aboard, as far as I knew, so it couldn't be someone in the throes of passion. I had my doubts it was that, considering the breathing.

My breath seized in my throat at the sight that awaited me. My heart thundered in my chest, my eyes widening slightly at the bare-chested man wielding a short sword and dagger, fighting an invisible enemy.

Sweat gleamed in the moonlight on his golden skin, sparkling like a prize, and his movements were sure and steady. He was so close I could hear the whoosh of the blade as he swung it near me. He couldn't see me, continuing his independent training. Anytime I sensed him turning in my direction, I switched to the other side of the mast.

I weakened, watching him with glazed eyes. Grayson Valle could be the most virile man I had ever witnessed in this way. Even growing up amidst pirates on my father's ship, I had never seen a man built like this. I couldn't recall any of them ever practicing swordplay shirtless in the moonlight.

"You can come out, Livie."

My mouth snapped shut at the same moment my eyes did. Having no idea how he could have heard me behind the mast, I'd made no sound at all. As if hearing my thoughts, his deep voice slid over me.

"I can smell you."

I opened my eyes, bolstering my defiance at those four words. Left with only a basin of water and not even a knob of soap, what did he expect? I stepped out, eyebrow raised at him. We swayed with the ship, still steady on our feet, staring at each other. He matched me, raising his eyebrow.

"I do not smell," I snapped, though after a few days with only water to wash with, I knew I did. I just wanted to be as difficult with him as he was with me. "And if I do, you could at least offer me a bath."

He bent, muscles rippling, and picked up another sword. Without a word, he tossed it to my feet, but when I reached out and caught the hilt, a slow smile bent his mouth.

"Did I tell you that you smelled bad?"

Er, no. I rotated my wrist, testing the weight and feel of the sword. Heavy, but I knew I would be able to handle it. Used to daggers, it had been quite some time since I'd held a sword. Swords were cumbersome, even for a woman dressed like a man.

"I can provide you with a bath, but you'll do it in my quarters."

Hmmm, tempting. I might do so just to be as clean as I could. It would be several more weeks before we reached Antigua. The men would bathe on the deck, especially when it rained, or they would jump into the water on a calm, much warmer day. I could do neither.

"Do you want me to fight you?" I asked, stepping toward him in a wide circle. "Is that what you want?"

He tilted his head, studying me. "You win, I'll provide you with a bath."

A laugh erupted from me. A man of his stature, I would never beat him. I wouldn't even be able to tire him out. He knew that, and yet he made a bargain I could not possibly win.

"Alone," I said.

"Very well," he conceded. "I've seen you fight. You are without fear."

"This isn't without fear," I admitted. "You could skewer me and hang me from the mast. It would never prove anything."

"It would prove me an idiot, for doing so would leave me without the leverage of your purpose here on my ship." He sighed. "Very well, if you win, a bath. Alone. If I win, a bath. With me."

My face flushed at the thought. Did I dare to take such a wager? I had to be out of my mind to consider it, but a bath sounded divine. I rolled my shoulders, stepping lightly to the side and watching him match my movements. Or did I match his? Either way, we danced around each other without touching, felt without feeling. We let our surroundings and each other guide us. When he lifted his sword, I touched mine to his in a ringing of steel against steel.

"You truly had no inclination that you were thwarting Percival? Rescuing me from a life of hell with a man who only wanted to possess me?" I asked, stepping lightly.

With a quick flick of his wrist, his sword met mine with enough force to send vibrations up my arm to the elbow. I held firm, parrying and sending my blade back against his.

His eyebrows raised, looking formidable.

"You have no wish to be possessed?"

I laughed genuinely. "By a man like him? I'd rather die."

Spinning around to avoid my blade again, Grayson laughed low. I admired his footwork, the way he held back whenever his blade slashed against mine. It only proved that he didn't want to harm his *prisoner*. Or he truly did not wish to bathe with me. I wondered if he even had a bathtub on board. And big enough for two? I doubted it wholeheartedly.

"Perhaps there may have been more to my offer than I originally let on," he said smoothly.

"Do tell," I murmured, slashing at him only to have him jump back.

"Did you know that your mother was from the south of France?"

I did. The soft lilt of her accent still whispered in my ears at night, especially after those difficult nights when I could imagine her running her fingers through my hair when trying to get me to sleep, telling me tales.

When I didn't answer, Grayson continued. "Our mothers were friends."

That knowledge slipped me up, but he knew it would and he did not take advantage of my weakness. If he had, I would have had a nasty gash on my arm when he could have brought his sword down and disarmed me.

My spine stiffened. "And yet I'm to be used as your bait."

"It's more complicated than that, and you know it."

"Explain to me why," I demanded, momentarily pushing him back with my wild swings, only to have him parry and force me back again.

"Your father is responsible for attacking my ship, stealing my cargo, and murdering my brother. I will avenge him. I will bring your father to justice."

A fair argument, even if I did not agree. That didn't mean I had to like it.

With all my strength, I jabbed, only to have him sidestep and spin around again. Each time he did so, he moved closer to me. I couldn't shake the feeling that he was trying to fluster me into making a mistake. I strengthened my spine, fighting against the feelings that were growing for him despite everything I'd been through the past week.

With each movement, each swing of my sword, step, and spin, I grew fatigued. I knew his tactics. He was simply wearing me down. Grayson knew he could best me in a fight, weapon or no, which made me wonder what he was trying to accomplish with this.

I could feel my heart beating erratically, sweat sliding down my back, yet I continued to deflect his swings. I couldn't comprehend why I was still able to resist him. He should have disarmed me by now. I would need a bath after perspiring this much.

Instead of stepping to the side, I stepped forward to surprise him, only to have him spin around and twist his blade, expecting it to fall from my grasp. But I held firm, refusing to be bested without a weapon. I twirled around, bringing my blade up against his until it slipped from his fingers. His back hit the mast with enough force to make him grunt.

Breathing hard, I had him chest to chest with my sword dangling from my fingers until it too dropped to the wooden planks beneath us. I felt every inch of my body against his, his strength radiating from him as though he poured himself into me. My lips parted. His eyes bored into mine, gleaming in the moonlight.

Achingly slow, his hand slid against my neck, drawing my mouth to his in a searing kiss. The feel of his mouth against mine made me realize why his smile was so devilish. Everything about him screamed wickedness as he kissed me thoroughly, our heavy breaths mingling together.

I tasted him. He tasted me. Warmth flooded my blood, liquefying my limbs into submission and gathering like a storm in the center of my body. Memories came rushing back, and it had never been like this. His lips demanded; I surrendered. When I should have pulled away from him, I leaned in for more, entranced by my own desires.

At the sound of a voice clearing, my eyes shot open, and I pulled away from him abruptly. Connor stood on the quarterdeck, his hands braced on the railing, staring down at us. Something must have woken him, and he now peered at us with his eyebrows raised.

I turned back to Grayson, his chest heaving but still leaning against the mast. His eyes were alight with desire, his tongue darting out to taste his lips.

"You'll have your bath, Livie," he said, pushing away and striding toward Connor.

Chapter Twenty Two

Grayson

The next day, as we entered the waters of the Bay of Biscay, I watched Livie closely on deck. True to her task, she recorded items needing repair and documented the happenings aboard the ship. When I leaned over her to review her markings, she quickly pulled the ledger away as though hiding a secret. But I'd already seen her meticulous recordings, so close to her that I felt the gentle stir of wisps of hair coming loose from her braid. Desire pooled low in my anatomy, dangerously becoming more frequent.

I allowed her on deck against my better judgment, knowing my men were watching her. I preferred that none of them looked her way at all, but this way, I could keep an eye on her rather than let her be alone in her cabin and at risk. Having seen her in action, I was aware that Livie could very well protect herself. Still, something deep inside me wouldn't allow me to leave anything to chance.

I couldn't stop thinking about last night under the moonlight, questioning my sanity for making such a bargain with her. While she was incapable of defeating me with a sword or by any other means, I recognized that her anger would find a better outlet in a fight than in being suppressed and allowed to spread. The fight, even though I controlled how far it went, had done us both good. Until I'd allowed her to win and push me against the mast. I could no more stop myself from kissing her than I could from breathing.

By God, I couldn't recall ever kissing a woman so deeply, nor having her return my kiss with such passion, yet trepidation. She couldn't realize how her presence affected me, making me stumble in everything I was known for: my strength, my resolve, and the goal that had brought her to me.

She'd been right to question my reasons for offering to take her away from London. Deep down, I couldn't bear to leave her there for the pompous Percival Monteclaire. I was sure my mother would agree. The spark I'd seen in her eyes the night we met would have faded as his wife.

I could no more stop the plunder of her mouth than I could halt my mission. Complications be damned. I was grateful that Connor had stopped us when he did. Kissing her felt like crossing a line I'd never be able to return from, yet that didn't stop my dreams during the night, which continued where we'd left off, as though she were still within reach.

The dream had been so real, with her small hands sliding up my chest, delicate fingers curling around my neck as if holding me exactly where she wanted me. A sigh escaped her lips, and I groaned, deepening the kiss. If I was going to go down in flames, by God, I would do it with her.

The softness of her curves beneath my hands urged me on. I wanted to pick her up, wrap her long, shapely legs around my waist, and bury myself in her. Thoughts emptied from my mind at the steady thrum of her heart against mine.

"Cap'n?"

At the sound of Kit's voice, I froze. Here I was, daydreaming about kissing the very woman I had stolen from her home, the very woman I should despise for half of her parentage, when I should have been preparing. Kit would think the worst of me for this, but if I were a good man, I would care. But I wasn't, and Kit should know that by now.

"What is it?" I ground out, arms crossed as I stood beside the helm, glancing at Livie instead of the course as I should have been.

"Storm's brewing," he said. "I can smell it."

The ship remained steady, but when I stepped away to look at the surrounding sky, lightning flickered within the darkness on the horizon. A storm could never be good in the middle of the ocean. Many ships couldn't withstand the turbulent waves and dangerous lightning, ending up at the bottom of the sea.

I looked back at Livie, cursing myself for the pleasure that surged through me at the sight of her. The crew knew her identity now, there hadn't been a need to pretend. Yet when the ship pitched, she grasped for the nearest stable object. It appeared to me that she still played a role, tricking the crew into believing she was a woman unfamiliar with life at sea rather than the daughter of one of the most feared men sailing these waters. She lied so convincingly.

Kit grimaced at the faint sound of thunder in the distance. A storm at night was worse when the inky blackness was illuminated only by flashes of lightning. Livie appeared innocently unaware of what would happen next.

"Aye, I smell it too, Kit." I glanced over at Connor. "Preparations begin immediately. The storm looks to be a few hours away, but it could miss us. Track it. Kit," I said, slapping him on the shoulder, "I need you to do something for me."

I allowed Livie to continue gazing out at the wide expanse of water while I assisted with storm preparations. Unbeknownst to her, she had played right into my hands last night. Never make a deal with the devil.

It was three-quarters of an hour later when I strode up behind her, pressing as close as I dared without touching her until I could feel her entire body tense. The laugh that escaped from deep in my throat was more sinister than I had expected.

"What are you doing?" Livie hissed, whirling around. "You're going to seduce me right in front of your men? That's hardly going to win you any favors."

I seized her wrist, tugging her with me as I strode across the deck. She resisted, but her strength was no match for mine as we entered the hallway leading to my quarters.

"I will not stay in your quarters during a storm," she snapped, until I opened the door to reveal the round wooden tub in the middle of the room.

Kit, Sully, and Wiley had hauled in buckets of water, though it wasn't warm and likely not as full as she would prefer. Nevertheless, it was a bath. For her.

The timing wasn't perfect, as I was hoping she'd bathe so we could empty it ahead of the storm, if it arrived. Storms were as unpredictable as a woman. Sometimes you get hit, other times, they completely miss.

Livie immediately stopped, her mouth falling open at the sight before her. If I could keep her in this room during the storm, it would be worth it. But for now, I'd give her what she desired, what I had promised, even if I had allowed her to best me in the fight.

"This . . . " She turned her bright blue eyes to me. "This is for me?"

"Aye, all for you. As promised."

For a moment, I thought she would begin undressing right there in the room. Instead, she whirled and threw her arms around my neck. I grabbed her arms, not to separate us, but to savor the feeling of her pressed against me. She expressed her gratitude, reigning in whatever thoughts she had of me and revealing her heart. A heart I never thought she would have.

"Grayson, I'm not sure what to say."

She pulled away, her teeth sinking into her bottom lip. The sight of the woman in front of me revealed a level of vulnerability I'd never seen. Drawing my spine straight, I nodded.

"Enjoy your bath."

No sooner had I turned my back to leave than I heard her belt hit the floor with a clank. As tempting as it was to turn around, I kept my composure and moved quickly before I could change my mind and join her without consent. The tub was barely big enough for one person, but by damn, I could manage.

After the door closed tightly behind me, I stood in the hallway for a moment. The splash of water, followed by a womanly laugh, drew a smile from me that lingered on my lips even as I went on deck to survey the preparations.

"You fool," Connor said when I joined him. "You won't get that vision out of your head, you know. I know *I* won't."

"Keep your tongue behind your teeth," I growled. "I left before she disrobed."

He tsked. "Doesn't matter, Gray. You'll envision it. And that's going to keep you awake for many nights to come, with no company but your own hand."

Lightning in the distance grew closer, dark gray clouds rolling in with it, accompanied by occasional claps of thunder. We were still leagues away from the storm, which would take roughly an hour to reach us. It would have been too close for comfort with her in the bath, and I hadn't provided her with a time frame.

Damn him and his words, I thought as I strode to starboard and raised the spyglass to the northwest. Aye, this storm would hit us, but it didn't look as bad as most. God willing, we'd stay afloat.

"Half the crew is sick," Connor mentioned.

"Not an excuse, and you know it well."

He made a face. "Don't blame them for your issues with women. She recorded it already, but many of them are too sick to be on deck when the storm hits us."

My eyes flashed. "And I said sickness is no excuse. Unless the men are dying, they pull their weight on this ship. I'll accept no less. We all work through it, or we die. Those are the options."

When he nodded, I knew he was thinking only of those who might not make it through. Failure to heed the monstrous storm gales could easily sweep men overboard. But I had to be firm or risk losing the respect of everyone. If that happened, a mutiny would soon follow. I had to complete my mission, and once that was done, I couldn't give a damn what happened to this ship.

I had spent years traversing these waters, first as a trader for our rare silks and more recently seeking the man indirectly responsible for my brother's murder. I would avenge Adam before retiring as captain and living out my days in peace. Despite being next in line following my father's demise, I had no desire to return home.

My father's relentless pursuit of control over me was met with my perpetual failure to satisfy him. I'd always come second to Adam. My brother never failed to do whatever he was told, honest and chivalrous to a fault. I would forever be my father's biggest regret for a son, even with Adam gone.

Once I captured Elias, my father would need to admit I'm as capable as Adam ever was. I didn't dare dream of more. I intended to live a quiet life in Barbados.

Kit hopped up the stairs, joining Connor and me with an impish grin on his face. Storms worried him, and if I were a better man, I'd have him stay with Livie in my cabin. But Kit was as stubborn as she was. Livie would probably disobey me, and Kit might too. But Kit had no choice but to obey me or risk punishment.

"Is she done?" I asked.

He shook his head, his cheeks blooming with color. "Could still hear splashin' when I put my ear to the door. D'ya want me to get her out?"

Connor burst into laughter.

While I shot him a glare, I placed my hand on Kit's shoulder. "No, laddie. I'll get her out of there myself. If I can convince her to stay in my quarters during the storm, would you stay there with her to ensure she doesn't get it in her head to come out?"

He stared at me as though I were asking him to commit murder. "Aye, Cap'n."

"Good."

I strode away, jumping down the stairs two at a time and rounding the corner like a man on a mission. Sure enough, the sound of humming met my ears at the door. I knocked twice before opening it, taking pleasure in the way her eyes widened as she covered herself.

"Storm's coming," I said. "You'll need to cut your bathing time short."

She sighed as she tilted her head to the side. "'Twas good while it lasted. Would you have a sheet of linen for me to dry off, or would you rather I stand as I am?"

Desire coursed through me at the thought of her rising from the tub, water sluicing from her glistening skin. I shook my head and moved toward the bed to grab the linen cloth I'd set aside and present it to her.

"This is as good as you'll get. Sully and Kit are tasked with emptying this tub before the storm hits."

She raised her hand, droplets of water falling back into the tub as she motioned for me to turn. With a grunt, I turned and listened as the water splashed around in the tub.

"This is highly improper," she said, her voice breathless. "I can't remember the last time I was unclothed in the same room as a man."

I nearly turned back around, but she tsked at me.

"I'm not finished yet. You'll wait."

"Rather demanding for someone gifted with a bath, aren't you?" I replied, folding my arms in front of me.

"Did you expect anything less? And I won this pleasure. It was not a gift."

The rustle of clothing filled the air, but I stood my ground with my back turned, giving her the respect she deserved. While I strongly desired her, even to an agonizing degree, I would never touch her without her permission. While I wasn't a good man, I was certainly not the scoundrel she painted me as. I didn't take without an offering. Not with women.

"All right, you may turn around."

When I turned, she wore her breeches and a tunic, but her feet were bare. I found myself looking at her petite feet before traveling up the length of her body. The tunic had grown damp from her hair, the thin fabric translucent under my heated gaze. Flushed from head to toe, I strode toward the table to roll up the maps and tuck them away safely.

"You'll remain here for the duration of the storm," I said.

"I hardly think so."

I turned, pinning her with my gaze. She was a vixen when in a fighting mood. It was no surprise she could go from a grateful woman to one who never admitted defeat in an instant. There were several ways I could think of to assist her in improving such a mood.

"I can help, Grayson."

"I said no."

She opened her mouth to argue, but I held up my hand, and she fell silent. A captain was to be obeyed in all things, and while she served as my clerk, she would never truly obey me. I knew that. But that didn't mean I wouldn't try to get her to listen to reason.

"I can't keep my eyes on you and ensure this ship stays afloat, Livie. Don't ask that of me. Please."

All at once, her gaze softened, and her stance relaxed. Had I finally gotten through to her? She moved toward the bed, sitting down to pull on her boots one at a time. I wondered if I should have Kit stay here with her.

"How do you handle storms?" I asked.

She shrugged. "It's probably best that I stay in here. Being swept overboard would not be good. I can't swim well."

My eyebrows shot up. A captain's daughter, likely raised on or around water, and she couldn't swim well? I could do nothing but laugh. This woman surprised me at every turn. I couldn't remember the last time someone had made me feel . . . lighter.

"Shall I send Kit in to keep you company?"

She shrugged again. "Only if he wants to. I shouldn't keep any men from aiding. I'd much rather this ship stay upright."

All I could do was nod. I wanted the same thing. But as I strode to the door, I couldn't help but picture her standing naked in the tub. The thought heated my blood like nothing else, intruding on my mind while I tried to maintain a sense of responsibility. Like a love-struck boy, I swung open the door and left before I did something foolish.

Chapter Twenty Three

Grayson

"Catch that rigging before it smashes into someone!" I shouted from the main deck, sideways rain pelting me like tiny pinpricks as the ship pitched back and forth.

The storm's violence tossed the vessel around like a rag doll, while the crew did their best to maintain order. Connor, at the wheel, struggled to steer in such conditions. As I often did during storms, I could only pray that the ship stayed above water.

No amount of preparation had equipped us for the onslaught of this Atlantic storm. I didn't have enough men onboard to contain its fury, with some ill and others either dead or injured.

For a moment, I thought about the woman in my quarters. She had been furious when I ordered her to stay there for the duration of the storm.

The fire in her eyes was a sight to behold, a fury I had seen before and selfishly looked forward to witnessing again. I couldn't be responsible for her safety while ensuring the ship and crew remained safe. Watching over her as well would have been too much to handle.

A snap caught my attention. The spritsail had torn free from the rigging at the bow. The rain-soaked deck made it nearly impossible to cross without slipping. Together, Wiley and I made our way toward the sail that threatened to come entirely loose and float away into the black sea.

Wiley, spry at twenty-two, climbed up to the jib boom like a monkey while I held my breath. With the ship tossed about, he would be lucky to hang on to such a narrow perch to rescue the sail. My unbound hair slapped against my cheek as I watched him re-tie the rigging to hold it in place.

Another snap split the air, but I waited to ensure Wiley got back down to the deck before turning my attention to another sail coming loose. I had promised the crew an entire cask of rum after we weathered this storm, a bottle for myself included.

As soon as Wiley's boots hit the deck, I spun around and squinted through the flashes of lightning to see a lithe figure, distinctly feminine, sprinting across the deck. One of the main topsails was flapping angrily in the air. My jaw clenched as I watched Livie take a flying leap at the rigging, climbing up the ropes as though her life depended on it.

"Damn it all to bloody hell," I shouted, charging toward the mainmast.

"Would you look at that!" Wiley said from behind me, apparently following my trek toward the determined woman.

Halfway up the mast, Livie paused and looked down at me. Lightning flashed, revealing the determination in her eyes. Unlike any man I'd seen before, she grabbed the rigging to propel herself toward the sail. I caught a glint of a blade as she tucked it between her teeth before yanking herself the rest of the way to the crow's nest.

My heart thundered as I watched her for another moment before running toward her at breakneck speed. Though my boots felt like they might slip, I ran as if my survival depended on it. If she fell . . .

A hand on my arm stopped me, and I looked at Kit, his hair plastered to the side of his head, water streaming down his cheeks. He pointed up.

"Damn vixen," I muttered. "I'm going to get her, Kit."

I grabbed the rigging, but Kit's grip tightened on my forearm. He shook his head and pointed at her again. "Look."

Livie was swinging from rope to rope, that damned knife still clenched between her teeth. Her hair had come undone, and her feet were bare. She wound the end of a rope around her leg to ensure she wouldn't fall and was bringing the sail in hand over hand.

She tied knot after knot with incredible speed to secure the sail, and I watched, captivated, before she began her descent. The ropes were slick with rain, and her hands slipped as she descended. Suddenly, she lost her grip and went flying until the rope around her leg stopped her.

"Get down here. Now!"

I didn't realize I'd shouted until her eyes met mine, right before she grabbed another rope and unwound her leg from the one she'd secured herself with. Like an acrobat, she grasped the ropes and flipped backward until she swung around and jumped down beside me. When she withdrew the knife from her teeth, I wanted to shake her until her teeth rattled. Instead, she gave me an impish grin and ran off down the main deck to help elsewhere.

Something shifted in that moment. I looked around at the men who'd witnessed her act of bravery, or stupidity. Equal admiration met my gaze, even when I looked back at Kit. He grinned knowingly.

After this storm passed, I vowed to drink an entire bottle of rum. Then I was going to tell her how reckless her actions were. But before I could think of what I would say, I was after her. Instead of being on deck, she needed to be in my quarters, dry, safe, not carousing on deck while the men handled the ship. We were all here to ensure her safety.

The flash of lightning blinded me for a moment before I saw the swell in the distance rising over the railing. It was headed directly for us, and if it crashed into the ship, it would sweep her overboard, never to be seen again. Even if she knew how to swim, the violent waves would overpower her.

Livie saw it too; her eyes grew wide. For the briefest moment, she pushed the wet strands of her hair out of her face and tilted her chin up as if choosing to meet the wave head-on.

Absolutely not, I thought, grabbing a rope from nearby and rushing toward her. I wrapped the rope around my waist as quickly as I could before reaching her, yanking her against me as I threw the rope around her waist.

"Brace yourselves!" I shouted to anyone who could hear me just as I felt her hands knock mine out of the way. She quickly tied the knot faster than anyone I'd ever seen, even with the swell arching over us.

She threw her arms around my waist and pressed her face against my chest, squeezing. I prayed while my arms enclosed her. The wave hit with such ferocity that I thought we'd all be gone. The ship would surely capsize after such a monstrous swell.

No matter what, I locked my arms around her torso, slipping my leg between hers for momentum. Her arms remained tight around me when the wave crashed against us. It took my legs out from beneath me, the rope tightening and snatching my breath as well. But we clung to each other, desperate to hold on for our lives.

The deck met my back with such force that I thought a lesser man would have broken bones. The waves tossed us around like puppets. Livie still had her face tucked against me, the top of her head just beneath my chin. Slowly, the wave receded and pulled us toward the railing. The rope jerked us to a halt, and when we finally settled, limbs intertwined on the deck, she lifted her head and our eyes met.

Bright blue eyes intensified my heartbeat, plump lips slightly parted in surprise. Wet strands of her hair hung loose, but her gaze held mine, threatening to be my undoing.

I couldn't help myself. My mouth crashed down on hers with the intensity of the wave that had just hit us. My fingers smoothed along each side of her jaw, grasping her face until her mouth opened to me.

The storm continued to rage around us, slowly easing as it passed. I held her in my embrace, continuing to kiss her as though branding her mine and mine alone, afraid that if I released her, it would be the end. The end of everything.

Chapter Twenty Four

"Who taught you how to do that?"

My head snapped up at Grayson's commanding voice from the doorway. Still thoroughly soaked, his tunic and breeches clung to his powerful body. His wet hair hung just shy of his shoulders, framing his piercing eyes. In his hand, he clutched a bottle of rum.

The kiss he gave me after the near-drowning and the look in his eyes when he ordered me down from the sail repair were unforgettable. When he kissed me, it felt as if he poured everything into it. That memory would stay with me forever.

The sail I saved from snapping loose would have been detrimental to our survival had it floated away entirely. While I understood that sails on ships were repairable, the absence of the mainsail would have been a considerable disadvantage. According to the ship's ledgers, we did not have a spare mainsail.

Promptly after the storm passed, Grayson steered me back into his quarters and left me there. Kiss be damned, he was furious with me for being on deck when he'd ordered me to stay below. I didn't know what had come over me. Ordinarily, I listened to orders, but when I went above to the main deck and saw the mainsail flapping, I could not sit idly by.

I sat on the edge of the bed, his bed, after changing into dry clothes. Kit had found a trunk below filled with mismatched garments, most of which were too big for me while mine needed laundering. I rolled up the breeches, my bare feet and ankles peeking out from underneath, and tied the tunic at the waist. Without a corset, the tunic fell to the side, leaving my shoulders bare.

Even after the storm had passed, the ship still rocked precariously with residual swells. Kit had lit a lantern in Grayson's quarters and left me with a change of clothes while the men surveyed any damage aboard. The storm had raged for hours. The sun rising on the horizon behind us, and my exhaustion had reached its peak.

Grayson ignored my state of dress when he stepped into the room and closed the door behind him with the heel of his boot. The finality of the noise kept my gaze on him.

"Did your father teach you how to do that?"

His question confused me. He knew my lineage, and I pondered the reason for his query until I understood that I had withheld my genuine self from the crew and Grayson during the voyage. Until now.

"Teach me how to do what? Can you be more specific?" I asked, watching him sit heavily in a wooden chair and pull off one boot, then the other.

He leaned back in the chair, pulled the cork with his teeth, and took a long gulp from the amber-colored liquor. I watched him tilt his head back for a moment before lowering his gaze to meet mine. He wasn't in the mood to play games.

"Save the mainsail. Tie ropes faster and more efficiently than I've seen any man do. *Climb* ropes like that. All equally terrifying to anyone unfamiliar with such tasks, let alone a woman."

He lifted the bottle, an unspoken offering. I slid off the bed and walked toward him with slow purpose. Did he wish to continue what we'd started on deck only a short time ago? A deep part of me did. Grayson could take me in his arms at any moment, and I would nearly swoon at his feet like any genteel lady of higher society. Because of that, I walked up to him and plucked the bottle from his grasp.

Darkness shadowed his eyes as he watched me tip it back, the searing liquid heating my insides, or perhaps it was the way he watched me. It felt as if he were waiting for me to make some sudden confession. But a confession to what, I couldn't know. He already knew everything he needed to know about me, didn't he? I was Elias Blackwood's daughter and his only offspring. I didn't know what else he needed to know.

"I've never seen such expertise," he murmured.

"Are you still speaking of my actions on deck?" I whispered. "Or the way I drink this rum? You see, you might have been expecting a perfectly poised woman of refined upbringing, never shouting, always behaving. I did that for three years. I'm not about to continue."

I took another drink, handing the bottle back to him as I relished the burn traveling down my throat. There were things I had yet to admit, things others were not privy to, such as my time spent between losing my mother and being discovered in a delicate position with Edward.

One small part of me was tired of living such a lie, but admitting it openly would only sink me further into retreat, and I'd done that my entire life. I spoke the truth when I admitted to not continuing. To protect myself, I suppressed my feelings, my history. With squared shoulders, I lifted my chin.

"I don't think I can do it anymore," I admitted in a whisper.

After he set the bottle down on the table beside him, he raised his hands to my hips and drew me down onto his lap. "Tell me, Livie." His voice, commanding and deep, sent flames through my body, burning hotter than the rum.

"Did you mean what you said when we were departing? Am I only a means to an end?"

Although I asked, I had no desire to learn the response. Surely what was happening between us was more than whatever bargain he had for me to fulfill. I had to believe it, though parting from Edward had nearly been my undoing. For so long afterward, I pined for a love I thought I felt. But had it been love?

"We aren't talking about that now. Tell me what happened after your mother died."

I closed my eyes for a moment, wishing I could tell him everything about my life. But I didn't trust him, just as he didn't trust me. Feelings surfaced, but they did not equal trust.

Even if it didn't have to be this way. He could chase as many destinies as he wanted, but he would never be happy. Pushing lightly against his chest, I stood, unwilling to be his decoy for the duration of our voyage. I couldn't.

Grayson watched me walk to the door. I could feel his eyes on my back as I left. I glanced back when I reached his door.

"I was on my father's ship."

His gaze burned into mine. "The entire time? Until you were sent to London?"

I nodded once.

"Why? Why would he allow you sail with him for . . . almost ten years, then suddenly bring you to London to live with your aunt?"

That was not a question I would willingly speak of yet.

"All you need to know, Grayson, is that my father taught me everything I know. If you need anything done on board this ship, there is no one more qualified for the task than me."

He seemed too shocked to speak, his mind racing behind his eyes. Many people underestimated me. But a person does not survive life on a ship with an intimidating father without coming away with something less than perfection. Even the crew did not have the same standards that I did. He expected so much more from me as his daughter, his blood, his namesake. And I would never escape it.

Chapter Twenty Five

Her parting words rattled me. Elias Blackwood had taught his daughter everything she knew. I should have known. I knew that he had imparted knowledge to her during her time on his vessel. What I hadn't expected was that she had been on his vessel for so long. Livie executed her tasks with such practiced hands, such precision, as if she had been doing them for years. It became clear that she had been doing them for years. She didn't just sail on his ship; she likely knew everything about it. It left me questioning how she had managed to stay concealed while everyone believed she had perished with her mother during the hurricane.

What other tricks did Livie have up her sleeve? From what I had witnessed today, she could be an asset to any crew. Her father's decision not to keep her left me puzzled. She had proven herself by helping to repair the ship after the storm, tying knots with lightning speed, and even stitching up a few wounds. While I admired her, the thought of taking her to bed was a separate matter entirely.

Because the storm had lasted for such a long time, the crew unanimously agreed to delay their survival celebration until they completed all repairs. Sully produced his fiddle, rum was retrieved from the ship's storage, and Kit fashioned a drum using rope, a damaged sail, and a broken cask.

With the sunset came the rum and music, fostering a joyous atmosphere that made my men smile. I wandered the deck, nodding at each of them as I strolled. While I pretended to survey the repairs, all of which I had overseen or helped with, my eyes searched for one person.

When I caught sight of her leaning over the railing, speaking with Wiley, I noted her rapt attention to whatever he was saying. Her focus did not waver. She remained completely engaged. But when he said something that made her laugh, her laughter brightened the entire deck.

Jealousy spiked through me, fast and deep. I had never been the type to feel discord over a woman. Women had always eased the ache. True, I had spent time with some more than others over the years, but no woman had captured my attention enough to make me envy other men.

The laugh that fluttered from her throat somehow made her seem even more vibrant. Her smile was radiant, and her eyes danced. Wiley said something else and laughed with her. It didn't seem he aimed to befriend her, and I knew him well enough to recognize when he was chasing a skirt.

Not that I could blame him. Being at sea for weeks at a time had its drawbacks. Days felt like an eternity, and nights felt even longer.

But as I gazed at Livie, something changed. She had come alive beneath my hands both times I'd not been able to control my rising desire, but this was entirely different. Her whimsical laugh drew me in. That was a genuine laugh, impossible to fake. The woman I stared at was the real Livie.

The moment her eyes lifted to meet mine, a spark shot through me. I knew then that this was no ordinary woman. I had sensed she was different when she completed tasks suited for a man and quicker, and weeks ago, she had been dancing in a ballroom filled with high society, her gown floating around her. This was a woman of many talents.

Her lips parted, laughter fading softly, causing Wiley to look my way with his auburn eyebrows drawn together. There was no sense in standing there pretending I hadn't been staring at her beauty. The look in the other man's eyes shouted disappointment. He would not war with me over her attention. He couldn't. Every man aboard had seen me kiss her during the storm, as foolish as I might have been to do so.

Every one of them knew that this was a prize I would not share. And a prize like Livie Blackwood was. A rare one that any man would be a fool to give up.

Clasping my hands behind my back, I dared to approach her. Her hair, still unbound but dry and whipping in the wind, made me want to wrap my hands in it and draw her mouth to mine. I wanted to smother the breathy sighs I'd heard each time I'd claimed her lips. Her eyes darkened demurely as she watched me move closer, as if we were dancing without touching.

The tilt of her head unleashed a merciless desire within me. She was unaware of the effect she had on me with her lips inviting a passionate kiss. Her eyes brightened with anticipation, perhaps a touch of fear, as she stared at me.

Two more steps and I was in front of her, and silence was all that was necessary. I was sure everyone had their eyes on us, but I didn't give one damn about anyone else. There was only her. Livie Blackwood, daughter of my enemy, bane of my existence, and the sole cause of my recent restless nights.

I extended my hand.

Chapter Twenty Six

Livie

Mesmerized, I stared at Grayson's outstretched hand for a moment before raising my eyes to meet his. It was an invitation, not a command. As dark as his eyes were, I sensed something deeper within them. He commanded his crew, his ship, and me, yet the way he offered his hand held no authority at all.

Hesitantly, I reached out, trying not to exhale in a rush the moment his skin touched mine. It was warm and persuasive. If Wiley had said anything, I wouldn't have heard it, so captivated was I by this man's gaze. I should count myself a fool for falling under his spell, whatever this was. But a fool I was, because I wanted him to show me more of the man behind the captain, even if I would not give him the same courtesy.

Hadn't this very thing happened three years ago with a much lesser man? I had been so ensnared by Edward's charm that I was too late to stop it. Caught between an unyielding father and a man who held my fragile heart in the palm of his hand, confusion plagued me when Edward blamed me for our compromising position. I couldn't believe Edward would do such a thing, even though we had navigated the situation together. Regardless of who might take the blame, the disappointment in my father's eyes was unmistakable.

"Livie," Edward whispered, fingertips trailing beneath my tunic. "Can you feel my heart?"

Almost afraid to answer him, my lips quivered. "Aye."

His mouth, steady and sure against my neck, sent shivers skittering down my spine as his palms flattened against the sensitive skin just below my breasts, rising higher and higher until cupping them.

"It beats only for you, love. Always for you."

Delirious from the feeling of his hands, his words went straight to my heart. The ship rocked beneath us, under my narrow bed where we lay with him wedged between my legs. This wasn't his first time entering my cabin secretly, with all the men having passed out from too much drink, and I doubted it would be the last. We'd been so careful.

"You will never leave me?" I asked, my voice breathy as I dragged my fingers through his hair.

"Never," he growled, hips slamming into me as his hand moved to cover my mouth from emitting any sounds that would betray us. "I will never leave you, Livie Blackwood. Someday you will be my wife. I vow it."

Those were the last words he spoke to me before my door crashed open and Edward was dragged away, leaving me bereft from the sudden emptiness. Rand's thick arm was around his neck, a pistol to his temple. The shadow of my father loomed over me as I scrambled to cover myself, his eyes colder than I'd ever seen.

How often I wondered if it had been love I felt for him or merely lust.

I pushed those thoughts aside as Grayson's fingers curled around my hand, gently tugging me away from Wiley, and a moment later, toward an opening on the deck. The drum thundered a beat as he spun me around, as though we were waltzing in a ballroom rather than beneath the stars.

Every man on the crew watched us.

Grayson's feet were swift and sure, leading me into a lively jig. Dancing had been a way of life aboard *The Executioner* during the long days and nights when little else occupied our time, and I knew enough outside of a ballroom to move along with him.

From the age of seven to sixteen, I committed the workings of the ship to memory, even during the times my father taught me how to fight. If he wasn't teaching me, his quartermaster or first mate were. Although his quartermaster, Nels, was well into the latter half of his life, he drilled it into my head how to tie and untie knots with a speed that rivaled any sailor.

Having small hands and fingers helped immensely, as did the hours I spent practicing. Rand taught me how to be quick on my feet and with a dagger. Only my father taught me with a sword. His intolerance for mistakes leaving me with a higher threshold for adventure. I wouldn't make a mistake. His words from when I learned how to climb a mast with such speed echoed: "Someday you'll thank me, lass. This world isn't for the weak. You'll grow up strong, self-reliant, able to protect yourself when the day comes that I can't."

Little did I know how true those words would prove to be.

While fighting was my preference over dancing, my father believed it important for me to learn both how to be a lady and how to be part of the crew. I tilted my chin at Grayson's reassuring smile. My father did me no favors when he sent me ashore. It spurned me, yet he was still my father.

"What are you thinking?" Grayson asked, spinning me into a wide circle before pulling me back into his arms.

"How much I learned growing up despite being aboard a ship surrounded by men. Dancing and whatever little education I could get was included."

The honesty that spilled forth surprised me. I hadn't intended to let Grayson into my life, my *real* life. In this moment, he wasn't commanding me to answer his questions. It felt as if he might genuinely be interested in knowing me.

"I count myself lucky."

"Why is that?"

"A beautiful woman to dance with on this starry night? I can hardly complain."

The compliment didn't go unnoticed. Not one for blushing, I felt an unusual warmth spread across my face and swiftly looked elsewhere, praying he wouldn't notice. I still had my pride, which was nearly all I had left.

"I'm quite certain you could find something to complain about."

"Is that so?"

His words struck me. I'd heard him say them many times before, but the way he said them this time made my feet stumble. It was as if he were challenging me to show him something to complain about. It flustered me.

As the fiddle whined and the drumbeat thundered, Grayson spun me around and around until I felt pleasantly dizzy. I couldn't help but laugh at his quick feet, the feeling of euphoria settling into my bones.

With the crew clapping in unison to the melody, some started dancing, and others soon followed, even without partners. Laughter bubbled up and out of me, louder than I could remember in years. Grayson's eyes lingered on mine, a desire deep within them mirroring my own.

I wondered how long I could hold on to him when all I could think about was his kiss. How long would it be before the day came for him to barter me away? I reveled in how my entire body melted into him, into his practiced hands as they slid down my torso, studying my every curve and dip. I groaned, sure he could see the desire reflected in my eyes.

Chapter Twenty Seven

Several days later, we were hit by another storm as we neared more tropical climates. The ship sustained only minor damage, allowing us to continue our journey south without further delay. I spent the day amid the bustling activity on deck as the ship glided smoothly through the calmer waters. I helped wherever I could on deck, under Grayson's watchful gaze.

After recording what had transpired during the latest storm in the ship's logs, detailing the repairs needed, losses incurred, and injuries suffered, I closed my books and wandered toward the railing near the cannon closest to the bow. Wiley was checking the machinery to ensure its durability in case of an attack. As the sun dipped below the horizon, it created a stunning sky that slowly faded into night.

"Good day to you," he greeted, his eyes lingering on me.

Whenever he had the chance, Wiley flirted shamelessly. He never crossed the line under Grayson's scrutiny, but that never stopped him from trying. His deep auburn hair, ruffled by the wind, peeked out from his red scarf, and his striking deep-set blue eyes made him an attractive man, if a woman were looking for a sailor who would never settle down. I'd had enough conversations with Wiley to know this.

He stood up and leaned beside me at the railing.

"You've been sailing with Grayson for many years, have you not?" I asked.

He eyed me suspiciously, but I smiled kindly. Toying with a frayed rope, he tilted his face up to the sun for a moment before glancing back at me.

"I have, but if you're looking to ask me anything about our captain, I'm afraid I'll have to decline."

I laughed nervously. "No, I'm not seeking information about your fearless leader. I'm just making small talk. I don't know anyone aboard except Grayson, and we don't exactly see eye to eye."

"It can be lonely for those on board, too," he murmured. "Do you want to tell me about yourself, Livie?"

That was where I drew the line. I didn't want to share the painful story of my childhood under my father's scrutiny with anyone. What good would it do? It was over and done. I shook my head and turned to leave, but he caught my wrist, much like Grayson had done before.

"Wiley," Grayson's deep voice cut across the deck, low and dangerous.

Wiley released me quickly, sauntering away without a word to Grayson. Suddenly, I felt bad that Grayson had chased him off. I genuinely wanted to get to know some of the men on the ship, even if it was just to have someone to talk to.

"You didn't need to do that," I snapped, leaning over the railing.

"Unless you want company in your bed tonight, it's good that I did."

"What is it that you want, Captain?" I retorted.

He clasped his hands behind his back, studying me for a moment. "I'd like to invite you to dine with me this evening. Kit has informed me you haven't eaten since this morning."

As easily as the words spilled from his lips, my resolve crumbled. He had interrupted my discussion with Wiley, and while I initially suspected jealousy, his reasons were actually different. It was possible those reasons would surface later, but I thought eating with him was necessary to get more information.

"Very well," I said, stepping closer. "I apologize for snapping at you."

The softness in his eyes nearly made me weak, and he offered me the crook of his arm with a lopsided smile. Grayson Valle, attempting to be a charmer, I mused as I entwined my arm with his and allowed him to lead me across the deck.

Stares followed in our wake, as though he were guiding me toward a dance floor again, making me wonder what those on deck might think of this sudden display. My chin lifted, a surge of pride washing over me as I sensed Grayson beginning to yield.

A white linen-covered table for two, complete with flickering candlelight and wine, awaited in Grayson's room. The room's light faded as the sun went down, intensifying the glow of the candles. I allowed him to lead me to the table, where he pulled out my chair. In front of me sat a simple bowl of turtle stew, thick with onions. Grayson's place was similarly set, aside from the mismatched bowls, with a tray of bread between us.

"Would you like a glass of wine?" he asked once seated across from me.

The ship lurched, and he moved effortlessly with it, unaffected by the sudden movement. I picked up my glass and held it out for him, equally unruffled. The red liquid splashed into the glass, sparkling in the flickering light between us.

I took a sip. The flavor of the wine burst on my tongue. "Where did you get this?" I breathed, relishing the taste after weeks at sea.

He chuckled, pouring himself a glass before breaking off a piece of bread for me. "I intercepted a Spanish merchant ship on my way to London. I sold everything but one cask that I kept for the right occasion."

My eyes narrowed as I reached for the bread he offered, sinking my teeth into it. Lightly soaked in broth, the bread was soft. But the lump in my throat, wondering what the right occasion was, had to be washed down with a gulp of wine.

"And what is the right occasion?"

He leaned back with his wine, ignoring the soup. "I thought it might be nice to treat you to an enjoyable evening after so many days at sea. Did you think of this as something more than it is?"

I pursed my lips and picked up my spoon. "Of course not." Meeting his gaze over the candlelight, I took a sip of my soup. "Did you?"

He chuckled. "No, Livie. We still have many days before we reach-"

"My father?" I asked. "Assuming he answers your summons."

As I watched him drink his wine, I waited for any sign of dishonesty. I needed to catch anything that suggested this dinner was more than he had led on. Nothing in his demeanor revealed his true colors. This was simply a dinner and nothing more.

"We'll make a stop in Antigua to unload our cargo," he replied.

"Oh?" I asked. "And if my father intercepts you before then?"

He shook his head. "Livie, we are having dinner. Whatever you're imagining, I have no motive other than to dine with an extraordinary woman."

The spoon slipped from my hand and clattered against the bowl. Extraordinary? He thought I was extraordinary? I couldn't help the warmth that surged through me or the heat rising to my cheeks. Demurely, I picked up my wine and looked at him across the table, wondering what was happening between us. I had a feeling, but I would be damned if I made myself comfortable here.

"On deck during the storm, both this storm and the last," he began. "You didn't flinch."

After another sip of wine, I set it down. "You don't flinch when you're on my father's ship. I learned that at a very young age," I whispered.

"Will you tell me about it?"

"I will tell you that not everything is as it seems."

"So you were aboard his ship for several years. How did no one know you were there?" he inquired, setting his wine down to eat, as if he needed the liquor first to gather courage. "You know there was a rumor that you had died."

"My mother died in a hurricane when I was seven in Barbados." I took a deep, unsteady breath. "His men picked me up shortly after. I was on his ship until after I turned sixteen."

"That's when he dropped you off in London?"

I nodded.

"That must have been difficult for you, so many years at sea with no other women. How did the men . . . treat you?"

"Some treated me like family, while others stayed as far away from me as possible. They were sworn to secrecy, or they died. No one could know I lived on his ship. Everyone we encountered was told I'd died in the hurricane with my mother."

"I remember that storm in September 1694. It was rumored to have taken the lives of over three thousand people and decimated over twenty British ships. I was very young myself."

"There are some who no longer sail with him who know of my status."

"Meaning?"

"The night you offered to rescue me from Percival? I ran into an . . . old acquaintance. I doubt Edward would tell anyone about me, but . . . he threatened to. As did Percival. It was good of you to take me away when you did."

Grayson's smile had the effect of softening my hardened heart. I resumed eating to avoid his heated gaze. "Perhaps you can explain the situation with Percival a little better. Help me understand why he insisted so thoroughly, including his attempt to threaten me, on having you as his wife?"

"I had no choice," I whispered. "He found out what I was doing in Wapping and around the docks. I had no choice once he asked my uncle for his permission. It was marry him or face the gallows."

He cursed, slamming his fist down on the table and making everything jump. "That bastard," he said. "Why did you not tell me?"

I laughed. "Everything I built in London hinged on my reputation, Grayson. No one could know what I was doing down at the docks. It would ruin me and my family. Uncle Winston and Aunt Marjory didn't deserve that after taking me in. Imogen, as much as she irks me sometimes, deserves to find a suitable husband, and William to find a woman with a good reputation, befitting his title. I would never do such a thing."

Silence enveloped us as we ate our soup and sipped our wine, our gazes meeting across the dancing flames more often than I cared to admit. His deep, intense eyes were a sight to behold, appearing dark one moment and light the next, such a myriad of colors.

When Sully shuffled in to clear our dishes, leaving us with the wine, I couldn't help but wonder about Grayson's scar. It made him look dangerous, even if I thought it didn't look that bad. He was fortunate that whatever had happened hadn't taken his eye.

"Will you tell me what happened to your eye?" I asked lightly.

Grayson stood, taking his glass of wine with him as he walked to the starboard window. I heard a sigh escape him before he took a sip.

"My brother," he said. "Adam and I were practicing after we had been drinking. It was an accident. As soon as he realized he'd connected, he pulled back, otherwise it would have taken my eye."

I stared at him, so many more questions plaguing me. But I needed to tread carefully. Asking so many questions of him would only lead to more questions about me.

"My father blamed me, though Adam was remorseful. It was an accident, after all," he continued. "I could never quite measure up to my father's standards. I still find myself lacking."

I stood, leaving my wine behind as I approached him. When he turned to look at me, drinking his wine to mask the grief I already saw in his eyes, I reached up and traced the scar with my fingertip. I wasn't sure what possessed me to do such a thing, but a wistful look lit his eyes before he caught my wrist in a punishing grip.

"How did Adam die?" I asked, barely above a whisper.

The color of Grayson's eyes seemed to shift, and the rigid set of his jaw tightened along with them. If there were to be trust between us, he would tell me this.

"Shot. During a fight near Jamaica about six months ago. A ship overtook us, many crew aboard injured or killed, and stole a significant about of money in rare silk from southern France." He looked directly at me, our gazes connecting and clashing.

"You want my father to pay for that, don't you?"

He looked perplexed, as though I had stumbled onto something he didn't want me to know. If he was after my father, then my father deserved it. Now I understood why he had convinced me to come along, though I didn't agree.

"Do you know, without a doubt, that it was my father's ship that attacked you?"

He stared at me but said nothing.

"I found evidence in London that suggested the cargo had been sold there." His gaze held me. "You, Livie. You led me right to it. Your father's insignia was stamped on the crates, which means that your father is, in fact, the ship that attacked us."

"It matters little what your father thinks of you," I said, my chin lifted. "You are a very capable man, and one only needs to look at your crew to know that. Thank you for dinner, Captain."

As I stepped away from him, his hand shot out to catch my wrist, preventing me from moving any further. With another tug, I was against him, and his hands cupped my face.

"You are telling me that I am in some way responsible for this, for your vengeance," I breathed. "And yet I'm here with you. You should hate me, and truly not speak to me until my father comes to claim me."

He shook his head. "I am not laying blame at your feet. Your father did this. It is your father who will pay for what he's done."

Reaching up, I pulled his hands away from my face. I couldn't quite understand how he could look at me with such longing in his eyes, kiss me with such rough abandon, knowing that my father had cost his brother his life. I knew my father. He was merciless. But in this moment, I dared not agree with Grayson. I couldn't. He was still my father, and regardless of what he'd done, I couldn't bear to see him hang for his crimes of piracy.

"I'll return to my own cabin now," I whispered.

"No," he snapped, his eyes and tone unyielding, even as he let me go.

"Why?"

I stepped back until I was next to the table before he could answer, a dizzying array of emotions raging through me. It was too much to bear. Being on this ship with him, desiring him as I did, while knowing he only meant to use me.

"Then you may as well take me to bed," I snarled. "What good am I otherwise?"

Shock registered on his face, his eyes darkening a moment later as they swept over my body, lingering on my waist and lower before finally darting up to meet my gaze.

"I have no intention of taking you to my bed tonight."

Chapter Twenty Eight

Livie

"No? Am I not to your liking? Is this not what you were expecting when you offered your protection? You did insist that I spend the journey in your quarters when we departed London, did you not?"

A growl escaped from deep in his throat, his eyes mirroring the displeasure my words had created. My, he was easily rattled.

"You want me to take you to my bed? This is what you want?" I barely managed a nod before he continued. "Once I start, I do not stop. I won't."

With deliberate slowness, he unbuckled his belt. Deft fingers pried the buckle apart until it hung suspended. He set his sword aside and stepped closer to me. I stood still, captivated as he eased the strap that held his pistol over his head and set it down next to the sword. The precise way he moved captured my complete focus, making my mouth go dry.

"Don't cry, begging me to be gentle." He shook his head. "I won't."

With quick jerks of his nimble fingers, he plucked the ties of his leather jerkin, opening it enough to fling it off as he continued to stalk toward me like a predator toying with its prey. I could have sworn his already ominous eyes grew darker.

Next came his tunic, which he yanked from the waist of his breeches. He swept it off in one swift movement and tossed it carelessly next to his discarded jerkin. With his chest bared to my eyes, I took in the sight of the dark swirls of hair on his chest, a narrow trail leading down, disappearing under his breeches. Another few steps, and he'd reach me.

Never one to run in the face of danger, I stood my ground. Not that I could flee now, I had backed up all the way to the door until I could feel it at my back. One long arm could easily prevent my departure, and by the look in his eyes, that might only spur him on.

"Don't implore me to stop when it hurts, and I will hurt you."

My eyes snapped up to meet his, just in time to catch the wry twist of his mouth. Of course, he thought I still possessed my virtue. I'd never told him otherwise. But two could play this game. Let him believe I was the innocent young lady her aunt had sheltered all these years.

I refused to lower my gaze as he untied his breeches, leaving them open while he took the last few steps to reach me.

A gasp tore from my throat when he seized my chin with his strong fingers, forcing me to keep my eyes on him. I was held so firmly that trying to break free would only result in my getting hurt.

"Tell me the truth. Is your maidenhead still intact?"

The question shocked me into stuttering. "Wh . . . what?"

"Surely you understand what I am asking."

My eyes widened.

"Are you a virgin?"

"How dare you ask me such a thing?"

"The truth, Livie. I will have it." His grip tightened almost painfully. "It matters little to me if you aren't. In fact, it makes this much more . . . enjoyable for both of us. But I'll know here and now if you carry another man's child."

I pressed my hands against his chest. His skin was so warm it felt like an inferno beneath my fingertips. The steady thrum of his heart caused me to pause, drinking in the deep desire in his eyes.

He may not have intended to take me to his bed tonight, but that quickly changed.

Throwing my head back, I yanked my chin out of his grasp. Discomfort be damned. I stared into his eyes defiantly. If there were any signs of bruises come morning, he would pay for it.

"You go too far, *Captain*."

He pushed his face closer to mine, our mouths nearly touching, allowing me to feel the warmth and smell the sweet wine on his breath. Our eyes locked. "Is that so?"

My chin lifted slightly. "You can be assured it's been quite some time since I've lain with a man. There is no chance that I'm carrying another man's child."

"Good."

He gave me no opportunity to speak further before his fingers plunged into my hair, bringing my mouth to his in an urgent meeting of lips. The touch sent a wave of heat straight down to the apex between my legs, rivaling the warmth still radiating beneath my fingertips against his bare chest.

Plundering my mouth, he gave me no chance to take a breath, as if he intended to mark me in a way that no one else would dare erase. His other hand tugged at my corset, attempting to untie it.

With a frustrated growl that echoed into my mouth, he finally pulled away enough to order, "Take this off."

I raised my hands to the ties, trying to unlace them as quickly as possible. Another growl of frustration erupted from him as he spun me around, pinning me against the wall with his hips. My hands splayed against the door, and I felt every inch of him flush against me, hard, unyielding muscles against my pliable body. This was no ordinary man.

"You'll find that I'm not a patient man," he murmured just below my ear, pressing his open mouth there and sending a shiver rippling through me. "I've a mind to tug your breeches down and take you like this."

My eyes nearly rolled back in my head at the raging inferno he ignited with that suggestion, flowing through my core and settling low between my legs. A gentle throb built in response to his arousal pressing against me.

I didn't remember it being like this before, no matter how many years had passed. My cheek pressed hard against the cool wood of the door, and I hoped to find relief from my burning skin. My hands pushed against the wall, a weak attempt to hold on to something.

He moved slightly back, enough to spin me around. My eyes widened when a dagger appeared in his hand, slicing up through every single lace of my corset until he lifted it up and over my head. With my corset gone, my tunic shifted to the side and fell to the crook of my arm. The feel of his mouth against the sensitive skin of my neck, moving lower to my shoulder as if he wanted to taste every inch, nearly unraveled me. My legs trembled where I stood, not from fear, oh no, but pure adrenaline setting me ablaze like I had never felt before.

When he lifted my tunic off, a sound tore from deep in my throat, caught between a gasp and a cry, just before his mouth claimed mine again. His practiced hands pushed my breeches down, shoving them over my curves while his mouth kept me otherwise occupied.

"Grayson," I gasped when he finally released my mouth.

Another growl, louder and more ferocious, rumbled from his throat as his hands traced my exposed flesh. "Keep saying my name like that, and you're unlikely to get any sleep tonight."

"My boots."

With a grunt, he bent down and yanked them off one by one, tossing them aside before rising slowly, the palms of his hands sliding over the skin of my legs while he did so. A sigh, my sigh, echoed throughout the room. My hands slid into the hair at his nape, pulling his mouth back to mine as his hands slid beneath me, lifting me until my legs wound around his trim waist.

"Tell me," he said, pressing me against the door.

One hand held me up while the other palmed my breast, drawing gasps from me when his thumb grazed over the sensitive peak, replaced quickly with his hot mouth. All I could do was cling to him, my fingernails digging into his shoulders. My head tilted to the side as his mouth moved on, tracing a line from my collarbone up to my jaw.

I felt his hand slide around to cup my backside, stifling a squeak when his fingers found the molten part of me yearning for release. His eyes danced with pleasure as the tips of his fingers teased me until I panted with desire.

"Tell you . . . what?" I asked breathlessly.

"Do you want me to take my time?" He nipped my ear.

"No."

A breathy scream tore from my throat as he pulled back for a moment, guiding himself with his hand, the feeling of pressure building until I thought I would shatter from intense pleasure. He'd promised not to stop once he started, and I didn't want him to, holding my breath until there was no separation between us.

Spinning, still filling me to the hilt, he carried me to the bed. Without breaking contact, he lowered me down and smoothed his hands along my arms until they were above my head, holding my wrists together as he found a steady rhythm.

My limbs felt fluid, every nerve ending threatening to spark as he took me to heights I'd never known. With my legs clutching him, I attempted to match his thrusts until he finally released my wrists and straightened his spine. His molten eyes took in the sight of me beneath him, my flushed cheeks and heavy-lidded eyes.

His hands slid down the length of my body, stopping at my knees, scorching my skin where they rested. When I reached out to touch his chest, he grabbed my hand and pulled me up until I was sitting on his thighs, his hands anchored to my hips as he tilted his head back.

I couldn't help myself. I lifted my hands to his face, my fingertips tracing the scar that stopped short of his cheekbone. Grayson stilled.

"What are you doing?"

"Getting to know you," I replied, wrapping my other arm around his neck and pulling his mouth to mine. "Scars and all."

"Livie," he growled, allowing me to take control of the pace until I could hardly breathe.

"Grayson," I managed with a smirk in my voice, though I barely got it out before my body threatened to explode. "I . . ."

"Livie," he growled again. "It's been many months since I've been with a woman. Find your release. Now."

And I did, letting wave after wave of profound pleasure wash over me until my limbs grew heavy. Grayson followed, roaring out a grunt, then tensing for a moment until he too became languid.

I eyed him but said nothing. He hadn't planned this, yet here we were. I couldn't help but wonder what might happen next, but I dared not ask. Instead, I loosened my grip on him and slid off.

Grayson's eyes followed me. "Sleep," he whispered. "While you can."

Chapter Twenty Nine

I woke alone in Grayson's bed, the sound of cannon fire filling my ears as if it were next to me. Bolting upright, I grabbed my clothing and rushed to the main deck as quickly as my boots would carry me.

"Liv . . . Livie," Kit called, catching up to me. "You shouldn't be goin' up there. Cap'n wouldn't like it."

I turned, remembering how innocent he was. "I will be fine, Kit."

"But—"

"I am the clerk, am I not?" I snapped, softening my tone when I saw him wince. "My duties require me on deck. Like the storm, I will stay out of the way of gunfire. As will you. Understand?"

He nodded vigorously.

I didn't wait for him to follow, turning and rushing into a cloud of smoke. Engaged at close range with a Spanish merchant trader, Grayson was on the main deck, his pistol ready for anyone daring to board us, shouting out commands to his men.

The blasts of gunfire between the two ships were deafening, the acrid smell of gunpowder burning my nose as I hurried up to the quarterdeck. Kit had followed me, but I turned and ordered him to stay low. There was no point in both of us being in danger of getting hit by grapeshot or cannonballs.

"What do you think you're doing?" I heard Connor shout, but I ignored him. "Get yourself below before you catch a round and Grayson ties me up by my thumbs for letting you on deck."

"I'll be fine, Connor," I snapped, my eyes finding Grayson.

As long as he didn't know I was on deck, his attention would be on the fight rather than me. It was early morning, and he likely thought I was still asleep, but I couldn't imagine how anyone could sleep in this racket.

Our cannon fire hammered the smaller ship repeatedly, splintering its wooden railings and beams as we pushed it back. They were no match for us, but before they waved their white flag in surrender, they fired one last cannon at us, hitting a man on the main deck right in the side. His name was Sawyer, one of Wiley's gunners. From what I'd learned, he had a wife and a young son in Barbados. My stomach plummeted.

The agonized scream that split the air made my eyes widen as I saw him fly back into the foremast, landing in a bloody heap on deck. Abandoning my ledger, I rushed down the stairs through the thick smoke. I didn't know Sawyer well, but I wasn't about to let him die alone.

Grayson's gaze followed me to Sawyer, his eyes locked on me as I fell to my knees and pulled Sawyer's head into my lap. He struggled against my hold, screaming in agony and thrashing his arms wildly. I was struck multiple times during his thrashing, all the while his screams echoing.

His blood darkened the deck beneath us, and his breathing grew shallow. I smoothed the damp hair from his forehead, looking into his eyes rather than at his wound. Even if we had a surgeon aboard, there would be no fixing the gaping hole in his torso.

He tried to speak, but I shushed him.

"I hear you," I whispered. "Listen to me. When I was a child, I traveled with my mother to many places. The clear blue ocean water and the waves washing against the shore like a caress.

Picture the sway of the palm trees. Did you know I used to climb them as a little girl, picking coconuts?"

This memory, both wistful and painful, emerged from a place so deep that I had almost forgotten it. My mother stood below the tree, laughing up at me. She used to tell me how much I was like my father, eager to please and even more thirsty for adventure. I hadn't been afraid to climb the tree, not as I had been the first time I had to climb a mast.

I looked down at Sawyer, a soft smile touching my lips to let him know he wasn't alone. Climbing trees, in a way, was worse than climbing a mast. I had no net to catch my fall.

Silently, Sawyer took his last breath, his eyes locked on mine. If I could have taken away the pain he felt until that last moment, I would have. Smoothing his hair back one last time, I closed his eyes. I sat with him for several moments longer, no one daring to breathe after such a heavy death, until someone picked him up to bring his body to the infirmary for burial preparation.

I stared at my trembling hands, his blood covering the paleness of my palms and clothing. It had been many years since I'd witnessed such a gruesome death. I bowed my head, tears welling in my eyes as I thought of my mother. On my father's ship, I had never been able to properly grieve her.

So many years had passed, and I still missed her terribly. I'd been so young, yet the memory that flitted into my mind felt like yesterday. My shoulders shook while I sat there until I felt strong arms wrap around my shoulders, holding me, patiently waiting for me to sob out my grief, for this young man who had lost his life so violently, for his wife and son, and for my mother, lost long ago but never forgotten.

I looked up into Grayson's eyes, grief that matched mine shining in his gaze, anchoring me. Swiping away the tears from my cheeks, I sat up, and his arms fell away.

"I have work to do," I whispered.

"It can wait," he growled. "Death is never easy, no matter who it was. You'll take the time you need before recording this."

He spoke the truth. It was never easy, but allowing it to sink too deeply into my mind would not be good for me. I knew my priority was to record the battle, the losses, and the repairs needed.

I struggled to my feet, Grayson rising quickly beside me. We faced off, him believing he was right and me knowing I was. I needed to work, or succumb to memories. I shook my head, turning toward the quarterdeck. He caught my wrist, and I looked down at our hands, dirty and bloody.

"I'll record everything now and rest later," I confirmed.

Grayson must have sensed my need to work, releasing my wrist and allowing me to walk away. I couldn't help but think he was beginning to understand me.

Chapter Thirty

Two days later, the heat had become oppressive, and the men's behavior reflected it as they continued to gamble onboard and collect debts from one another. The prize from the battle with the Spanish ship sparked an argument between two men over fair shares. Grayson's rules were firm: no man shall fight over prizes taken. He acted swiftly, announcing ten lashes each as a fitting punishment for insubordination. Connor administered the punishment while Grayson leaned against the railing, his arms tightly crossed and his jaw set grimly.

He disliked disciplining his crew. I could tell that much when I joined him at the railing. Neither of us flinched, nor did we take delight in the screams of agony that followed. Unlike my father, who seemed to take immense pleasure in punishing those who disobeyed him, Grayson reacted with a clenched jaw, folded arms, and eyes that were focused but not hard. The situation felt worse for men caught in circumstances they couldn't help.

We stood together long after the wounded were taken to the infirmary. Grayson said nothing, and I wasn't inclined to break the silence. After several minutes had passed, he merely strode away to speak with Connor. We hadn't addressed the subject of the night we had dinner together, and it hadn't happened again.

It was as if giving in to our desires had driven a wedge between us. Grayson had not voiced his regret, and I didn't regret it for a single moment. It had happened, and I would not take it back despite our tenuous relationship.

The day had been exhausting following the punishments, and I slipped into my cabin undetected late in the evening. My cabin was my refuge, a solace for collecting my thoughts without the humdrum of the ship's crew around me. Grayson had not come to my cabin since the day he had barged in, and I didn't expect him to. As the captain of a massive vessel with so many men to command, he was a busy man.

After I'd gone to sleep for the night, I was roused by the sound of my door being jiggled. My ears picked up the noise of someone trying to break in, the telltale sign of metal against metal, followed by the creak of the doorknob turning.

I froze, wondering if Grayson had finally come to carry me to his much bigger and more comfortable bed. Heat be damned, I missed his company. I had only spent one night in his bed, but I was already craving him.

The realization that Grayson would have knocked instead of picking my lock came too late. When the door burst open and two men entered without invitation, I was already reaching for my dagger beside me. I recognized one man as a gunner who served with Wiley. The other man was part of the carpenter's crew under Connor's command.

They seized me instantly. Their intent to remove me from my room rather than to harm me was obvious in how they tried to pull me up. Terror seized me as rough hands grabbed me while I wrestled back, a futile attempt at best. Clutching my dagger, I had no chance to wield it when the gunner knelt painfully on my arm to prevent me from fighting back. Little did they know how well I could handle men like them. My free arm came up, and my fist connected with the gunner's jaw, distracting him for only a moment. Two men against me were not ideal odds, but I'd be damned if I went down without a fight.

"Trent, grab her arm," the gunner grunted. "The skiff is waiting for this prize."

Realizing that I had more weapons than just my dagger, I screamed as loudly as I could and continued to fight them off. I had already kicked the meager blanket to the edge of the bunk, and my bare legs kicked mightily against the intrusion. I did everything I could to thwart them from carrying me away.

The moonlight shone dimly through the small window, casting shadows around the room. But there was no mistaking the shadow that filled the doorway. A moment later, one man was torn from me and thrown against the desk with a resounding crack. Then, the other was yanked away from me, the glint of metal reflecting in the moonlight.

I heard a gurgling sound a second later, watching the two shadows scramble quickly to vacate my cabin. Even in the dark, I could see the danger shining in Grayson's gaze as it swept from my feet to my face, registering the dagger clutched in my fist. As I unclenched my fingers, the dagger fell to the ground, and then his arm encircled me. My cheek pressed against his bare chest, the warmth doing little to ward off the chill I felt creep over me when I thought about what might have come to pass if he hadn't heard my screams.

He didn't remind me that he had warned me against this. That it would be dangerous to be in my own cabin, that his was much safer. He just held me, although I hadn't asked for comfort. I knew my worth, and it was much more than the two men had thought. When I met Grayson's eyes, I saw my worth reflected there, but he would never admit it. I was worth enough to trade for whatever he deemed more worthy. Nothing short of what these two men had obviously thought.

A grim reminder, indeed. Grayson, with minimal effort, held me and walked to the door, finding Connor and Wiley rubbing their tired eyes. His muscles were tense, fury still rampant, when he ordered them away.

"Bring Gregor and Trent to the main deck. I will meet you there."

It stood to reason that punishment would follow. Grayson had issued a command for no one to touch or harm me while I was onboard, and they had both ignored it. He couldn't let it go unpunished, and I did not want him to. I was certain I'd be sold if I were removed from the ship. I'd choose death over being sold into slavery.

I allowed him to carry me to his quarters, placing me on the bed and staying with me for a moment. He released me, turning away as he passed a hand over his face.

"Livie," he whispered, his voice etched with emotion.

"I know," I replied. "You need not tell me again how unsafe I am in my own cabin. I had it under control, Grayson."

He whipped around to face me, his eyes hard. "Is that so?"

I knew better than to argue with him right now, with his rage rolling off him more than I had ever seen. "God forbid your bargaining chip be marred."

Ferocity lit his eyes. "You are more than that."

Swallowing the lump in my throat, I nodded.

"You should know it after a few nights ago."

He rose from the bed, raking a hand through his mussed hair and stalking around the room until a knock at the door caught his attention. The men waited on deck as commanded.

"You will remain here," he said tightly. "I will return shortly."

I opened my mouth, unsure of what I could say. There was nothing to say, not even a nod, since he was already striding toward the door, his footsteps echoing through the cabin.

Once the door closed, I curled onto my side and tried not to think of what might have happened if he had not come when he did. I knew how to defend myself, and yet I hadn't come close to being able to in that situation.

Chapter Thirty One

Grayson

Fury barely described what I felt as I watched the two men put their hands on Livie. If Connor hadn't been right behind me after hearing her screams from the cabin, I might have torn Trent and Gregor apart with my bare hands. Floggings and other punishments were one thing. This was entirely different. Or so I thought.

Yet as I stared at the two men on deck, I was reluctant to be short of crew after having dealt out punishments to two other's just days ago. Still, I could never let this assault go unpunished. If Livie hadn't screamed, I would have remained oblivious to what had transpired in the cabin below mine.

Seeing her clutch the dagger in her hand, rendered useless by the force of both men, I had no doubt that had it been just one of them, he would have met his demise. Her wide eyes, filled with terror, nearly immobilized me, and I refused to witness that kind of fear in her again. I had already damned myself for what happened in my cabin that night after dinner.

When Livie became more of a target for my protectiveness, I couldn't say. There was so much more to Livie Blackwood than I had ever dreamed, and I had known for a long time that she was nothing like her father. Strong and capable, yet not unfeeling or rash. Like me, she harbored compassion beyond the demands of command.

When Sawyer died, I saw it in her eyes and could almost feel her touch as she gracefully guided him to his end. The gentle caress of her hands and her soothing voice eased his painful departure, a memory that lingered. Many of the men had noticed it as well, removing their hats to observe her compassionate care. Her heart, as tough as her resolve, made the weight of gold seem insignificant. Apparently, Trent and Gregor thought otherwise.

Then again, didn't I? After all, I was using her to draw her father out.

Connor and Wiley had the two men already standing on deck when my boots echoed in the darkness. The moonlight and the lantern's glow revealed Trent's remorse, while Gregor remained unrepentant, almost proud of his actions.

"Did I, or did I not, issue a direct order to keep your hands off my prisoner?" I asked, my voice low and threatening.

I paced in front of the two men as Connor and Wiley flanked them, keeping them in place. No reply came from either man, and judging by their expressions, it seemed Gregor had orchestrated this appalling act.

"Judging by the ropes I saw in her room and the skiff at the ready, I'm assuming you had plans to sell my prisoner?"

Gregor scoffed. "Prisoner. She warms your bed and nothing else. You're chasing a dream. Her pa ain't coming for her."

My eyes flashed. "If you had succeeded in your intentions, I would have found you and killed you both immediately. As it stands, I could string you both up from the foreyard by your balls."

Trent paled at the suggestion. Such a punishment would cause most men to collapse under their own weight, a torturous fate I had never inflicted and never would. But given the gravity of their crime, it was worth stating.

"That would deter anyone else from trying, would it not?"

"Captain, sir," Trent said, his voice trembling.

My gaze locked onto his. "Whose idea was it? Was it yours,

Trent?"

Slowly, he shook his head, effectively condemning his accomplice. Cowards, both of them, I thought. I was so angry that no penalty could ever be enough for what they had done. I could inflict any punishment, but it would never suffice for daring to touch her. I thought of her soft skin, unblemished except for the paleness turning to a golden color from time spent on deck, and how it felt to slide my rough hands over it. And her brilliant blue eyes, filled with fear, something I never wanted to see again.

"Put them in the brig," I ordered curtly. "They'll be flogged tomorrow morning for all to see, then suspended by their arms from the foremast, left to whatever weather befalls us throughout the day."

"'Tis your fault for bringing her aboard in the first place," Gregor sneered as soon as my back was turned. "No woman should be here on this ship."

It took every ounce of control not to throw him to the sharks. I would gladly flog him and then throw him into the water if he continued to speak. They would tear him apart in no time with a bleeding back.

I shook my head. "Take Trent to the brig. I'll handle Gregor."

Connor and Wiley seized Trent by the arms and hauled him away, leaving me to stare at Gregor, outraged by the man before me. The baldness of his head and the reddish-brown of his full beard were as ugly to me as the hatred in his eyes. I had heard grumblings from the crew about his treatment of new crew hands, gambling and taking their money without remorse. I didn't involve myself in the men's games. Connor managed that as part of his role as quartermaster.

But I would not hesitate to put Gregor in his place, knowing what kind of man preys on the weak. The kind who would force his attention on a woman. That thought alone propelled me toward him as I yanked him by the tunic to meet my glare.

"She's clouded yer judgment," he declared.

My fists clenched tighter, lifting him higher with my arms. I would not allow blasphemous comments aboard my ship, especially not about Livie, whom I wanted to protect. Rage coursed through me at this man and what he represented. I would not have such a man as part of my crew.

"Do you know what that woman's father would do to you if he knew of your treatment of her? You'd be begging for mercy at the hands of Elias Blackwood."

His eyes widened.

"I don't care what she says. Her father will come for her, and he will be furious. And you've just laid your filthy hands on a woman worth more than all our lives combined. You knew the mission we were on. We're taking back everything he took from us, and more."

When he threw his head back and laughed, I released him and swung. My fist connected with his jaw, sending him stumbling into the mast, still laughing. This would be the way of it, I thought, as I readied to pummel him. I vowed to rip him apart.

"Worse than what he'll do to you for taking his daughter to your bed?" he sneered before charging at me, but I was ready and swung with a ferocity I didn't hold back.

Bone crunched against bone, and he landed one strike on my jaw before I pushed him back with purpose. I had loved fist fighting with Adam, who had taught me everything there was to know about boxing. We practiced almost daily when we were younger.

Within minutes, blood gushed from his nose and mouth, yet he still tried to come at me. Bruised and bloody, my knuckles were a mess, and my jaw throbbed from the single effective blow he'd delivered. He should count himself lucky I didn't order his lips sewn shut. Under my command, I had every right to do so.

No, that would be too good for a man like him, taking and taking, selfishly believing it was owed to him. The fight had pushed us to the railing, and I wasn't finished yet. If I were in my right mind, I would place him in the brig with Trent and hand him over to Elias Blackwood, but that wouldn't matter. I would just as soon bring Elias back to London for judgment, unless he died fighting me.

As we reached the railing, Gregor bent backward over it, looking me in the eye.

"I hope the piece is worth it, Captain," he said, implying that Livie was nothing more than an object.

With a roar, I lifted him and threw him overboard. A moment later, a splash echoed, and I straightened, unable to believe I had actually thrown a man off my ship. Gregor was a liability I couldn't afford aboard. No matter what punishment awaited him in the morning, I knew he would have tried to reach Livie again, especially after I had revealed her identity. Though the crew should know who she was already, I had not specifically announced her to anyone. It could be that some were unaware of whom we carried. Or perhaps I was reminded myself of the precious cargo.

I stalked across the deck, suddenly eager to check on her and any injuries she might have sustained during their attack. As I reached my door, Connor and Wiley emerged from below.

"Where is Gregor?" Connor asked.

I shook my head. "Gregor will not be with us going forward."

Wiley's eyes widened before he huffed out a short laugh. "You threw him overboard?"

"I did, and I would do so again for his actions."

The truth couldn't be more straightforward. I acted not only for Livie but for the crew who had suffered this man far too long.

"And Trent?"

"Will face the punishment I ordered." I straightened my back. "It will be known tomorrow that I am true to my word. I will not have my orders disobeyed. By anyone."

Both men watched as I disappeared into my quarters without another word. My mood had soured considerably, leaving no room for further irritation. Heart still racing from the fight on deck, I shook out my stinging knuckles and strode toward the decanter of rum.

As frantic as I had been to hear her scream, I hadn't bothered to put on anything but my breeches. I drew them off and tossed them aside before pouring myself two fingers of rum, tossing it back as I gazed at the beauty in my bed. How had she gotten under my skin so quickly that I would kill for her? Abandoning the need for more rum, I strode toward the bed.

Livie looked peaceful, curled on her side with her arm beneath my pillow and her full lips parted in slumber. A bruise bloomed high on her cheek, and my fury held firm. She hadn't awakened to my footsteps, but the moment I sat down beside her, I felt her stir.

After a moment, I stretched out beside her on my back, feeling her small hand slide across my abdomen. The gasp that escaped her when I caught her hand warmed me, and I brought it to my lips, pressing a kiss to her palm.

She sat up, awake suddenly as if realizing where she was, and gazed down at me. Worry clouded her blue eyes as they swept over me, catching sight of my scuffed knuckles. She took my hand, studying the scraped and bloodied skin.

"Are you well, Livie?" I whispered.

"I think the better question is: *are you*?"

With my other hand, I reached out to caress her jaw, my thumb gently sweeping over the bruise that would show in earnest tomorrow. Her eyelids fluttered closed at my touch, and I pushed myself up to capture her lips with mine.

She sank into me with a sigh, my arms wrapping around her and pulling her close. So resilient, yet so soft. With me, she opened like the delicate petals of a flower. But I wouldn't ruin what was between us with the horror of what could have happened still fresh in my mind.

Instead, I lay back, bringing her with me, pressing a kiss to her temple and inhaling her unique scent. Content with her in my arms, my eyes closed as feelings swirled within me. She pressed her cheek against my bare chest and released a breathy sigh.

"Thank you," she whispered. "For saving me."

Chapter Thirty Two

Grayson

"When did you first notice it?" I asked Connor, extending my palm.

He slapped the spyglass into my hand with unnecessary force. At my glare, he turned back to the helm and resumed his position. As the quartermaster, the death of another crew member weighed heavily on him, yet he trusted my decisions.

"A quarter hour ago. I sent Kit down to notify you immediately. It hasn't moved," Connor replied.

Raising the spyglass to my eye, I braced myself against the ship's pitch. In the distance, another galleon appeared to be anchored, bobbing gently. My gut churned at the thought of another battle with Livie aboard, though she had proven herself fully capable of handling herself. She had stayed out of harm's way during the last battle, coming out only to ease Sawyer's death. That didn't mean she would continue to do so, even if she knew it was in her best interest. It was undeniable that she was a valuable addition to the crew. She had already shown her hand during the storm, and I couldn't help but admire her.

Battles stirred my blood, adrenaline spurring me on. Having spent time on her father's ship, I knew Livie had seen her share of bloody skirmishes. If I closed my eyes, I could almost picture her on the main deck in the heat of battle: legs braced, blue eyes focused, her defiant chin lifted in pride. That passion boldly manifested in my bed, for which I should be ashamed, but wasn't.

I handed the spyglass back to Connor and looked down at Livie near the railing, helping Wiley untangle netting. She had changed into the clothing she wore when she boarded, the torn tunic from after her makeshift bath tucked into snug breeches. I wondered how one woman could invade my thoughts so deeply.

"Captain?" Connor stepped up next to me, glancing down at the pair on the deck below. "Something troubling you?"

Not something, *someone.*

"No," I cleared my throat, finding it unnecessarily rough. "Has Wiley said anything to you about Livie?"

A short laugh burst from deep in his throat, cut off abruptly when he frowned at me and scratched his temple. "You think he would sweep her off her feet right before your very eyes? Especially when she's been sharing your bed? I don't think so, Gray."

It was my turn to frown.

"Everyone knows you're starting to have feelings for her." I opened my mouth to interrupt, but he cut me off. "Don't bother denying it."

My eyebrows raised. Connor rarely called me anything but Captain, even though we were family. He would never betray me, and I trusted him implicitly. He used only my given name when we were alone and speaking seriously.

"We've all seen the way you look at her. She's not quite what you expected, is she? Not what *we* expected."

I didn't want to answer him. I didn't need to. Connor knew me well enough to understand he was merely questioning what I had already thought. He had been at the ball and had seen what I had seen. The woman I had assumed was merely posing as a genteel lady was exactly who she appeared to be, and more. She might have believed she was fooling everyone, but Livie had truly become that woman.

In one moment, she was a fearless and skilled sailor braving a fierce storm on the ship's nets and ropes, and in the next, she was gracefully dancing in an elite ballroom, as if she had been born to such surroundings. She possessed a fierce resolve, ready to put her dagger to a man's throat and use it again if threatened.

No, Livie Blackwood was not at all who I had expected. My redemption for Adam loomed large in my mind, knowing that Elias would answer the call and rescue his prized daughter. He had believed her safe in London and would never let this go unanswered, just as he would never let an attempted sale of his daughter go unpunished. If he knew I was involved with her in more ways than just bait, he'd slaughter me. But I didn't want to exchange her for riches. I wanted to exchange her for justice.

"Have you spoken with her?" I asked abruptly.

My question flustered Connor. "About?"

I grunted. "When you speak with her, do you get the feeling she isn't being truthful?"

"What could she possibly be lying about?"

She could utter any number of falsehoods. Building trust had been difficult for me, yet I found myself trusting her. Trusting in her. I questioned whether a pretty face had deceived me, but I realized it hadn't. She was so much more.

I shrugged. "She could be lying to us all. Do you see the same woman we saw at the ball in London?"

Connor snorted. "Listen to yourself, Gray. That woman climbed to the crow's nest amidst a storm that could have thrown her like a rag doll from that height, and she did so without fear. Do *you* get the feeling that she isn't being truthful?"

The answer stuck in my craw. I wanted to distrust her. I wanted to dislike her. But none of that happened. Every moment I spent in her company made me crave her presence, her body, more. Hell, when I wasn't with her, I wanted to be with her. Never in my life had that happened before. I wondered how I could let her go.

Connor moved closer to me, our eyes drifting down to Livie just in time to see her laugh gaily at something Wiley said. That man could charm the undergarments off any woman, even those twice his age. His smile, his tone, everything about him was captivating.

"There isn't a man aboard who hasn't seen how you look at her," he murmured. "The only one denying it is you."

He tilted his head to the side, dark hair blowing in the breeze.

"She may be sharing my bed for now, but if I asked her to stay with me beyond that, she would deny me. Not once Elias comes for her. Not once she figures out that I'm prepared to kill him, should it come to that."

A loud, deep laugh escaped him, drawing attention in our direction. He leaned closer, as if sharing a secret. "By the looks she gives you, I somehow doubt that. A woman like that, capable and fearless, a siren in bed. If you're questioning what comes out of her mouth, I could think of some ways to keep her mouth-"

"Finish that sentence, Connor, and see what happens."

He drew back but then laughed again, strolling back to the wheel and resting his arm over it. "It's best if you keep her occupied, Gray. We're still days away from land. The men are getting restless. Keep her in your cabin. No one would dare take what's yours."

If I hadn't heard her cries, the two who had already tried to abduct her might have managed to get her off this ship and away from me. We were close enough to land for them to have made a fearless attempt to sell her on the nearest island.

When I set out to avenge Adam, I hadn't meant to spend my days at sea. I had experienced much adventure, yet once my mission was complete, I would cease my journey. I had a small house in Barbados, and despite what my father thought, I had no intention of returning home to resume my role as his heir. I couldn't help but wonder if things were different, would she consider staying with me? Would I ask?

My thoughts strayed to Livie. Would Elias send his daughter right back to London to marry the baron, or would he keep her sailing the seas with him? What would she do?

It suddenly dawned on me that Elias might rescue his daughter, but he might not be pleased with the outcome. Not if she was working for him in London. If he punished her for getting tricked to begin with, I'd never be able to live with myself. He had sent her to live with his sister after nearly ten years for a reason.

I needed to know that reason.

As I stepped away from Connor, he caught my arm. His eyes blazed with intensity. "Have care, Gray. She might appear strong, but beneath the surface, something lingers. Someone may have hurt her."

I scowled, questioning how he could observe something I couldn't.

Instead of staying with Connor to contemplate my choices, I jogged down the steps to the main deck and strode toward the laughing duo. At my approach, their laughter died. The faintest smile lingered on Livie's lips, making her look far more innocent than I knew she was. Her smile made her radiant.

"We're approaching a ship," I said, my voice rougher than I intended. "We should prepare."

"Are they flying their flags?"

At her breathy question, my resolve toward her softened. Connor's parting words echoed in my mind. Who could have possibly hurt her? She hadn't yet reached her twentieth year. Her mother's passing was long ago, yet Connor made it feel that something more recent had happened.

"None that I could see. We'll be upon it within the hour."

Livie tilted her face toward the slowly rising sun in the east, the sunlight dancing in her eyes and washing her face in a warm glow. Seeing her like that took my breath away, stunning me for a moment.

"I'd like a word with you before we approach."

Wiley snorted, nodding to both of us before striding away with his hoard of knotted ropes. I watched his swagger for a moment before turning back to her. She looked defensive, the light in her eyes diminishing.

"If you're about to tell me to stay below, you know where you can stick that nonsense."

My lips quirked up.

"One condition." I held up a finger. "You answer a question."

"A question?" she repeated.

"Why did your father send you ashore?"

Instantly, she took a step back, her face stricken. I knew she would be defensive about it, but I couldn't stop thinking about what might have happened to lead to such a thing. Everything I had deduced made sense except for one thing.

She placed her hands on her hips, standing tall before me. "The crew swore to keep my identity a secret," she said. "They were also sworn to keep their hands to themselves when I started . . . growing up. Having a seven-year-old girl aboard is far different from a sixteen-year-old."

My eyes followed her as she turned, leaning over the railing with a heavy sigh. Part of me regretted dredging up those memories, but this was something I felt I needed to know.

"There was a man," she said. "Edward."

My eyes widened, not having expected that.

"My father realized he had two choices. He could control his crew, or he could control his daughter." She turned back to me, her eyes full of fire. "He couldn't have both."

"He chose wrong," I said flatly.

"What would you do in that situation?" she asked. "I fancied myself in love and made myself believe he had the same feelings for me. Perhaps he did."

My heart broke for her when she shook her head sadly.

"I didn't have time to explain it to my father after he caught us in a delicate situation. He refused to speak with me, locked me in my cabin. Edward was lashed, beaten, and left on a deserted island. I was released from my confinement only when we sailed away from the island."

"And you were sent to live with your aunt."

She nodded shakily. "I was telling you the truth when I told you that I do not know where he is, Grayson. If you believe anything I tell you, please believe that. All communication I had with him was through his agent."

Her gaze remained fixed on me, searching for any sign of emotion her confession might trigger. I could only think of her on his vessel, ultimately alone despite being surrounded by crew. He was her father, and that only intensified my desire to kill him.

I ventured to ask a question that might catch her off guard. "If you did know where he was, would you tell me?"

While I expected her to remain firm and refuse to answer, I couldn't help but sympathize with her for having her future foretold without any choice in the matter. Regardless that it was the way of life with every woman, Livie made me feel differently. I was compelled to consider my own predicament.

"No," she whispered.

Elias had taken away my choice as well. By murdering my brother and hearing Livie's story, albeit different from how my brother lost his life, I knew without a doubt that Elias was a monster who needed to face justice. It didn't matter that I had enough proof. I would be the one to ensure he was brought to justice.

Chapter Thirty Three

The conversation with Grayson left me shaken, though I had answered truthfully when he questioned whether I would betray my father. I did everything I could to mask my discomfort at that single question. Asking questions about my father was one thing, but his pointed inquiries about me provoked an entirely different feeling. I didn't like it. I didn't like probing questions while in London, and I didn't like them now. Yet he'd asked them with such gentleness that I couldn't help myself but to answer truthfully.

I had little time to dwell on my unease as we approached the ship with surprising speed over the last few leagues. Grayson, standing beside Connor on the quarterdeck, snapped the spyglass shut and handed it back to the quartermaster.

"There are no men aboard that ship," Grayson announced. "All hands on deck! Pierre, Sully, prepare to board."

I reached out and grabbed Grayson's forearm. His muscles flexed beneath my touch. "It's a trap. We should leave it alone."

He laughed. Laughed!

"Is that so?"

"That is so!" I shouted. "I've been sailing longer than you! This. Is. A. Trap."

When he moved, I gripped his arm tighter until he turned back to me, a flash of challenge in his eyes. Woman or not, I didn't care.

The devil could take me here and now if that ship wasn't staged to ambush an unsuspecting vessel.

"Grayson, listen to me."

His hand covered mine, his thumb making small circles over the sensitive skin on the back of my hand. "I appreciate your concern and your experience, but I will not pass up this opportunity. We'll at least check."

"And if you're sending your men to their deaths?"

He straightened his spine. "I'll face mine as well."

My eyes widened, and he released my hand, moving away. The pit in my gut remained as I watched him jog down the steps to the skiff being loaded near the gangplank. Several men climbed into the small boat, and I held my breath when Grayson looked at me before getting in.

"Connor," I said.

"Livie." He rested his arm casually on the helm, my name slipping from his lips almost lazily.

"I need a pistol."

A short laugh escaped him. "The captain wouldn't agree with me giving you a firearm."

I turned to him, my eyes blazing. "On my word, that ship is about to open fire on us. Do you want me to attempt to save Grayson and the rest of the crew going over, or would you prefer to watch them become part of Davy Jones's crew at the bottom of this ocean?"

He released the wheel and stalked toward me. "If I give you a pistol and you accidentally shoot the men in that boat, you won't have to worry about Grayson punishing me. The crew will keelhaul me."

I set my jaw. "I give you my word, Connor. I have been on this vessel for weeks and done nothing but help. My aim is true. We are close enough to that ship that I can shoot anyone aboard."

He still looked distrustful.

But he reached behind him, withdrawing a pistol from his waistband and handing it to me. As if needing a final guarantee of my promise, he gripped it tightly and looked into my eyes before its release.

As soon as he let go, I dashed away from him down to the main deck and positioned myself near the rail, the pistol cocked and ready for the first sign of movement aboard the ship. While I might be taking a chance on pistol range, I was determined to try.

Grayson spoke the truth when he said there were no men aboard. None in sight, at least. It appeared to be a ghost ship, sails tucked in, bobbing in the water as if it had been there for some time.

I considered the possibility that I was wrong. Perhaps the crew aboard had died from a plague, and we were the first to come upon it. But I doubted it as my eyes scanned from the bow to the stern.

The skiff carrying Grayson and part of the crew rowed steadily toward it, Grayson at the stern with his boot propped up on the seat in front of him. I made the sign of the cross, hoping we wouldn't be surprised and that no one in the skiff would die.

Not Grayson. Despite how much he tore me apart sometimes, I didn't want him to die. The memory of him last night, making me ache with the merest touch, flashed before my eyes, quickening my heartbeat. No, we still had things to discuss between us, Grayson and me.

Just as I shook the memory from my mind, a man appeared on the deck of the other ship, a pistol aimed straight at Grayson. I took my shot, and the man fell back, a hole in his chest. How Grayson had missed him, I didn't know, and I didn't much care.

Grayson turned to look at me for the briefest moment before the rest of the ghost ship came alive. As quickly as the skiff between the two massive ships tried to retreat, the rain of bullets and cannon fire proved overwhelming.

I watched Grayson and the crew abandon the skiff and attempt to swim back to us while I reloaded and took another shot. To look back at Connor in pride overwhelmed me, but I continued to put my focus where it belonged. I could only triumph that we were close enough for pistols.

"Cannons at the ready!" I shouted, pointing at a young deckhand. "You there, climb up to the crow's nest and shoot at anything aboard that ship that moves!"

I wasted no time, giving orders to every man who came my way while I hurried across the deck to help with the cannons. Wiley had raced below, directing his team of gunners to open fire on the ship.

Being taken by surprise was the most unfortunate outcome for this scenario. One I tried to warn Grayson about, but he wouldn't listen, damn him. But that would be something to discuss later.

"Defend!" I shouted, aiming my pistol at those firing into the water.

My eyes scanned the dark water quickly, spotting Grayson helping Sully onto the rope to climb up. He would ensure every single man went ahead of him before he climbed up himself, and I would make damn sure to pick off anyone trying to prevent it.

"Fire!" I shouted down at the main deck cannons, smoke from the blasts filling the air and burning my nostrils. "Again!"

"Connor! Cover me!" I shouted, racing up toward the quarterdeck and taking aim at another threat.

"My God," he breathed, not paying attention to those on the other ship but focused on me. "Where did you learn to shoot like that?"

"I will defend this ship," I answered, evading his question.

"Fire!" I shouted again, and returning cannon fire hit the wooden deck beneath my boots, making it shudder.

I needed another pistol, one for each hand. "Connor, do you have another pistol?"

"Grayson has pistols in his cabin."

"Get them!"

I fired again, the blast from the pistol ringing in my ears. I disregarded the pain and fired again, successfully taking down a man attempting to board. Not while I lived and breathed.

Grayson finally made it up, soaking wet and looking formidable. He met my eyes briefly before someone handed him a pistol, and he strode away with vengeance.

Connor returned with a pistol, handing it to me before I slid down the railing of the stairs. My boots hit the main deck, and I ran toward the cannons at the far end, where Kit, who was not supposed to be in the thick of battle, was trying to load the shot. I tucked the hot pistol into my waistband and helped him load it in, catching a glimpse of a cannon aimed right for us out of the corner of my eye.

"Down!" I roared, but the boom, followed by the cannonball's path toward us, was too quick.

I threw myself over Kit, feeling the sting of burns on my arms and side as I thrust my arms out to shield him. Memories of the cannon fire Sawyer had taken the brunt of flashed in my mind, but the searing pain brought me back and took my breath away as Kit and I hit the deck in a tangle of limbs. When I lifted my head, my eyes burned from the smoke-filled air, and I saw that part of the railing was gone.

"Livie!" Kit murmured, pushing himself up and reaching out toward whatever wound was burning my chest.

"I'm fine," I muttered, not realizing I'd betrayed my own silence. "You will not die today, Kit. I won't allow it."

"Nor will you! But you're . . . you're bleedin'."

I bet I was.

"Ready! Aim! Fire!" I leapt up, refusing to let a minor wound keep me down, no matter how badly it hurt.

I would have whatever wounds I sustained checked later. We had a battle to win, and I would be damned if I let the other ship triumph. I shouted at Kit to reload, to man up and handle those shots himself. When I turned, Grayson stared at me with wide eyes. I looked down at the scorched marks in my tattered tunic, several of them seeping blood. Devil take me, my heart raced at the sight of the injuries I'd suffered. Not from cannon fire, but from shrapnel.

Grayson strode toward me. "You will go below immediately." He tore off his tunic, attempting to wrap it around my arm, where the bleeding seemed heaviest. "Go, Livie. Now."

Everything I had learned in life urged me to stay, but Grayson's command said otherwise. His eyes, his jaw. He meant it.

"We're winning this battle. Because of you. Now, go!"

Chapter Thirty Four

Grayson

"Connor," I said, lowering my pistol when I was certain the sounds of the blasts had faded. "Survey the ship for damage. Livie is hurt. I need to . . ."

"Go," he said tersely, knowing what I needed to do.

The other ship pulled up anchor, putting as much distance between us as possible, despite its heavy damage from the battle. I had a feeling we had suffered an equal amount of damage, if not more.

Pistol still gripped in my hand, I flew down the stairs to Livie's cabin, only to find a hole looking out to sea instead of a window. Debris littered the floor and bed, rendering the cabin completely unusable.

I found her lying on the bed in my cabin, the right side of her body, from shoulder to waist, bloodied, her shirt in tatters. When I saw her shield Kit from the cannon shot, I thought my heart had lodged in my throat. Telling her to go below while the battle raged on without following her had been one of the hardest things I'd ever done. The only other time I felt so helpless was when Adam died in my arms, and I resolved not to let it happen with Livie.

Not knowing how grave her injuries were, I needed to ensure the battle had subsided before I could seek her out. Now, I could do nothing but fall to my knees at her side as her eyes fluttered open and a weak smile curved her luscious lips.

"I might tell you that there is something wrong with my cabin," she murmured, her eyes half-closed.

"We'll speak of that another time." I reached out, hesitant to touch her for fear of causing her more pain. "Livie, I must see to your injuries."

She sighed. "My arm hurts. Chest . . ."

"I know," I whispered. "I'll make it better, love."

With shaking fingers, I touched the frayed edges of what remained of her tunic. Parts of it were stuck to her skin, leaving me no choice but to cut it away. I heard the door to my quarters open and glanced briefly at Kit.

His face was smudged with cannon smoke and dirt, concern etched deep in his eyes. He looked older than he was, worried for the woman lying in my bed who had stolen all our hearts.

"Water, linen, and bandages, Kit," I cleared my rough voice. "Now."

"Right away, Cap'n."

He backed out of the room, closing the door as I turned to my task. With my dagger, I cut away what I could of her tunic without lifting it off her. There would be no saving it, soaked with blood and grime as it was. A groan escaped her lips, her eyes remaining closed.

When pieces of the cloth stuck to her skin, forcing me to tug, she grimaced but otherwise remained silent. I admired her strength, but wanted to tell her it wasn't necessary to be brave in this instance.

I would have averted my eyes from what I'd already seen, but I didn't care, peeling away the shirt and flinging it aside. Nothing we had done in the last few weeks could be considered moral. I couldn't help but tell myself this was highly improper, having a partially conscious, half-naked woman lying in my bed. But I would be damned if I let anyone else tend to her.

While I studied her skin for the numerous wounds, Kit returned.

"Leave it by the door," I commanded.

"But, Cap'n."

"Kit," I growled. "In her state of undress, no one is allowed in this room. Do you hear me?"

"Might I help you? I . . . won't look."

Against my better judgment, I thought two pairs of hands might be better, especially if she woke and decided to struggle against me. I looked back down at her closed eyes, seemingly peaceful. Dark eyelashes brushed against her cheeks, flushed from what I assumed was fever setting in.

"You won't be able to not look," I said, my voice terse. "It can't be helped. Bring them here and let's get to work. If she awakens, you'll need to hold her down."

Kit set the bucket of water down between us, gasping when his eyes swept over Livie. "Captain," he breathed. "Is she . . . is . . . will she die?"

I held out my hand, a piece of cloth resting in my palm a second later. After dipping it in the water, I began gently washing away blood and grime, starting with her stomach and working my way up. It looked worse than it was. I needed to dig out any shrapnel that had embedded in her skin, otherwise infection would set in, and without proper medicine and an actual surgeon onboard, she would likely die from it.

"If a fever is setting in, I don't know," I had to be honest. "But she's strong, Kit. Let me wash the blood and dirt away so we can see the extent of her injuries. It appears mostly just flesh wounds, but some of the shrapnel went deeper."

"She pushed me out of the way." His voice trembled.

I glanced up at the boy beside me, younger than Livie but just as faithful. This woman I'd tricked into captivity defended my ship as though it were her own. I couldn't help my wandering eyes, memories of molding my large hands over her subtle curves. The gentle slopes of her breasts were a sight to behold, blood and grime aside.

Kit and I made quick work of washing away what we could to reveal several puncture wounds, some shallow enough not to need stitching, while others required me to send him to the infirmary for instruments. Luckily, only a few moans escaped her lips while I worked to dig out the metal. There were slight burns on her skin, which gave me reason to pause. While Kit ran to get burn ointment from the infirmary, I smoothed my fingers over her brow.

Her eyes opened at my touch. She didn't struggle or push against me. Instead, she allowed me to run my fingers over her hot skin while a hint of a smile curved her lips.

"How bad?" she asked, her voice scratchy.

I smiled, hoping to give her some optimism. "Just some scrapes and burns. Kit went to get ointment, and I'll bandage you up as soon as he returns."

Her cheeks flushed; I wasn't sure if it was fever or embarrassment until she asked in a hushed whisper, "Am I naked?"

My laugh escaped before I could stop it. "Only partially."

"Did Kit see?"

"Aye, but he won't tell a soul. I would apologize, but I didn't know if you would struggle against me, Livie."

"I forgive you." Her eyes fluttered, and I thought she would close them again, but she just looked at me. "I could use a bit of rum."

Not one to argue, I stood just as Kit returned. Seeing that she was awake, he did his best to avert his eyes as he brought over the salve. I poured a small glass of rum and brought it to her lips, helping her to sit up a bit. She winced but did not utter a sound while she sipped.

"This part may not be very comfortable," I said, sitting back down and opening the tin of salve. "I apologize in advance, but you will start to feel better."

She nodded, her eyes on Kit while he looked everywhere but at her. I took a deep breath, dipping my fingers into the salve and gently touching her reddened skin. She jerked, again not making a sound. After rubbing it in and wrapping bandages around her shoulder and torso, she visibly relaxed.

"Thank you," she whispered.

I handed the cup of salve back to Kit, who hurried to clean up our mess. The poor lad seemed eager to be done with this task.

"Go on and get yourself cleaned up," I told him. "You did well here, Kit."

Humbled, he backed out of the room, leaving us in silence as I looked down at her. She looked tired, but her eyes remained on mine. My gut told me this night would be long. I'd be damned if I moved her anywhere else, and I didn't dare share it with her, not when she was barely lucid.

"I hated my father for leaving me," she whispered, her eyes closing. "Everything I did, everything I do, I do for him. He couldn't even give me the courtesy of sending me word. Not a single word from him in the three years I've lived with my aunt. I'm tired, Grayson."

A pent-up sigh released from deep in her lungs, and her eyes opened. Bright and vividly blue, she stared at me. I decided then and there I would never tire of looking into her eyes. They were so beautiful . . .

"He'll kill me," she whispered. "My father."

I remained silent as she continued.

"I may not know where he is, but he would send missives through his agent. It's all I could do to prove my value to him. Less because I'd allowed myself to become a fallen woman. Edward managed to get away. I often wondered what had become of Edward, I just knew he hadn't died on that island. Then I saw him in London that night. No matter, my father will kill me for leaving London."

I found it hard to believe Elias would kill his daughter, yet I wished to question her, to explore her history and understand what molded Livie into the person she had become. But I dared not, fearing that she would close up after having already revealed so much.

"He taught me everything I knew, then ripped it all away. When he comes for me, I will face his wrath. And it won't be pleasant."

"He will not touch you, Livie. Not while I live and breathe."

I found myself drawn to her, unable to deny what was between us any longer. When I leaned down, pressing my lips to hers, her hand rose and curled around my neck. Neither of us could stop it.

We shared a kiss filled with longing, deep denial, and weakness. I welcomed the built-up passion. Kissing her amidst the storm was nothing compared to this. This was the point of no return, and it was just beginning.

Chapter Thirty Five

Grayson

The sea's color shifted to turquoise, and birds began circling days after the ghost ship encounter. The smell of land filled our nostrils as we approached Antigua. What I'd seen in Livie's eyes, her trust and the control she'd ceded to me while the ship slept, churned inside me like a foul corruption.

The crew's anticipation was palpable as we neared land, and I shared their eagerness. Yet, the closer we got, the more guarded I became. After dropping our cargo in Antigua, the next stop would be to see if Elias showed up to intercept us. Livie would learn of my plans and hate me for it; she would never understand my need to avenge Adam. Elias had taken more than my brother. He'd taken the lives of countless other crew members in addition to rich cargo.

When the time came, I hoped she would understand, but I doubted it, and therein lay the crux of the problem. I didn't want to hope. I wanted two things that I could not have: Livie or vengeance. I couldn't have both.

I spread open the map and placed it on the flat top of the quarterdeck while Connor lounged with his boots propped lazily on the wheel. There was nothing in the distance as far as the eye could see, but squawking birds flew overhead as Sully hauled in nets of fresh fish for supper. We would reach land by tomorrow.

A man stepped cautiously up the stairway toward us, hands clasped in front of him and eyes darting nervously. Instantly, I straightened. The crew did not usually come up to the quarterdeck unless there was an issue or one of us had beckoned them. Connor's feet struck the deck with a thud as he rose from his perch.

The man's name was Otis, one of the gunners under Wiley's command. If there had been an issue with any of our weapons, Wiley would have brought it to my attention as the master gunner. I frowned, ignoring the map.

"What's your trouble, Otis?" I asked.

He stopped at the top of the stairs, gaze shifting between me and Connor. Abandoning the map, I strode toward him, my eyebrows drawn together. Something about his approach set my instincts on high alert. Something was amiss.

"Cap'n, I must confess," he said, his voice trembling.

Connor cursed colorfully beneath his breath. "What did you do, Otis?"

Otis took another step forward, thrusting out his hand, palm up, and opening it. In his palm sat a signet ring, solid gold and heavy-looking. I plucked it from his hand, studying the ring with the heavily scrolled initial B.

I swallowed thickly. "Where did you find this, Mr. Beckett? Is it yours?"

He shook his head. "No, Cap'n. I found it in the woman's trunk."

My eyebrows shot up, eyes darkening. "You were snooping through someone else's belongings?" He nodded. "Why is that?"

He reached into his pocket, producing a small rolled parchment tied with a string, which looked fairly old. Wasting no time, I untied it and rolled out a small map of the Caribbean Islands. Jamaica, Barbados, Cuba, and near Puerto Rico was a red X.

I glanced up at Otis.

"I found that as well." His eyes gleamed with unnecessary satisfaction, though the information he had brought forth only curdled in my stomach.

"Who else knows of this?"

He shook his head emphatically. "No one."

I clutched the ring in my fist, but kept the map intact. Livie had lied to me. She knew exactly where her father's hideout was. I trusted her.

"Very good, Mr. Beckett. You will keep this to yourself."

As hard as it was for me to release him, the news of her betrayal sank my mood into the depths of despair. Otis perked up, appearing delighted that snooping wouldn't lead to his punishment.

"We can sell her when's we reach land, Cap'n. Money made for the capture of Blackwood's daughter." His tongue darted out to moisten his lips, but he stepped back at my dark gaze.

"That will be all. You will keep this to yourself or be fed to the sharks. Do you understand me?" I asked, the ring digging into my palm as I gripped it.

He nodded vigorously and disappeared back down the stairs. Connor turned to me, a wry tilt to his mouth. Knowing her father's whereabouts changed everything. We would still need to unload our cargo, being lighter in the face of battle. But I could perhaps catch him unaware. I would deal with Livie later.

"Gray?" Connor asked lightly. "What will you do now?"

I grunted. "She lied to me. She looked me in the eye and told me she did not know where her father's hideout was. And I foolishly believed her. This, Connor, is what I wanted to hear. And yet, I didn't."

"And Mr. Beckett?"

"After dark, when everyone is asleep, have him confined to the brig."

His eyebrows shot up. "Why?"

"You heard the man. He wants to sell Livie onshore." My gaze met his. "I cannot allow that to happen, or this entire mission is at risk."

"And Livie? What will you do with her?"

"Nothing. As far as she knows, we don't know where that bastard is hiding. When the time comes, and I confront her father, she will harbor such hatred for me that it won't matter."

Even as I said it, my heartbeat quickened and my stomach churned. I had wanted to trust her so badly, to believe she was nothing like her father, and she had deceived me entirely.

Chapter Thirty Six

Livie

I couldn't shake the feeling that something was bothering Grayson. We reached land the following day. Though he'd allowed his crew to stay ashore for a night of carousing once the cargo was unloaded, it was not safe for me to do so. I disagreed with his excuse, but I knew it was because he did not want to lose me when we were so close. And that hurt.

Grayson had gone ashore with his men to unload while I remained behind, bored to tears as I listlessly paced on the main deck. Connor had returned with a few other men before darkness fell, but the majority of the crew was still ashore by the time I went below and curled into myself amid the otherwise empty bed.

A loud thump jolted me upright, clutching the thin blanket to my chest. The heat was suffocating, even though I'd lived most of my life accustomed to it. Yet, despite my clammy skin, the emptiness of the bed beside me chilled me.

"Grayson?" I called out.

It was the middle of the night, and the ship was quiet, swaying gently with the tide. It was unusual for Grayson to leave me alone at night, but we both knew that no one would dare enter his quarters without orders or permission to do so.

Quietly, I climbed out of bed and dressed before heading to the main deck. There were a few men in the lookout, as cargo had been taken ashore for payment. The deck remained cloaked in darkness, with only the sound of waves gently lapping against the ship.

"Livie." Wiley approached me on the main deck, breathless from his jog from the hull.

"Ho, there!" I smiled. "Do you know where I might find Grayson?"

Everyone knew that Grayson and I shared a bed each night, but no one dared speak of it. Wiley stared at me, his expression cautious.

I had given it some thought and wondered when my father would come for me. I knew he would, though I'd led Grayson to believe otherwise. I'd rather not know if he still intended to trade me away. If he did, I would leave here with my head held high.

"Two men deserted."

My eyes widened. "Did he find them?"

"He's gone ashore to see if he can track them down." He reached out, grabbing my wrist before I could walk away. "Livie, your father's ship has been sighted."

Devil take me!

"You won't win against him, Wiley." I shook my head, wondering if this was worth anything. "Perhaps Grayson should cut me loose and save the crew the hassle."

"He would never do that."

Fury boiled over as Wiley confirmed what I already knew. It didn't matter what happened. When faced with the choice, Grayson would choose vengeance. He would choose it over his own crew, even. I held no value, not even to Grayson.

I raced back to the cabin and slammed the door, pacing until I thought I would wear a path in the floor. Hours later, in the dead of night, I heard footsteps along with several others, but whoever was coming passed by and continued down below deck. No doubt men returning from shore.

After several minutes of waiting, I snuck out of the cabin and made my way to the berth, where hammocks were strewn about and cannons were ready. The berth was largely empty, as many hadn't returned yet, so it was quiet.

Then a crack split the air, the sound of someone being punched, followed by a grunt. Slowly, I made my way down the wooden floorboards, using the voices to guide me. I wound my way through the hammocks strung up in the room, sidestepping casks used for gaming when the men were bored and wanted to escape the sun.

At the far end of the level, toward the hull, I spotted another cabin with the door slightly ajar. No one else seemed to be around as I walked steadily forward.

"I'll ask you again," came Grayson's voice, his tone menacing. "Where is Elias Blackwood? He can't possibly be at his hideout. I have his daughter, and he knows it."

"A pox on you." I heard someone spit.

Another punch followed by the creaking of wood. "There's still time to string you up by your balls," Grayson ground out. "You'll tell me everything you know. I know where his hideout is. Don't lie to me."

I drew nearer, peeking into the room where Grayson had a man by his tunic. Thick ropes bound the man's hands behind his back as he was tied to a chair, and Grayson lifted him and the chair clear of the floor. My eyes widened.

Muscles in Grayson's arms and back rippled with the effort, but the set of his jaw nearly made me back away. I knew him to be a formidable captain, but I'd never seen him physically punish someone himself. Nor had I seen him this angry.

"Kit, ready the deck for our . . . guest. The seagulls are about to have a feast."

The chair hit the floor, tipping precariously for a second before righting itself. "No."

"You have one more chance to tell me what you know. I have what is rightfully his, and I know he's bound to come for his daughter. I won't be caught by surprise. You will tell me here and now where he is."

"Last I heard, he was in the Cayman Islands."

"And Livie?"

I stiffened at the mention of my name.

"He won't let her go. Not to the likes of you. You'll have to kill him first."

"Oh, I intend to."

My hand clamped over my mouth, smothering a gasp. If my father wouldn't let me go, why had he left me to begin with? He cared nothing for me. I knew he didn't. A father who dropped his daughter off with a family she'd never met would have sent word now and again. He never had.

Confusion swept through me, and I backed away from the room. All I heard were things that brought more questions racing through my mind. I didn't need to hear more. I needed answers. Grayson had told the man he knew my father's whereabouts, which meant only one thing: he'd gone through my belongings and found my map.

Turning around, I stumbled through the room to the staircase. Wiley called out to me, hearing me stomping through the hallway, but I ignored him until I reached the next level and raced into Grayson's quarters.

Surely he must have it among his possessions. It was mine. It belonged to me. I slammed the door behind me, immediately dropping to my knees in front of one of his trunks. I dug through clothing, weapons, and toiletries, trying not to make a mess. Doing it this way, I found nothing.

The top of the trunk came down with a thud. Disappointment speared through me, hot and bitter. I pushed myself up, wandering about the cabin I had shared with him for several days now, since the last battle had rendered my cabin useless.

I threw myself into the chair, slouching and crossing my arms as my eyes swept over the stack of maps tucked into a corner. Wasting no time, I ran over and pulled out the rolls of maps, only to find several books tucked behind them.

Journals Grayson had written in.

I hadn't seen him writing in any journals since I'd been around him. After looking at the dates of each of them, I noticed they ended just after we'd left London. He must have stopped, fearing I would discover what he had recorded in his quest.

I sat on the floor, journals surrounding me, soon forgetting all about my map.

Greedily, my eyes scanned the first dated journal. He had indeed written about what had happened to his brother, Adam. He was killed when a pirate masquerading as a privateer intercepted them, although he couldn't identify the privateer. From the words he wrote in these journals, Grayson blamed my father for his death. My father was known for not always flying his colors. Tears pricked my eyes as I read about Grayson barely surviving by swimming with Adam to shore, his brother dying in his arms.

When the door opened, my head snapped up, and my eyes immediately connected with Grayson's. Bleak, dead eyes stared back at me. I closed the last journal and laid it aside, not bothering to move until he closed the door.

"You think you understand now?" he asked, his voice unusually low. "Understand me?"

I got to my feet, clutching the last journal in my hand. "I might understand you better than you understand yourself. Why?"

"Why what?"

"Why do you think it's your right to be judge, jury, and executioner?"

Grayson strode up to me quickly, his jaw hardened and his eyes flashing. "What if your father had a hand in your mother's death? Would you not want her avenged?"

My eyes widened. Had my father had something to do with her death? He'd left us on that island. Nothing could have prevented that hurricane, and even I could have perished from it. I shook my head and raised my hand to slide over his set jaw.

"Leave him be, Grayson."

His hand caught my wrist, brutally punishing in its grip. "He'll be held accountable for what he's done. Adam was not the only innocent man to die that day. We suffered tremendous losses in men and in cargo. Cargo that I found traces of in London, *with* your father's insignia."

When he released my wrist, I kept my hands to myself. Grayson would never believe otherwise, and I didn't know the truth to argue it. Instead, I walked past him and out the door.

Chapter Thirty Seven

When she walked past me, a torrent of emotions in her eyes, I let her go.

Livie would never understand my need to see her father brought to justice. She could read every journal I'd kept and still never comprehend. Adam hadn't just been my older brother; he'd been my savior. He protected me from our father's temper, guiding me through life and helping me find courage within myself. He never could convince my father that I was more worthy than he believed. But Livie was the one who made me believe I was more than second-best. With her, I didn't have to prove myself.

When he left to sail the seas, my father ordered me to find the man responsible. Anything less would be seen as a failure in his eyes. Always second to Adam. My determination was to avenge Adam and the men who lost their lives to Elias, and to earn my father's respect, even though deep down I knew I never would.

Just as Livie would never earn her father's. We were more alike than either of us thought.

I turned and hurried out of my cabin toward the main deck, where I found her standing in the rain. Her golden hair hung down her back, gloriously loose. Her black breeches and tunic clung to her slender body as she watched the rain strike the water. It was a gentle rain, refreshing.

As I approached, she whirled around. What I might have missed behind her eyes when she walked away was clear now: anguish and hurt. What did she expect me to do? Choose her over vengeance? I didn't know if I could.

"Don't do this, Grayson," she said. "Give over what you have on him to the authorities and let them handle it."

She'd read what I'd written. I wouldn't have lied in my journals. Things may have shifted for us, but I still wanted her father to face a reckoning, my reckoning.

"It's your intention to kill him?"

"Livie, let me explain," I started. "My brother meant everything to me. It broke my mother's heart to hear the news of his murder."

Her arms hung at her sides, resigned to the maelstrom of emotions swirling within her. I doubted she would listen to my reasons, but if she was willing to hear me out, that was a step forward.

"Don't you understand?" she cried. "Avenging your brother will not bring him back, even if it were true that my father attacked your ship. So I ask you again: was it your intention to kill him from the start?"

I could never deny that, even though it pained me to see the anguish in her eyes. She'd lived with her father and learned from him. She still worked with him. Of all the people who knew what he was like, she did. How could she ask me to admit it?

Like a coward, I couldn't say anything. How could I do this to her? She'd never hurt anyone, least of all me. She'd given herself freely to me, offered herself to this ship, all behind a cloak of secrecy and lies. But now I was about to take it all away. Her map be damned. I didn't care.

"Yes," I whispered.

"If I asked you to turn this ship around, to leave my father alone . . . would you?"

This time, my silence dug my grave. Anguish turned to regret in her eyes almost instantly. This time, when she walked away from me, I let her go.

Chapter Thirty Eight

Livie

I stayed in my old cabin the rest of the night, despite its need for repairs, but I couldn't sleep. As I lay in my empty bed, emotions swirled in my mind. I tried to sever those feelings the moment they began, unable to reconcile Grayson's need for vengeance when he couldn't possibly win.

The rain made the bed wet and uncomfortable. I stared at the gaping hole in the wall for hours, contemplating my life and where I would go from here. When I'd left London with Grayson, I hadn't expected it to be like this. I'd thought Grayson and I would dance around each other at first. I might end up in his bed from the undeniable pull I'd felt since meeting him. But this? Whatever this was, I didn't know.

What had happened to bring me to this point? What would happen next?

If Grayson succeeded in luring my father, I couldn't stand idly by and let anyone get hurt. Despite the past between my father and me, I wouldn't allow Grayson to kill him. Nor could I let my father kill Grayson.

This left me in a bind, one that only I could resolve.

There was one way out, and I'd be foolish to think I would get far. I'd have to be light on my feet, stealthy enough to sneak past anyone to do it. In the dead of night, anything could happen on the water.

It would be an incredible risk.

One worth taking if it meant no one I cared about would die.

Decision made, I braided my hair and covered it with a scarf. The crew had already returned from shore. Rather than risk anyone hearing my footsteps, I stepped forward with determination into the darkness of early morning.

Dawn was only hours away. I had one shot at this.

I'd almost breathed a sigh of relief while creeping past Grayson's quarters when a hand clamped over my mouth so viciously that I had no time to make a sound. My attacker's arm slung around my waist, lifting me off my feet. Not much taller than me, it wasn't Grayson. Grayson was much more muscular than whoever thought to strike. Whoever it was had been watching.

Not again, I thought. Would the men aboard this vessel stop at nothing to try to harm me? One of the men who had tried before, I'd never seen again. I kicked and thrashed against my captor, earning only a quiet grunt before another locking hold caught my legs.

"This is for your own good, love," the words murmured against my ear had me frozen.

Edward. He must have left London about the same time we had. But how he'd come to be on this vessel, I couldn't venture to say. Currency weighed differently based on who had more to gain. I could only question what Edward would have to gain from this.

The two men carried me up to the main deck, despite my struggles. In fact, they both had a firm grasp on me. I tried to look around, convinced the lookouts would see this and stop it from happening. My eyes fell to the helm, absent of Connor or Sully.

"Liv, we're going to set you on your feet. Should you struggle, I will not hesitate to knock you out. You will not want me to do that, and I would rather not hurt you. Nor do I want to alert anyone to my presence here. It was difficult enough to sneak aboard."

I dared not agree or disagree. If the man holding me would take his hand away from my mouth, I could let out a scream loud enough for someone to realize that this was happening yet again. Edward released my legs, and the other man clasped me so tightly I could hardly move.

"Livie," he growled.

He was sorely mistaken if he did not expect me to fight for my life. Whatever they intended, it could not be good for me. I got in one solid kick, followed by a grunt before something struck my head and everything went black.

My head ached fiercely when I cracked my eyes open to the light of a sparsely furnished room. Lying on the single bed, my gaze fixed on the thatched and caned roof, I found my hand immobilized by a tie to the bedpost, allowing only a foot of movement.

As much as I tried to yank myself free, I only rubbed my wrist raw. A single window across the room was my only indication that day had come, the palm trees in the distance waving in the slight breeze, though the room itself was oppressive with heat. I could hear the waves against the beach, longing for something to quench my thirst.

"You'll not get free anytime soon."

My eyes darted to the doorway behind me, craning my neck to see Edward strolling in. He sat down beside me, shifting my legs over as he did so.

I glared at him, though it hurt my head immensely when I did. When he reached over to brush the hair from my face, I pulled away. This was not the same man I'd fallen in love with. He'd hit me. Whether to render me unconscious, I did not care. He had hit me.

As if reading my thoughts, the corner of his mouth quirked up. "I'm sorry, love," he whispered. "If there had been any other way, I would not have hit you."

"Why did you kidnap me?" I asked through clenched teeth.

When his head tilted to the side and his eyes grew soft, all the memories of how I'd fallen in love with him came flooding back. "Do you know the story of your father and mother?" he quietly asked. "How your father rescued your mother after she'd been abducted?"

I drew in a heavy, irate breath. "My father won the prizes on a ship he'd overtaken. My mother was part of that prize. Do you mean to tell me that you think you are repeating history somehow?"

He laughed, a soft, lilting laugh as though he were innocent in whatever this was. "Perhaps I'd like to think of your father as rescuing your mother. Your father knows I escaped from that island."

Of course he did, I thought. My father knew everything that happened to the point that sometimes I thought he knew things before they even happened. I knew what Edward was trying to do, even though it wouldn't do any good. What had been done was done.

"He won't forgive you," I whispered. "Just as he won't forgive me."

My words didn't stop Edward from running his finger down the side of my face, and I let him because being nice was all I knew how to do at the moment. With my wrist tied to the bed, I wouldn't be getting out of this mess. They had removed my daggers, which is why they only tied one of my hands.

"You think you'll give me back to my father and he will forgive all our transgressions?" I asked.

"Don't you? I rescued you from your captor. It's the least he can do. Perhaps he'll allow us to marry, as we'd always said we would." I opened my mouth to recant my previous promises, only to have him smooth his thumb over my lower lip. "You cannot tell me you have not thought of me these past few years. I've thought of little else. And when I saw you in London, I knew I couldn't let you get away again."

"Release me," I demanded. "I can't properly talk to you unless you untie my hands. This is extremely uncomfortable."

He looked doubtful. "You promise you will not run? I have men posted around this hut who will stop you if you try, but I'd rather not hurt you again."

I shook my head. "I'm too exhausted from your unanticipated strike to run anywhere."

Leaning over me, Edward worked the knots in the rope around my wrist until I was finally free. True to my word, I slowly sat up and rubbed my wrist.

"Did it ever occur to you I left London for a reason, Edward? My father is going to be furious when I'm brought back to him." I lifted my chin. "You bringing me to him is only going to cause him to think you have done this."

Edward rose from the bed, and I followed. "Everyone knows you were abducted, Livie. Whether you realize it, Grayson Valle took you from London to draw out your father."

I frowned. "How do you know that?"

"Like you, I had eyes and ears all over London. Grayson Valle was looking for any information regarding stolen cargo, rare silks that were taken when his ship was attacked and his brother murdered. When you turned up missing, all fingers pointed to Grayson."

"But I left letters for my family."

He shook his head. "It does not matter. Percival Monteclaire-"

I took a step back, my mouth popping open. "No."

"Apparently, he did not take kindly to his fiancée going missing. Grayson was immediately accused of taking you, forcing you to falsify letters to your family."

"That is not what happened!" I cried, immediately grimacing at the ache in my head. "Please, Edward, do not take me back to my father."

When his shoulders sagged, I knew it was a battle I would lose. Edward was firm in his resolve to take me to my father, believing it would lead to forgiveness. I knew my father better than Edward did. He would not forgive and forget, and he would certainly not allow Edward to marry me.

"How much?" I asked.

His head snapped up, bright gaze meeting mine.

"I will gladly pay it if you return me to Grayson's ship. I'll take my chances there rather than being returned to my father. You may have escaped with your life, Edward, and I am glad for that, but he was harder on me than any of his crew. He will not forgive me."

Edward took a step toward me, grabbing my hands in his and squeezing them. "It only seemed that way. That was not the way of it, Livie."

"Return me to Grayson's ship, Edward."

If I needed to beg, I would. Edward had been through enough at the hands of my father. If I could save him from further harm, I would. That and I couldn't help but to think of the letter I'd left behind for Grayson to find. Surely, he would think I had left in pursuit of saving anyone involved. And I had. I just hadn't planned on being intercepted.

"It's what you want?" Edward asked, his voice oddly cracking.

"Aye. I need to return, and you need to forget me and move along with your life. I will never be happy unless I choose my own path forward. You know that."

Chapter Thirty Nine

As soon as Livie left me on deck in the light rain, I marched to my cabin to clean up the mess she had made with my journals. While tidying up, a thought popped into my mind that I couldn't shake.

Lying in bed, a bed that smelled like her, my mind raced through my options to salvage the only relationship I'd cared about since my brother's murder. Dawn was just beginning to break when I rose and dressed.

I opened the ledgers that had been carefully maintained during our voyage, her penmanship neat and orderly on the pages. Page after page displayed her elegant swirls, every detail exact. It made me wonder how a woman who'd spent most of her life under the watchful eye of a pirate father had such refined skills. From what I knew, she garnered most of her education aboard *The Executioner*, achieving the rest in London.

Either her aunt had worked miracles, or she was truly more than met the eye, as I'd already been thinking.

I could no longer stay silent. I had to speak with her.

"Livie, please open the door."

I closed my eyes, leaning my forehead against the hard wood panel, a single object of separation, yet so much lay between me and the woman on the other side. My palm pressed flat against the surface, and the words I longed to say threatened to spill out.

"Livie," I whispered, her name a burn in my throat, an ache. "I never meant to hurt you. I . . ." I couldn't say it.

The depth of what I felt, the way it had fundamentally changed me, was indescribable. What kind of man would this crew follow if they knew?

I knocked again, only to be met with silence. If she kept this up much longer, I'd have no choice but to open the door without her permission. I'd done it before, many weeks ago, and if my eyes fell on her as they had that time, I would take her in my arms and profess my feelings.

"Please."

Silence.

Clenching my jaw, I grasped the doorknob and yanked it open. The room was empty. Had she gone up on deck without anyone noticing? I spun around just as Kit came charging down the steps, alarm in his eyes.

"Cap'n, it's gone."

Panic surged from deep in my stomach. "What is gone, Kit?"

"One of the skiffs. That's not all that's missing." He looked sheepish, as though reluctant to say it. "Pax and Rodney are gone, too."

The two crew hands whom I never would expect to stab me in the back, I thought. When I found the two gunners, punishment would be imminent. No sooner had Kit spoken than I was running past him, taking the stairs two at a time before I burst out into the blinding sun with Kit on my heels.

"Has anyone seen Livie yet this morning?" I threw the question behind me.

"No," he replied.

I grabbed the nearest crew member by the shoulder and asked if he'd seen Livie, Pax or Rodney. No. Everyone I asked hadn't seen any of them, which meant only one thing. They'd abducted her and taken her inland. I could only imagine why.

Regardless of Elias Blackwood's reputation, she would fetch a fair price for anyone in search of a slave as exquisite as she.

With a growl, I stormed up to the quarterdeck and grabbed the spyglass. I knew I wouldn't see anything out of the ordinary with the line of other ships bobbing on the northern side of the island, but I had to try. If I could not spot her aboard any other ship, I could only assume she had been taken to the island.

Dread filled me as my thoughts drifted to the worst. If a ship that had already departed had taken her aboard, the chances of her being recovered were slim, if that was indeed what had occurred.

All options put her in immediate danger. I would rather lose her back to her father than see her live a life under someone else's thumb. Or worse.

"Cap'n." Kit stood on the stairs, holding out a piece of folded parchment.

His fingers shook as I took it from him, the look on his face mirroring my own terror. Anything could happen to her out there. She had daggers, but those were only effective when close enough to wield, and that gnawed at me. I didn't want anyone getting remotely close to her. I couldn't bear the thought of her being hurt somewhere.

I opened the letter, noticing clear marks in the ink from water droplets against Livie's handwriting. My gut turned. She'd been crying when she wrote this. As I scanned Livie's last words, Kit and Connor, now joined by Wiley, waited to hear what she had written.

"She says she cannot choose between me and her father."

I crumpled the letter in my fist. She thought to escape, conning Pax and Rodney into accompanying her away from my ship. A territorial growl escaped from deep in my throat as I stared at the island in the distance, my silent vow to find her echoing my own demise.

Immediately, I started barking out the names of men I wanted to accompany us to the island. I dared not leave the ship vulnerable, otherwise I would have taken every single able-bodied crewman with me. Connor joined us, knowing Livie's temperament when she was angry. Wiley also came along.

Rowing to shore seemed to take much longer than it should have. My boots hit the water the moment the skiff hit the sandy beach. I heard Connor calling out behind me, but I dared not wait. The island was vast, and finding her would be like searching for a specific seashell among so many.

I stopped in my tracks when the familiar, fair-haired vixen stepped out from beneath the shade of the trees with a man I recognized as the one who had accosted her in London. The same man she'd held a dagger to his neck. My breath seized in my lungs when she laughed at something he had said before looking my way, her surprise halting her steps.

Possessive had never been something I considered myself to be, and it shouldn't be something I suddenly felt now, but seeing her in the company of this man, laughing with him, brought a rush of it through me. I strode up to her, my hand firmly on the hilt of the dagger at my belt.

"What are you doing?" I snapped, resisting the urge to reach out and pull her away from him.

While she looked up at the man, as if questioning her answer, my gaze swept over her to ensure she was uninjured. The moment my eyes caught the redness on her wrist, I lunged at the man.

"Grayson!" Livie said, trying to push her way in front of him. "This is not . . . Please allow me to explain."

"Were you going to leave with this man?" I asked, incredulous at her recklessness.

"No!" she cried out. "Let me explain, if you would just leave Edward be for a single moment."

Edward. The very man who had stolen her innocence, getting her evicted from her father's vessel for his wrongdoing. Had he professed his love to her, wooing her away from me with his pretty words?

"It was a misunderstanding," she said tightly. "Edward was escorting me back to your ship. That way, you can continue with your plans to bait my father. He merely wanted to give me a choice."

My eyebrow raised, and I couldn't help but think this was a silly ruse to get me away from my ship. I glanced back at Connor and Wiley, both of them ready to fight if the need arose.

Edward crossed his arms in front of him, his gaze narrowed at me.

Livie turned to Edward. "Be happy, Edward. Live your life as you should."

When she took a step toward me, he caught her uninjured wrist and spun her back around. I moved, wrapping my arms around her waist and lifting her off her feet before he could think to lay his mouth on my woman. Kicking against me, she fought, but I turned and set her down.

"*Captain*, you have no right!" she yelled.

Her words slapped me. She was right. I had no right to feel this way. But one way or another, Livie would be returning with me.

"Say goodbye," I ordered, my tone hard and unyielding.

When she moved to walk back to Edward, I slashed out my arm to stop her without catching her injured wrist.

"Without touching him," I growled.

Satisfaction at the way her eyes widened at my words speared through me. I couldn't help the corner of my mouth from lifting when she raised her chin in defiance and looked at Edward.

"Goodbye, Edward," she said lightly. "Thank you for trying to rescue me. It shall not be forgotten."

Edward did not look as though he liked me much, but his gaze toward her softened, and he gave a brief nod before turning and striding away. I would have turned to leave, wanting to put distance between us and this island, but Livie waited while watching him depart.

I couldn't imagine what she thought while watching him walk away, but I would get the story from her later. It wasn't something she owed me, but I would ask anyway. When she turned to leave, I tried to grab her elbow, but she yanked away and created distance between us.

"Don't," she snapped.

Chapter Forty

Livie

When the skiff reached the height of the railing, I jumped out and strode past Grayson. The fury in his eyes mirrored my own, but I refused to give him the satisfaction of acknowledging it. Let him suffer the demons and ghosts he allowed to haunt him.

"Livie," Grayson shouted after me, his voice carrying an edge I had never heard before. "Bloody hell, stop."

If there had been any doubt about my feelings when I crossed the deck in response to his commands, those doubts were laid to rest when I ignored Grayson. Aware that Grayson was following, I quickened my pace until he reached out and grabbed my arm.

My eyes blazed when I turned to face him. If I had thought I would get away with slapping him, I would have. Grayson was far too agile for me to even try. I knew the way he moved as surely as I knew my own movements. The way his fingers wrapped around my arm, possessive and controlling, only spurred my anger higher. Where he touched, I burned.

"Let me go," I said, my voice eerily calm.

"No," he snapped. "We'll have this out, Livie."

Instead of releasing me, he hauled me toward the narrow passage that led to his quarters. I could have sworn I heard a few chuckles and guffaws as we passed. I stumbled after him, realizing that he'd taken care not to grab my sore wrist when he drew me into his cabin and slammed the door behind us.

"You had no right," I said. "None at all."

"*I* had no right?" he yelled. "You know my mission, and yet you decide to leave. Knowing the dangers out there that you face, you still did so! I can't decide whether your recklessness will get you killed, or get *me* killed! When I took note of your absence, when I saw you on the beach with that . . . that . . ."

"Edward," I supplied, my voice turning breathy.

He clenched his jaw, moving toward me a step. "The man who threatened you in the street in London the night before we departed."

My eyes widened as I recalled that night, my memory after running into Edward when Grayson had found me sitting at my usual table in *The Captain's Quarters*, realizing that he'd watched me that night. He had watched Edward toss me against the wall like a rag doll and hadn't intervened. He'd known I would and could defend myself. My resolve faltered.

Grayson took another step toward me. I took one back, then another until my back hit the table, my eyes widening at the realization that I'd met my match.

"I meant to do murder when I found you gone," he breathed. "And then I find you with him."

I shook my head. "A misunderstanding. Edward was returning me to you."

"Even though I mean to use you to get to your father?" he questioned, taking another step toward me until we were less than an arm's length apart.

I swallowed the thickness in my throat, barely nodding before his hand slid against my neck and brought my mouth to his. The heat between us nearly undid me. A whimsical sigh escaped my throat as his lips feathered kisses across my face and down my neck, his hands coming around to grasp my backside and draw me closer.

"I never wanted you to be hurt," he whispered.

"That's a bloody lie," I retorted, my voice still oddly breathy.

Grayson drew back, his eyes hooded. "It's the truth, Livie. From the moment I met you in that ballroom, I expected someone different. A pirate's daughter. Ruthless, immoral, unrefined. But that's not what I found. You're cunning, intelligent, daring, and poised."

I hated that my hands trembled, longing to believe him. To believe in him. But how could I when he intended to let me go? It broke my heart to know he would seek his revenge rather than choose me.

I hated that I tried to leave instead of confessing to him. I knew it wouldn't do any good. I knew that. What could a woman professing love to a man set on vengeance accomplish? I couldn't handle another love lost, though Edward had returned. He was too late. I had already given my heart to Grayson, but I could never admit it to him. It changed nothing. It couldn't.

"You are everything I didn't know I searched for in a woman, Livie Blackwood."

My heart squeezed. My lips parted.

That was all it took for Grayson to seize my mouth in a searing kiss I felt all the way to my toes. This man, I thought, devil release me, but I wanted him. There wasn't anything I wouldn't do under his command, even if it meant returning to my father's ship. If he could have his vengeance, I would do it. My father would face the consequences of his actions. That was the price to pay for his unlawfulness.

The strength of his mouth stole the very breath from my lungs, waves of warmth growing beneath his masterful touch and weakening me to my core. My hands pressed against the edge of the table as he plundered my mouth. When he grasped my breeches and yanked them down, removing my boots next, I smiled. Slowly, he pressed kisses to my bare leg on his way back up, stopping to pay homage to my sensitive core until I gasped.

Sliding his palms up my thighs and around me, he lifted me into his arms until my legs snaked around his waist. In that moment, I knew I would never get enough of him. Not when he commanded me without care. He demanded, but he also gave.

"Don't you dare ruin another corset," I murmured against his mouth, waiting until he carried me to the bed before setting me down.

I worked the laces as quickly as I could, my practiced hands that were fast at tying knots now quick with the laces. Not quick enough for Grayson, who growled as he divested himself of his own clothing while he waited.

"Quicker, Livie," he demanded, his voice sending shivers across my skin.

Once blissfully free of the corset, he whisked away my tunic. The heat of the morning only contributed to the rising inferno between us. When he pushed me onto the bed, my hair splayed behind me, he stepped back and surveyed me with heavily lidded eyes. I watched him lean over me, prowling toward me, his skillful mouth igniting my skin wherever it pressed against my body.

His hands worked down my torso, teasing me into fitful moans until he pushed my legs apart and settled between them. Holding my legs, he extracted every breathy sound from my lips as he filled me completely, keeping his eyes locked on mine.

"You will forever be mine, Livie Blackwood," he growled. "Say it."

As he began to withdraw, drawing a groan from my throat, I tried to look away, but he grasped my chin, forcing me to meet his gaze.

"Say it."

"I'm yours, Grayson."

"Forever."

"Forever," I whispered just as he slammed his hips back into me, a gasp escaping my lips so forcefully it came out as a cry.

Grayson caught my hand when I reached for him, peppering my palm and the red ring around my wrist with kisses while together we showed each other what we meant. No words were needed as he took what I gave him, demanding in his careful way, while I took everything he had. Even if there wouldn't be much time for professed feelings later, I would take this. And take I did.

Chapter Forty One

Livie

There he was. *The Executioner*, sailing proudly toward us as we approached the waters around Puerto Rico, his banners flying high, a dagger entwined with roses. As much as I would have welcomed the sight after three long years, I despised it now. I feared it. I had to resolve not to show my fear.

All the emotions slammed into me as I stood at the bow, the warm breeze teasing wisps of hair from my braid. I had forgone the scarf, but still wore my black breeches and tunic, with the only corset I had cinched down to reveal the tops of my shoulders.

Grayson approached from behind. I knew it was him by the very air that seemed to pull me toward him like an invisible force. I glanced over my shoulder, wondering what he might be thinking. With a determined jaw, his gaze swept over me before focusing on the distant ship.

"What is your plan?" I asked.

He shrugged. "See if your father sends someone. If he does, I'll hear out his terms and reject them unless your father comes himself."

"He won't."

Grayson laughed, pressing behind me and hooking his arms around my waist. His dark, deep voice in my ear sent a shiver up my spine. "You said he wouldn't come. Yet here he is."

Tense, I turned in his arms. "Don't be fooled. I meant very little to him when he left me before. I doubt his regard for me has changed."

"If you could change your future, Livie, would you?" he asked, his expression sullen as he gazed down at me.

"I have already changed it," I said. "Otherwise, I'd be the Baroness of Vensworth, warming Percival's bed rather than yours."

He leaned down to kiss my lips softly. "I thank my lucky stars for that. But now, we need to deal with what I've brought to our doorstep." I agreed, but before I could say anything, he continued. "I have something that belongs to you, and before you charge at me with accusations, I am not the one who took these from your cabin."

He opened his palm, revealing my father's signet ring and the map. I grabbed them from his hand, my eyes blazing. "Where did you find these?"

"One of my crew took it upon himself to search your belongings while you were otherwise occupied." He tilted his head, offering me a chance to explain.

"And this man, what happened to him?"

"In the brig. I confined him while we were at port, ensuring he wouldn't cause any more trouble. I consider theft to be a serious offense, especially when one of those items is a map that clearly marks a hiding place. Care to explain?"

Reflecting on the fact that these items would not have been found had I not left my cabin served no purpose. Someone could have snuck in and discovered them while I was on deck. Grayson suspected I was keeping secrets, the map only confirming his mistrust.

I unfurled the map and looked at it. "You would never believe me if I told you."

"Try me."

"When I found this map three years ago, I marked the spot where I *thought* my father's hiding place was. I never knew for certain that this is where he hid, and Niles would never confirm it when I showed him. He told me it was best for everyone that I never knew. That no one knew."

Grayson was silent for a few moments before he sighed. "I believe you, Livie. God knows there was a time when I didn't believe a word coming from your mouth. But so much has changed, hasn't it?"

"Aye," I replied. "Everything has changed."

When I looked back at the approaching vessel, I tucked the ring into my corset. It wouldn't be long before *The Executioner* reached us. They were too far away for me to see anyone on deck, least of all my father. I could look through the spyglass, but suddenly I didn't care.

While Grayson had been attentive enough last night to make me think he might change his mind about letting me go, the look in his eyes now told me otherwise. And suddenly, I didn't want to be released. I wanted to remain with him, though with my father's appearance, that wouldn't be an option. I put my hands on his arms, pushing them down and away from me before walking off.

We waited for my father's approach, milling about the decks and preparing for battle if it came to that. Given that I was on board, I didn't think my father would open fire on us. Perhaps I had upset him back then, but I never imagined it would put me at risk.

I helped Wiley ready the cannons before checking how far away *The Executioner* was now. Surprised that they were nearly upon us, I glanced at the quarterdeck where Grayson stood with Connor.

Just as I did, the sound of a cannon blast echoed in the air, rocking the ship from the hit. My eyes widened, realizing that my father indeed intended to fight us. Running, I hit the forecastle deck and grabbed the rigging to hang on. I could hear Grayson shouting at me from across the ship, but I ignored him.

If my father could see me on deck, perhaps he wouldn't fire continue to fire at us.

Another cannon blast hit us, and the rigging jerked beneath my palms, threatening to shake me overboard. I held tight, even as we returned fire. Kit helped the gunners while Grayson shouted commands to return fire. Even when he met my gaze, as though asking for permission to fight back, I confirmed with a nod. My father was firing on us, and we would respond in kind.

My greatest fears had materialized, and as I dangled from the ropes, I desperately hoped everyone would survive. I jumped down, dodging shards of wood from the blasts hitting us. Besides rowing to my father in the skiff, I had no other recourse. I could return fire or stand here and wait.

My feet hit the deck, but I stayed where I was. If I persuaded Grayson to quit, it still wouldn't guarantee our salvation. I'd never seen or heard of my father bowing down to anyone. Elias Blackwood was undefeated in battle. There may have been close calls, but he always emerged victorious. He showed no mercy.

I ducked when another cannon blasted us, sending debris showering down around me, but I started running toward Grayson. He had to know that I would stay with him regardless of the outcome.

He tucked his pistol into his waistband when I reached him, gathering me in his arms for a moment before pulling away to look into my eyes.

"If you're going to betray me, do it now," I said. "I won't have this ship blown out of the water for me. He'll never surrender. He's got a bigger ship and more cannons. We will never win this. I thought I had lost Edward to his retaliation. I won't lose you."

Our eyes clashed and warred, and eventually, he drew a deep breath. He looked down at me. "For you, I would do anything."

My heart soared, but another hit had me stumbling.

"Raise the white flag," Grayson told Connor grimly.

"Grayson!" Connor shouted. "You can't be serious."

"We won't win this unless Elias comes over here himself, Connor. Hoist the flag. Do it now."

Connor whistled down to Kit, who scrambled over to the mainmast to raise the white flag. It flew in the air, all hands on deck looking to Grayson, even though we were still very much under attack.

Suddenly, everything stopped as if the world had paused. I waited, my breath held, while I watched those on my father's ship. Clearly, they'd seen our surrender. All he had to do was sail away. But he wouldn't.

My eyes swept the deck, searching for my father and finally spotting him as he strolled toward the railing directly across from me. He looked much the same as the last time I'd seen him, his lengthy brown beard and hair equally long beneath a tricorn. I could almost see the beads he'd threaded through his beard, the glint of his blue eyes, the same color eyes I'd inherited.

I could see his solid, unyielding stance. Why wasn't he giving the order to retreat? He'd won. He could disappear back into hiding with no one the wiser. We would leave, wherever that may be, and no one had to die. He wanted me, I thought. He would not sail away unless he had me.

As quickly as everyone had held their breath, the sound of fire resumed from *The Executioner*.

"No!" I shouted.

Despite our surrender, my father made the decision to continue shooting at us. Despite me. I didn't understand, jumping down the stairway to the main deck while we were riddled with cannon and pistol fire.

Grayson met my gaze through the haze of smoke. While he'd set this event in motion, I was the only one who could stop it. And I would do so.

I handed Kit my pistol and dove into the water.

Chapter Forty Two

Grayson

"Livie!" I bellowed as soon as I saw her dive into the water between the two ships.

My heart pounded with fear, and anger simmered just beneath the surface, emotions crashing through me like a net. I couldn't breathe as I watched her surface and swim with expert strokes. That cunning vixen, I thought. Why she had told me she wasn't a strong swimmer, I didn't know, but I aimed to find out.

If she thought this was how to save us, she was mistaken. Nothing would save us if Elias didn't accept our surrender. I glanced across the expanse and saw Elias watching his daughter swim toward him.

I raised my rifle, having a clearer shot at him than I would likely ever have again. The bullet would go straight through his chest if I took it. The woman in the water would be better off with me than with her father. I loved her, though I'd never said it to her.

My hesitation cost me. Elias suddenly moved, disappearing from my sight. I held my breath, waiting for him to show himself again. When he became visible again, a rifle of his own at the ready, I was too late to react. He took the shot. Wood splintered just below me. I returned fire, missing him. We were not close enough for this exchange.

"Bloody hell," I muttered, lowering my rifle and preparing to jump in after Livie.

If Elias wanted to kill me, he would have taken another shot, but instead watched his daughter swim. Thankfully, she appeared to be a skilled swimmer, already more than halfway to his ship.

"Don't you dare, Grayson," Connor strode up beside me, hand reaching out to grab my arm. "You will not jump in after her. You reach that vessel, Elias will kill you for touching his daughter."

I scoffed. "He doesn't know-"

"Grayson, you do not carry a woman across the ocean and not touch her. Especially after seeing the two of you together. He'll know it instantly. You are fooling yourself to believe otherwise."

For once, I didn't know how to respond. Part of me wanted to fight to get her back; the other part wanted to wait it out and see what would happen. I wondered what she'd been thinking when she leaped into the water and abandoned my ship. Abandoned me. Did she reconsider her circumstances after our heated confessions? Vengeance and proving to my father that I was not second best had consumed my thoughts since Adam had gone. I didn't need them. I needed her.

"Captain?" Connor asked again.

I glanced at him. "I need a moment."

"They've ceased firing at us."

"For now. We wait."

"Until?"

"Until I damn well give you orders," I ground out.

The crew relied on me for direction. Some were looking at me, waiting. Others were watching Livie reach her father's ship and climb the rope. Any of us could take aim, shooting her and her father. It felt as though both ships were lying in wait.

We all waited for Livie's next move.

"Lower the white flag," I murmured. "If they choose to continue fighting, we shall fight."

Connor followed me down to the main deck, waving at Wiley to take the helm in his place. Now was not the time to hesitate, but someone was demanding answers. I needed them, too.

"What about Livie?"

I spun around so quickly that Connor took a step back. "She's made her choice, Connor." I shook my head. "It's done. We cannot get her back."

"So you're giving up?" Connor shouted.

"She's just made her choice, and it wasn't me."

"You don't know that!"

"I do know that!" I shot back. "And if you continue to challenge me, I'll send you the same way Livie decided to go. I won't be questioned on my own damn ship."

This was spiraling into a disaster. I wanted to smash my fist into everything and everyone around me, drown myself in a bottle of rum, and run after the woman who had stolen everything from me, tying her to my side.

"They're leaving."

I looked at the other ship Livie had boarded. Sure enough, they were sailing toward the rock formation and would soon be out of sight. My heart felt heavy, knowing I had just let the one woman go that I shouldn't have, and would likely never see her again.

Worse than heavy, it felt dead. Panic rose as I wondered what Elias would do with her now that she was back in his clutches. I didn't know her past beyond what she'd told me, but no father would leave his daughter without a word.

I watched the ship for several minutes, pondering my next move.

"We have company," Connor said, jerking his gaze toward the other side of the rock formations.

Sure enough, another ship had joined us. From the flags, I could see that it was *The Sea Serpent*. Captain Jasper Stone, a noted ally of Elias Blackwood, albeit a tenuous relationship, I wondered what he wanted. A moment later, cannon fire split the air.

Chapter Forty Three

Livie

When I plunged into the water after my father's attack, I knew there was a chance I might die. Though my fear was palpable, I didn't believe my father would kill me. Hurting me was a possibility, but execution was not. This was the only way I knew how to fix this, and even as I reached the railing and swung a leg over, I felt as though I would have a pistol aimed at me. The crew encircled me while I straddled it, but I saw no pistols. My father stood with his legs braced and arms folded across his chest. His blue eyes, mirroring my own, watched me intently, while the grim set of his mouth beneath his neatly trimmed mustache sought to intimidate me.

"Give me a good reason why we shouldn't shoot you where you are," my father said, and I noticed the pistol in his hand, tucked in with his arms crossed.

"Because your blood runs in my veins, though why you would fire on a ship I was on raises questions," I replied, tilting my chin up to show no fear.

For several moments, we stared at each other. Years slipped away, and memories flooded back. Bitterness sliced through me, mingling with heartache at having to leave Grayson. I glanced back at *The Retribution*, as the sails overhead snapped in the wind, echoing our departure.

"So the prodigal daughter returns," he said, holding out his hand. "I want my ring back."

I swung my other leg over and jumped onto the deck, water dripping from my braid and clothes. My eyes narrowed. How dare he call me a prodigal daughter? I may be reckless, but I always had a purpose. Everything I'd done, I'd done for him, yet it had brought me nothing but grief.

I pried the ring out of my corset and slapped it into his waiting hand.

"Weapons?" he asked.

Jutting out my chin, I withdrew each dagger from my belt before reaching down to remove those tucked in my boots. A nearby crewman I didn't recognize snatched them from me, leaving me defenseless.

"Lass, give up the rest."

I nearly groaned before reaching around to withdraw the sheathed dagger from my corset, snug at my side. A woman could never be too careful about whom she might encounter. The man snatched it from me.

"Bring her to the brig, Quartermaster," he said tersely.

Incredulous, I watched him turn away from me and walk toward the quarterdeck. I looked around at the crew, some of whom I recognized. Nels, with his familiar grey hair and beard, smiled at me, missing more than a few teeth but still possessing that familiar twinkle in his eyes as he nodded in greeting.

"Come, lass," he said, reaching out for me.

I dodged the old man, rushing after my father and wishing I had the courage to swipe a dagger to use to stop his angry strides away from me. Being here didn't give me the sense of belonging I'd hoped for; if anything, I felt like a stranger.

The back of his white tunic mocked me as he moved swiftly away. His hair, still dark and not yet grey, was tied with a leather strip beneath a perfectly set tricorn. He was a wealthy man, though I didn't know where he kept his riches, nor did I care. I wanted none of his blood money, especially if some of it was from the attack on Grayson's merchant ship.

Reaching out, I grabbed his arm. He turned to me, eyes blazing.

"Don't you dare, lass." He shook a finger at me. "If it weren't for me, you wouldn't be in this world, and I'll damn well take you out."

"You didn't do anything for me," I shot back. "My mother brought me into this world. She cared for me when you abandoned us."

Grabbing me by the arms, he pushed me until my back smacked against a mast. I winced at the sharp pain, resolved to keep my mouth firmly shut or show weakness. He wouldn't hear any weakness from me, but he would hear what I'd been holding in for years.

He released me and resumed his path. "Nels, show her to the brig."

"I deserve some explanations."

When he stopped, he didn't turn around. "Once you've had a chance to calm down, I *might* provide you with some. For now, you will seek solace in the brig. After all, you were on a ship meant to capture me, were you not?"

Exasperation washed over me as he disappeared into the hallway below the quarterdeck. He wouldn't listen to reason until I obeyed his orders. Gently, Nels touched my arm.

"Livie," he rasped, "come now."

Nels led me down the stairs into the bowels of the ship, where the air was rank and thick. He nudged me into a corner space with bars from the ceiling to the floor. A crude bench, clearly wet from the sea air, and an empty bucket were all I had for comfort. The metal door closed behind me with a clank, and Nels locked it.

Before Nels turned to leave, I snaked my arms through the bars and hung my hands limply on the other side. "How have you been, Nels?"

His lips quirked when he looked back at me, his eyes sorrowful for having to lock me up. "Good as I'll ever be."

"You haven't retired yet?"

"Never. The sea will take me before land does." His jaw set. "My life is here. With yer pa."

It didn't have to be that way, I wanted to tell him. He could retire on a beach somewhere, never having to follow someone else's orders again. After all the years he'd spent with my father, Nels deserved a life of relaxation, swaying in a hammock on some island.

"You rest now."

I said nothing as I walked to the bench and sat down heavily. Still soaking wet, I had nothing to do but wait. Without solid walls, there was nothing I could remove without the possibility of someone seeing.

I waited for hours, eventually curling up the best I could on the hard bench and closing my eyes. Sleep wouldn't come. I stared at the ceiling and the supplies in the space beyond my bars, my thoughts swirling into a storm of emotions. I wondered how long it would be before my father dragged me back to London or, worse, tied me to the mast. When we last parted, he'd been furious with me. So very angry.

Now, I had to confront him once and for all.

He could drop me off on some island, and I would find my way in life. I would never return to London, perhaps never return to the sea. My heart felt hollow at the thought of Grayson. He chose me, and I'd leapt off his ship in a weak attempt to save him. I had to carve my own future, and I would do so, but first, I had to face my father.

Heavy footsteps on the stairway jolted me upright. My skin felt raw from the wet clothing that would never dry in this suffocating heat, but I stood and immediately went to the bars. A man with hair a similar color to Wiley's stepped down, cut short without the flamboyancy of Wiley, a wicked gleam in his eyes as he strode over.

"What is it?" I snapped.

He flung a dress at me through the bars. "Captain wants to see you."

I lifted my chin defiantly. With another unsettling sweep of his gaze, he backed up and crossed his arms as though intending to watch me strip.

"I will not undress with you standing guard," I said sharply. "Turn around, or better yet, leave. It will take me time to get out of this wet corset and into this dress."

With a smirk, he turned and left me alone. I waited several moments to ensure he was gone before I began unlacing my corset. Free from the damp fabric, I tossed my clothing onto the bench before reaching for the dress.

This was no ordinary dress. As I stepped into it, the midnight blue skirt brushed my ankles, while the laced bodice barely cupped my breasts. Indecent, but Grayson would like it, I thought. The small sleeves were made of the same material as a white tunic and rested lightly against my biceps, with a sash tied low around my midsection as though designed to hold weapons I didn't possess.

As soon as I put it on, I wanted to take it off. The men would only gawk at me. I turned to look at the damp clothing on the bench, wishing I could have just stayed on deck to let the heat of the sun dry me. But no, my father was angry enough to have locked me up. I decided to face him with courage as footsteps thundered down the stairs again.

"Cap'n's waitin'."

I shot a glare through the bars before he unlocked the door and swung it open for me. That dark gaze traveled over me again, and I swore, if I had the courage to endure even more anger from my father, I would carve out this man's eyes.

"Take me to him now, and you'd best pray I never get the chance to bury a dagger in your belly."

"Fancy words from a woman who went against us in battle."

I did no such thing. They fired at us first, but I wasn't about to argue with this man. Instead of leading me to the captain's quarters, he took me into the dining hall, where a long table set for ten dominated the room.

My father sat at the head of the table, already eating from a full plate in front of him, brandishing a turkey leg and beckoning me to sit beside him. Pride be damned, I drifted into the room with my head held high.

"You couldn't have found something more appropriate for me to wear?" I asked as I slid into the chair beside him.

The man pushed my chair in before my father waved him away, leaving us alone.

My father leaned forward, his eyes menacing. "You are not in a position to be challenging my decisions, lass. You're lucky I provided you with that to wear. I could force you to parade around naked, but I wouldn't trust any of my crew not to take their turn with you."

Appalled, my eyes widened. "I am your daughter."

"Then act like it," he snapped, leaning back and tearing off a piece of meat with his teeth. "No daughter of mine would cavort with a man intent on delivering me to the magistrate. No daughter of mine would betray me with one of my men. But here we are."

"Is that what you think?" My heart shuddered. "Edward and I were in love. And yes, I cavorted with Grayson, and he had good reason to seek justice for the man who killed his brother and stole his cargo. But know this," I leaned toward him, "everything I did in London was to appease you. To prove to you that I am more than just your daughter."

His eyebrows raised. "And I should believe what you say just because you say it? Because you're my flesh and blood?"

"Yes! I did everything you ever asked of me for over ten bloody years. And you just dropped me off with a family I didn't know because of my behavior. Could you not have let Edward and me be?"

His fist slammed down on the table, causing everything to jump from the force. "By God, lass, do you not understand what your actions did? My very daughter, having a clandestine affair right beneath my nose! That could not go unpunished."

When he set the piece of meat down on his plate, I thought he might reconsider everything he had believed over the last three years.

"Have I not righted the wrong?"

"By your activities in London?" He shrugged. "You may have, but here you sit in the same position as you were three years ago. This time with a man who wants to see me hanged!"

"Did you not murder his brother and steal his rare silks?"

He laughed. I watched him tip his head back, his throat bobbing with mirth. Sliding my hand beside the plate, I clutched the cool metal of the knife. "Lass, I did not attack that merchant ship in which the Valle brothers sailed. Jasper did."

I started, nearly releasing the knife. "What?"

"Jasper," he repeated. "He overtook the merchant ship and stole their cargo. That anyone died is warfare."

"Then how did you come to have the cargo in London? Your markings were on the crates."

"Jasper, as much as he hated to, asked me to take the cargo to sell on his behalf. For a percentage of the cut in my favor, of course. The plague overtook his crew shortly after that, and he would not have made it to London to sell. I took it, hoping to regain favor with the Crown."

The knife slipped from my grasp, landing on the table with a dull thunk as I leaned back in my chair. Dear God, Grayson was after the wrong man. I looked at my father, meeting his gaze, the mirth still lingering at the corner of his mouth.

"Now that the mystery has been solved, you still must answer for your crimes against me, lass. You came here intending to have me arrested."

"You fired first," I pointed out. "And then promptly threw me in the brig like a common criminal. I am your daughter. Did my mother mean so little to you?"

The flash in his eyes told me I'd hit a nerve. A big one.

"You dare bring up your mother to me?"

"I am sure she was a saint compared to me, but you rarely spoke of her when I was growing up. Did she make the same mistake as I did with Edward?"

He rose from his chair so quickly that it fell over with a bang. Grasping my biceps, he hauled me up and pushed his face close to mine. The breath caught in my lungs. I had never seen my father so angry.

"She would never have," he whispered. "Your mother was the most angelic person you would ever meet. You would have done well to inherit her qualities. But you did not."

I tilted my head, ignoring the throbbing in my arm where he gripped me. He had no idea just who I was, who I'd become. Surely, I would see bruises by morning. "I did better. I took after the most feared, elusive pirate sailing the seas."

He released me so abruptly that I fell back into my chair. Confusion swept through me. Wouldn't he have wanted me to take after him? I didn't consider myself completely like him. I knew my mother had done her best to help anyone she could, which was how she'd died. Trying to get me out of the way, saving me. I helped those in need, didn't I?

"You truly don't know me at all, do you?" I whispered. "Why do you hate me so?"

"Hate?" he growled. "Disappointed in your actions, but I do not hate you."

"You don't love me! Did you ever?"

Beneath his coat, his chest heaved. "Let us get something straight, *Livie*."

I leaned back in my chair, crossing my arms over my chest. "Yes, let's."

"When your mother . . . died." He took a deep breath, as though he couldn't bear to say the word, righting his chair and plopping down. "I had no choice but to take you with me. You, a girl of only seven, with the biggest blue eyes I'd ever seen. I knew within days of bringing you onto my ship that I would stop at nothing to make sure you were protected. But no one could know that. To show it would be considered weakness."

My eyebrows raised.

"She never should have died," he whispered, his eyes hard. "But she did. And I would be damned if I left you defenseless again. Until you . . . and that blackguard Edward." He shook his head. "It broke my damn heart that you'd given yourself to him. I'd sooner see you with a man who challenges you like I did, who respects you enough not to sneak into your cabin with lovely words."

When I simply stared at him, he stared back. "You haven't the slightest idea of how much she meant to me." He shook his head. "How much *you* mean to me."

I never understood my father, not this side of him, anyway. He was never one to be tender, and I couldn't recall a single memory of him telling me he was proud of me or that he loved me. It was always anger, commanding me like one of his hands. Now I knew why.

"You could have sent me to live with Aunt Marjory after retrieving me from the storm. Why didn't you? Why allow me to grow up among men, learning the ways of a sailor, only to abandon me the moment it became too much for you?"

His eyes flashed. "If you couldn't be raised with the grace of your mother, by your mother, whom I loved with every part of my being, then I chose to raise you alongside me. Think of how powerful you could become."

"I don't want power," I cried, meaning every word. "You stole my childhood, forced me to make decisions I should never have had to make, then abandoned me to a foreign world."

"'Twould seem I'm at a point where you have a say in your own future."

The heart in my chest beat uncontrollably, trying to regain control of my spiraling life. Everything felt chaotic. I could not be the daughter he wanted, and I realized that I didn't want a life at sea. I dared to allow myself to dream of a home. Children.

Grayson.

"I don't want this life," I whispered, looking down at my hands.

All this time, I had longed to return to the sea, only to discover that I no longer wanted it. A rush of relief swept through me, followed by panic. I had nowhere to go.

At his heavy sigh, a sound of resignation, I looked up to see his eyes glistening with unshed tears. In all my life, I'd never seen a single tear in his eyes.

"What do you want, Livie?"

He rose from his chair, came around to mine, and sank to his knees. When he reached for my hands, clutching my much smaller ones in his rough grip, he bowed his head. Where was this man when I was just a child? Frightened of losing my mother and worried I might lose him too, I huddled in my cabin bed, shaking with tears. He could have comforted me when no one knew he did. But he had not. He had molded me into a hardened woman, taught me to be cunning and daring.

"Grayson."

Immediately, he stiffened and looked up at me. "The man who has been trying to bring me to heel, dragging me back to London to be hanged? The blackguard who abducted you?"

Surprise shot through me. "Where did you hear that?"

I watched him push to his feet, pacing around the table. "Word came from London about the time I received a message from Grayson Valle that he wanted to make a trade. You went with him willingly?"

He was becoming angry again.

"I did. To escape from the Baron of Vensworth." I shook my head. "Grayson offered me a way out, and I took it. Though I knew you would be angry about me leaving."

"The Baron of Vensworth?" he asked.

"Percival Monteclaire. I believe you are familiar with the name, as he was my mother's betrothed when her ship was intercepted." I purposely left out that Percival had found out about my activities down at the docks. There was no need for him to know that.

He slammed his fist back down on the table, though not as forcefully as before. "There is no man who shall be good enough for my daughter. And Niles can handle London, although you did very well while you were there."

"Did you not just tell me that you want me to find a man who challenges me? Who respects me? Grayson is that man." I swallowed thickly, a feeble attempt to suppress the tears welling in my eyes. "I love him. He challenges me at every turn and does not woo me with sweet words."

My father cursed, stalking toward the door and throwing it open. "Arthur! Tell Mr. Nels to bring the ship about. Set the course back to Port Royal."

I jumped up from my chair. "Why?"

When he turned to look back at me, my heart sank. Something else had happened, something I did not know about.

"What have you done?" I whispered.

"I couldn't very well let the blackguard who stole my daughter get away without punishment, could I?" he yelled. "If I failed to kill him myself, I made a backup plan. When I received word that

Grayson Valle is a wanted man in London for your abduction, I called in a favor."

"And?" I asked, panic rising.

"Jasper was not far off when we engaged in warfare, close enough to capture Grayson's ship, which I had anticipated would be heavily damaged." He shrugged. "Until my reckless daughter decided to take matters into her own hands and abandon his ship. By now, he's likely in Jasper's brig, bound for the gallows."

Dread speared through me as he left the room. Pursuing the Royal Navy or any of Her Majesty's subjects would put my father in a perilous position. Going to Port Royal? My father would be arrested on sight. I'd already lost my mother. Despite what he'd subjected me to my whole life, I didn't intend to lose him too.

But having to choose between his life and Grayson's . . . I couldn't. I needed them both.

Head snapping up, I charged after him into the hazy sunshine on deck. He looked around at his crew, eyes hardened, challenging anyone to disobey him. None did.

"If Jasper has a valid letter of marque, charging after him will only get you sentenced to hang," I pointed out, stepping up beside him.

"My dear lass." He laughed low. "Do you really not have enough faith in my abilities to evade imprisonment? Death? *The Sea Serpent* came to collect Grayson and bring him to Port Royal, where he will face his crime. Jasper owes me enough favors not to turn me in."

"There was no crime!"

"Be that as it may, the Crown believes he committed a crime against an innocent young woman. He may not yet be in the clutches of Queen Anne's magistrate, and thus we may still stand a chance of retrieving him."

Chapter Forty Four

Livie

Dread filled me as I sat at the bow of the ship, my back against the foremast, knees drawn up, and wrist hanging limply over my knee. It had been days since I'd leapt from Grayson's ship. Days since I last saw him.

My father had stopped confining me to the brig and given me my own cabin, but it was all the same. Worrying about Grayson's circumstances prevented me from sleeping. If Jasper's ship had attacked Grayson's, had anyone been hurt? And if they'd lost the fight, was he already in the brig on that ship? The possibilities plagued my thoughts, making me restless. I dared not think that Grayson could have perished in battle.

Even with my father taking the risk of going to Port Royal, a town that had once been a haven for pirates but was now known for bringing them to justice, I didn't know the chances that we would find Grayson. Unless he had fought back and won, I could be worrying for no reason. I felt like I was still very much caught between the two men in my life who meant the most to me.

I hadn't endured hell and back only to lose my father, even though I was angry with him. He could have told me years ago about his feelings, but he waited until now. Until I forced his hand. That night, after the crew had long since gone to bed, we sat up with a bottle of rum between us. He admitted that he had left us on the island because he couldn't bear the thought of us becoming targets because of him.

He also confessed to spreading the rumor that I had died alongside my mother to ensure no one would take me to get to him. Recognizing my vulnerability, he believed leaving me with Aunt Marjory offered the best opportunity for a semi-normal existence. By then, he knew I had adopted a pirate's perspective to such a depth that he could only guess I wouldn't end up a lady.

He was pleased, however, that I possessed enough inherited traits from my mother to provide me with an advantage. I could easily play any role.

My father's gravelly voice beside me straightened my spine.

"We'll reach Port Royal soon."

Port Royal, I thought. I didn't want to go there, but if that was where Jasper would head to turn Grayson over to the authorities, I would yield to his knowledge. Enough time had passed for my thoughts to slowly drive me mad. Thoughts of whether Grayson lived, was hurt, or was angry with me for abandoning his ship . . .

"You cannot be a part of this," I said. "You have already put too much at stake by coming out of hiding. What if the Royal Navy has a ship at the ready?"

The smile that curved his lips promised darkness, a darkness I had seen my entire life. Whatever he planned, he intended to go down swinging. If I had anything to say about it, he wouldn't have the chance to be caught.

"Let me take a skiff," I said. "Someone can come with me to ensure it gets returned."

Rocking back on the heels of his boots, he laughed. "You'll never reach the island in a skiff from this distance, lass. We need to get closer, and they may have already caught wind of our approach. No, Livie. You will wait. Calmly."

"Calmly?" I barked. "When have I ever done anything calmly?"

"You convinced everyone in high society London that you were a lady, did you not? Surely, you can remain calm at this time.

We'll approach, and I'll consider our options at that time. And not before."

I turned, but he reached out to prevent me from walking away.

"As it is, Jasper and I are not on the best of terms. He took on Grayson for me because of you. He could betray me, and I cannot have that. As it is, we might already be too late."

"Let me take the bloody skiff!" I cried. "I can row that far. I can!"

"Livie," he started. "As hard as I've been on you in the past, I can't have my daughter attempting to row that far in a small boat. We shall get close enough, and if I decide you should go, you'll go, but by damn, if you get caught, I will come for you."

I laughed. "I won't get caught."

Resigned, I waited by the mast, trying to gauge the distance between us and the island with a heavy heart. Who knew what I would find when I got there? If anyone hurt Grayson or anyone on his crew, I would unleash hell.

Nels drifted toward me, and I raised my brow, wondering why he wasn't commanding the helm as he should be. I glanced back to see my father, legs braced apart at the wheel, looking every bit the captain he was. It momentarily stunned me to see him like this, even after growing up with him.

"They won't arrest him."

Years of sun exposure had left Nels with wrinkled, tanned skin and crow's feet around his eyes. At times, he was more fatherly to me than my biological father, tending to my injuries and showing me a kinder approach to life.

"They won't?"

He shook his head. "The cap'n is a cunning old man. He'll not let them get close enough to catch him. Not gonna happen, lass."

I laughed, not having considered that. One could never know if other ships in Queen Anne's fleet were loitering. It would be a full-blown battle should that happen, but I knew my father would fight back. And he would win.

But that didn't make me feel any better. I needed to figure out how to keep my father safely away while I rescued Grayson.

"Did you know my mother, Nels?"

"Aye, gently reared she was. An heiress."

I sighed. "I know that. What I don't understand is how her family will not answer any messages sent. Am I not her flesh and blood?"

"She was snatched right from a ship on her way to her betrothed," he explained. My father had rescued her from abduction, but Nels's description changed my perception. "Terribly mistreated she was until your father sailed right up, battling that ship for its riches only to find the most invaluable prize. They fell in love, they did. Never seen the Cap'n so happy, other than the time you were rescued from that awful storm."

The story filled me with warmth, a sense of completeness I hadn't experienced before. Like Grayson, he'd saved her when he hadn't realized it. If he hadn't, I would never have been born. If my mother had made it to her betrothed . . .

"She wrote to them, your mother did. Sent her parents a letter, explaining her situation. By then, she'd fallen in love with your pappy. They cut her out, refused further communication. No surprise they did the same to you."

I looked back out at the shimmering water, the sun setting quietly behind us. We had to be close enough to the island now for me to get into the skiff and rescue Grayson.

Nels followed me across the expanse of the ship, stopping halfway up the stairway to the quarterdeck and looking at my father for permission.

"Yer certain about this?" he asked. "This is what you want?"

I nodded. "I have no doubt in my mind. If Grayson doesn't want me, then the least I can do is save his life. Only he can choose his future."

"And yours?"

"Freedom," I murmured. "My own choice in this life."

Chapter Forty Five

It was fully dark by the time the island came into view, and I held my breath as we slowly weighed anchor in that cloak of darkness. Not long after Nels's departure, my father approached me, announcing his decision to send someone else to make inquiries instead of me. He didn't dare risk my life.

So upset was I that I ran to my cabin and slammed the door like a child, hard enough to rattle the walls. He would send someone in the morning to make those inquiries, but I couldn't sit idly by and let someone else return with nothing. I needed to see for myself.

Even while docked, the lookouts presented a challenge to leaving the ship. They'd be watching for anyone sneaking aboard to commandeer my father's vessel. As elusive as he was, it wasn't a matter of if, but when.

In my haste, I had dressed in the ridiculous dress my father had given me shortly after I boarded, cinching the corset until I could scarcely take a full breath. Beneath my skirt and at my waist, I'd secured as many daggers as possible, but I went without boots when I left my cabin. Boots would only slow me down. Fill with water if I needed to jump into the water.

Sneaking cautiously up to the main deck, I kept to the wall beneath the quarterdeck until I reached the railing. A skiff already bobbed precariously in the water below, as though my father had sent someone to shore. With a quick glance at the lookouts, I couldn't see if any men were stationed there. They wouldn't see me until I began to row to shore.

Once I started rowing, the alarm would sound. I cursed my ridiculous planning. My father would pluck me out of the water before I could make it halfway. This needed to be done differently. I'd need to swim for it.

Flattening myself against the wall again, I shimmied out of my undergarments and gathered the dress around my thighs. I hoped no one could see my indecency, but this would have to do. I tucked as much of the skirt into the sash as I could and hurried to the railing.

Jumping would create a splash large enough to alert others, so I nimbly swung over the railing and grabbed the rope ladder, sliding down until the deck could no longer see me. I sucked in a breath at the rope burns on my palms, grasping the rope and to climb the rest of the way down.

My fervent hope was that no other ship lookouts were gazing in this direction, because a woman with her skirt gathered around her thighs as she climbed down to the skiff was bound to generate questions, as if I were attempting an escape. When my bare feet hit the skiff, I released the ladder and climbed over the side of the skiff, easing myself into the warm water.

Bobbing up and down with the waves for a moment, I looked at the dim lights scattered across the island. I could swim part of the way and float some, but it would still take time to reach the shore. Taking a deep breath, I began to float slowly away, thankful that my dress was a darker color. Aside from the sleeves and my light hair, I might get away with this.

Halfway there, since no one had alerted anyone to a woman swimming under the light of the moon, I stopped for a moment to catch my breath. Why I'd lied to Grayson about my swimming skills was precisely for this reason. I needed a trick up my sleeve, and now that he knew, I doubted he thought I would be swimming in an effort to rescue him.

By the time I reached the beach, my dress was heavy with water. I quickly ran for the line of trees before I squeezed out as much as I could. A quick pat-down on my thighs ensured my daggers were still there. I would need every available weapon if Grayson were here, and he had to be. I'd seen *The Sea Serpent* anchored in the bay. My worry stemmed from not seeing Grayson's vessel, but at least I had a path to follow.

I unbunched the skirt and released it to where it should be. Getting caught here would be detrimental to my plan, and having my skirts up would be damning. No one on my father's ship knew I'd escaped, and there was no one else who would rescue me.

Walking through the rowdy streets as a woman here had to be safer than walking in the seedier parts of London in a dress, so I sauntered toward the city where the taverns and bawdy houses were, hoping to engage someone in conversation about who might have been brought in to face the Crown's judicial system.

I caught many backward glances as I went, keeping my daggers within reach. Those at my waist would be much handier than those beneath my skirts. I had those ready in case someone grabbed me. I would need to free myself, and I doubted anyone would look beneath my skirts. Especially with bare feet and no undergarments.

Several whistles followed me when I ducked into the closest drinking establishment, gliding into the fray with my eyes scanning every way out of the place. No one paid attention to me, as several other serving wenches and ladies of the night mingled within. I wedged my way to the barkeep, who wiped his hands on his dirty rag and sauntered over.

His bald head gleamed in the light from the sconces behind him, reminding me of Boon. Wistfully, I presented him with my best smile and folded my arms over the scarred wooden surface of the bar.

"What can I get ya?" he asked, bracing his arms against the surface.

"Information, if you would, please."

A dark eyebrow rose. "It'll cost you."

Devil take me, I thought. "It's a matter of life and death, sir."

He crossed his arms in front of his chest, causing his round belly to protrude. "Coin or gold bars. Your choice."

Not much of a choice, I mused. I would need to use my name as a bargaining chip. With nothing to pay him and certainly not about to offer favors, my bloodline was all I could offer.

I raised my chin. "I am Livie Blackwood," I announced. "I'm assuming you know who Elias Blackwood is. Would you by chance know if Jasper Stone and his crew have been here?"

For several moments, he stared at me. Unfazed by my declaration of identity, I could only pray he would at least answer my question. That shouldn't cost me, at least not much.

With a jerk of his chin, he said, "In the back."

I pushed away from the bar, only to change my mind and lean back. "If I collect my payment, I will provide you with the cost of that information. Thank you, good sir."

With that, I moved further into the establishment that reeked of sour ale and sweat. This deep in the tropics, the stench of unwashed bodies was much more pronounced.

The barkeep had told me the truth: Jasper and some of his crew were at a long table in the back. Boisterous laughter threatened to deafen me when I approached, but as soon as I stepped closer, a man slid an arm around my waist and dragged me down onto his lap.

Though I struggled, the opportunity must have been too good to pass up. I pulled out the dagger closest to my hand and pressed the flat tip to his nose. His brown eyes widened, his head drawing back.

"I can think of better things to do with your hands," I murmured. "But none of them give you leave to have them on me."

I dared not glance toward Jasper, who sat in the corner, until I had this blackguard well under control. The man laughed but did not fight against me nor surrender to my weapon. Instead, he sat back but refrained from putting his hands on me again, sliding his fingers around his ale to take a drink instead.

"What's a wench wandering about here that doesn't want a hand up her skirt?" he asked, his voice impossibly thick and low.

"Rolf, leave her be," I heard from the corner. "State your business here, or suffer more than the attention of my quartermaster."

I rose from Rolf's lap and turned, keeping my dagger palmed. Jasper, his chestnut hair feathered away from his handsome face, leaned back in his chair as Rolf did, his hand around his mug of ale.

In a white tunic that looked as though it needed a good washing, pushed up to his elbows, his eyes danced with merriment. I wondered if he knew who I was. My father had said they hadn't been on the best of terms, so to tell him my business, I would have to admit who I was. Or did I?

"I'm looking for a man you might have captured."

The corner of his mouth quivered until it finally tipped up in a half-smile. "Livie Blackwood," he said, my name on his lips like a resignation, the light in his eyes to be wary of. "My, you've grown up, dove. I'm assuming if you are here, your father is-"

"Gone," I lied. "I escaped from his ship and begged passage here. You've captured an innocent man, Captain."

"Call me Jasper. After all, we're practically family." He grinned, sweeping out his hand. "Join us, Livie Blackwood. I'm most interested in hearing how you think Grayson Valle is innocent."

I remained where I stood. "I know he's innocent. He did not abduct me from London as you were told. I went with him willingly."

The table of men erupted in laughter, and I looked at each of them in confusion. A more rowdy group I'd never been in the presence of in a tavern, and I wasn't about to get comfortable now. If Jasper were here, Grayson had to either be in jail, still on his ship, or . . . No. I refused to believe that he had already been tried and sentenced.

"Where is he, Jasper?" I asked.

"You'll not get to him."

My chin raised in defiance. "Watch me. Where is he?"

"Likely still in a cell, being held by the authority of Her Majesty, Queen Anne," he finally answered, though his men still laughed around me.

I whirled, but a hand caught my arm. My eyes widened as Rolf tightened his grip on me, preventing me from taking another step toward freeing Grayson.

"You can't just run off to the jail and break him out, dove," Jasper said, though he hadn't moved from where he sat. "There are far too many authorities on this island now. Even if you get him out of his cell, you'll not get far."

Roaring in my ears had me spinning around, smacking my hands on the table and leaning toward him. "Then help me. You owe him that much."

"Aye?"

"Aye. You were the one who battled and took the merchant ship with rare French silks, were you not? Killed his brother?" He held my gaze unblinkingly. "You owe him."

With a sigh, he gulped down what remained of his ale and stood. He shocked me with his sudden willingness to help. If they caught him, they'd hang him without a trial. Grayson, luckily, had a letter of marque and a fighting chance. I wouldn't leave anything to chance, though, and I would take any help offered.

Chapter Forty Six

Grayson

Since I last saw Livie, I'd only been able to think about her smile. If the memory of her could get me through whatever awaited me on the other side of the bars holding me in this tiny cell, it made everything I'd ever done worth it. She deserved so much more than I could offer, yet I'd be willing to try if I just had a single chance.

I lay on the narrow cot, staring up at the ceiling marred by water stains. My eyes traced the lines back and forth. I would do anything to keep my mind off disappointing my father again. But after Livie, it didn't truly matter what he thought. Resigning myself to never being good enough for him, I vowed to avoid returning home as his heir if survival was possible. By the sound of it, I wouldn't see many more days, likely headed for the gallows.

The sound of jingling keys caused me to look up. In the middle of the night, my jailer would not be strolling down the aisle. No one could get in or out of these cells without the guard stationed at the door.

A moment later, a man strode in and faced me. I recognized him as the quartermaster of *The Sea Serpent.* He hadn't harmed me, other than giving me a hard time after they overtook my ship and took me aboard. The captain had laid out the charges against me, though I knew they were false. Without Livie to corroborate my story, I was as good as guilty, hence my confinement here.

"You'll live to see another day," Rolf said brusquely, hurrying to unlock my cell.

I jumped to my feet, wasting no time and asking no questions when he held the door open for me. Only when we reached the doorway did I see that the guard had been knocked unconscious. I looked back at Rolf.

"If you linger, we'll likely get caught. And nothing would anger me more, so best to get a move on, aye?"

We took the stairs quickly, passing another unconscious guard as we went. I knew it wouldn't be long before someone spotted us. We moved quickly, another man joining us from the shadows until it was the three of us charging down the corridors of the fortress.

"You aren't going to provide me with a weapon to defend myself?" I asked. "And why the sudden change of heart?"

Rolf growled, "Quiet, or they'll hear us."

We rounded the corner, facing two more guards who clearly thought something was amiss. Simultaneously, they drew their swords, and Rolf and the other man immediately rushed toward them with a ferocity I'd seen in few men. Three against one was easy. As soon as one guard's sword clattered to the ground, I retrieved it, and the other guard was disabled.

"No time to waste now," Rolf tossed over his shoulder as we hurried forward. We ascended another flight of old stone stairs before reaching an overpass. Looking over, my eyes widened. If we jumped from this height, we would surely break our legs.

"This way," he ordered, leading me away from the ledge and toward a turret. Three guards intercepted us this time but were easily outmaneuvered. Clearly, they wanted to get out of this fortress as much as I did, but when I looked beyond him, I saw another man, missing two of his teeth, grinning at us.

"About time," Rolf growled. "The woman?"

"Awaits below with Jasper."

Livie, I thought. It couldn't be anyone else. Only she would be brazen enough to charge in here for my release. I wondered what had happened with her father. Surely, he wouldn't have allowed her to come here and risk all of us.

Rolf looked at me then. "Your freedom awaits."

With wide eyes, I watched the three men rush through the turret before I followed closely behind them. On the other side, a rope had been secured to several barrels of gunpowder. They each went over, climbing down quickly. When I heard shouts behind me of more guards closing in, I swung over the side and climbed as quickly as my bruised ribs would allow.

When my feet touched the ground, Rolf yanked on my tunic, and we sprinted toward a copse of trees. We ran for miles, it seemed, my lungs burning, undetected by any more guards. Apparently, being the only prisoner made them lax in their duties. I could never be ungrateful for that, as we made our getaway.

When we neared the beach, I skidded to a halt in the sand. I would have breathed a sigh of relief upon seeing the one woman who held my heart so securely that she could crush it in her fist, but Jasper had her clutched to him with a dagger at her throat.

"Unhand her," I growled.

Jasper smiled. "I think not, heir to Jeremiah Valle."

My heart thundered, my pulse racing with fury. "She isn't part of this. This is between you and me, Captain."

The fear in her eyes rooted me to my spot in the sand. There could be guards after us, but we were standing here because one man was too greedy to leave well enough alone. Those were my thoughts as we stared at each other.

"What do you want?" I finally asked.

"Her," he said simply.

"You can't have me," Livie growled. "What is this, Jasper? You helped him escape, for what?"

Jasper laughed. "I helped you, and you are payment for my services."

From the look in her blue eyes, I knew that if she could reach the daggers hidden beneath her skirt, she wouldn't hesitate to bury them in his chest. The sheaths at her side were empty, either already used or taken from her. Having been relieved of my own weapons, I only had the sword I'd taken during our getaway.

"If you take her, you'll be hunted down," I threatened.

That only made him smile more. "I certainly hope so, Captain Valle."

Jasper nodded at the three men near me before they attempted to turn and run, but I wouldn't give him the satisfaction of leaving with Livie. I would fight for her, as I should have done weeks ago.

Rolf knew I wouldn't let them go, raising his sword to mine in a clash of steel. I would have this out with him, I had no choice, but Jasper would still escape with Livie. I could hear her angry curses directed at Jasper while he dragged her away as Rolf and I circled each other, our swords meeting viciously.

As I disarmed Rolf, I knew Jasper could already be in a skiff on his way to his ship. I didn't have time for this as I parried, struck, parried, struck. The stifling heat, combined with being confined for days, had weakened me, but I would never give up. I changed tactics, using moves he hadn't seen me use until I finally shoved him back with force.

"You see," I said, my chest heaving as I defended and spoke, "there is a reason I am a captain and you are a quartermaster. Although I thank you for releasing me from my imprisonment, I cannot allow your captain to escape with Livie. I won't."

With a quick flick of my wrist, I circled his sword with my own to disorient him until the tip grazed his arm, causing him to release it. I threw myself against him, kicking it away.

"Concede," I demanded.

Rolf held up his hands. "You won't catch them."

I shoved him again, bending down to retrieve his sword before spinning and running toward the beach. No sooner had I broken through the trees and I stopped. Jasper hadn't gotten Livie to one of the boats to take her back to his vessel.

Elias Blackwood stood on the beach, his pistol pointed directly at Jasper, who still had Livie in his clutches. The man looked even more formidable now than he had when he'd been firing at me and his daughter. Clearly, he'd reconsidered where she was concerned.

"Stay where you are, Captain Valle," Elias's voice rang out, deadly low.

Chapter Forty Seven

Livie

"Do not move, lass," my father said.

How could he remain so calm? The last time I remembered him stepping off his ship was to rescue me after my mother died. And here he stood, risking everything to ensure Jasper did not leave with me.

I couldn't see Grayson behind me, but my father's warning for him not to move had my heart thundering in my chest. If I could reach a dagger beneath my skirt, I could disarm him myself, but the dagger pressed against my neck brought back memories from the last time this had happened. I had escaped unscathed except for a cut on my neck that hadn't turned out to be as shallow as I thought. But I had gotten away.

This might not end the same way.

"Jasper," I whispered. "Don't do this."

I felt his lips near my cheek as he bent down. "My dove, as fetching as you looked sauntering into the tavern, I knew I had to have you. I will have you."

Despite more men joining us on both sides, Jasper held firm. He would never have me willingly, if that's what he thought. I would fight as hard as I could to return to Grayson, and if he hurt Grayson or my father, he would be beyond redemption. I would stop at nothing to make sure he paid.

"Release me," I whispered. "And I will go with you willingly."

"Livie, no!" Grayson shouted.

Jasper chuckled. "Even if I had your word, your father would shoot me as soon as I release you. I'd have better success trying to get around him. But as it is, I have both of them at a disadvantage."

"You won't kill me," I challenged, hoping to call his bluff. "If you truly wanted me, why would you risk killing me? As soon as you drive that dagger into my neck, my father will kill you. And if he doesn't, Grayson will. In fact, they both likely will. Your best option is to release me and find a willing woman."

He scoffed, then sighed, and I felt him ease his hold slightly. The dagger still pressed against my throat hadn't moved, but he contemplated it, and that was all I needed.

Everyone stood frozen to see what Jasper would do. He wouldn't escape this. I wasn't sure if I would, either, but he definitely wouldn't. Not facing off with my father.

"I need your word that you will not shoot me, Blackwood," Jasper said. "If I release her, my men and I leave here without injury."

I watched my father lower his pistol. "You have my word."

Jasper's arms and dagger fell away from me, and I stumbled just as Grayson rushed toward me, catching me up in his powerful arms. I nearly cried out trying to reach him, but a single shot rang out in the night's quiet. My eyes widened as I turned to see Jasper fall to his knees before landing face-first in the sand.

Smoke wafted from my father's raised pistol. Grayson clutched me to his chest as I looked back at my father.

"Thing about my word is, I protect what's mine."

I looked up at Grayson, a blooming bruise high on his cheekbone and a split lip, but otherwise he looked satisfactory. His clothes hung loosely, as if he had been left out in the elements during the days we'd been apart.

"Tell me where you're hurt," I whispered against Grayson's chest.

"A few punches won't keep me down," he replied bluntly.

"They left you outside in the elements."

"Not even a bit of sun can keep me down. You, however . . ." His nose brushed my temple, and I heard him breathe in deeply. "Watching you jump off my ship took the life out of me, Livie."

"You there." My head shot up at my father's voice. "Take your captain back to your ship for a proper burial, and let it be known that the next man who touches my daughter dies."

Grayson tensed, but I smiled and kept my arm around his waist as we walked toward my father, his arm slung over my shoulders. I felt him tense again before we reached my father, both of them eyeing each other with dangerous malice.

I watched my father tilt his head, raising an eyebrow.

"I was not the one to betray you," my father spoke first. "Although I've done my fair share of misdeeds."

My eyebrow raised.

"Fine, I am the blackguard everyone claims I am. Had I been the one to intercept your ship, I would have. Jasper is the one who attacked you and your brother. I cannot lay claim to that misdeed. I can only lay claim to having taken his cargo for him and sold it."

The tension in Grayson eased. If he had gone through with his plan to trap my father, even kill him, he would have targeted the wrong man, and his vengeance would have been incomplete. He might never have known it.

"You will find your ship in port beside Jasper's, although I suggest leaving first if it needs repairs. Repair later if you can."

Releasing Grayson, I ran toward my father, not knowing when I might see him again. I threw my arms around his waist. After a moment, just when I thought he wouldn't return my embrace, his arms slid around me, and I felt him press a kiss to the top of my head.

"Go, lass. Live your life," he whispered.

I looked back up at him once more before releasing him. He motioned to his men to return to the skiff, and within moments, they were rowing away from the island. I imagined he wanted to put distance between Port Royal and himself.

"Take care of my lass," he shouted at Grayson, and winked. "And do let me know where you end up so that I might consider dropping in from time to time."

I turned in Grayson's arms, gazing up at him. He smoothed my hair away from my face with his fingers, pressing a kiss to my forehead. "You'll need to tell me whatever gave you the idea to attempt breaking me free."

Laughter bubbled from my throat. "I will tell you everything, but like my father, we need to put distance between us and this island, lest they bring you back. I'm not sure I can ensure your escape a second time."

Chapter Forty Eight

Grayson

Dark lashes fanned out against her pale skin, a slight rosy tinge highlighting her high cheekbones, which led down to full lips, lips that had driven me to the brink of madness the moment I had her in my clutches again. My gaze swept lower to the swell of her breasts tucked beneath the blanket, my desire to taste those subtle curves between them rising eagerly. This exquisite woman in my bed had risked everything to save me.

All her secrets spilled freely in an instant. I could only repay her in the one way I knew how, if she would have me.

When her eyes blinked open, revealing the brilliant blue I'd grown to love, words eluded me. She mesmerized me, drawing me into the light and holding me there. She had taught me that chasing a ghost would prove pointless, that I was the best man I could be, regardless of my father's judgment. In the end, justice had been served regardless.

I lay on my side behind her, not touching her. Not yet.

While she had succumbed to my arms last night, finally back on my ship where she belonged, few words had been spoken. They didn't need to be. We communicated with our bodies, quickly like the fury of a storm threatening to consume us, then slowly like the rising sun at dawn.

She might have chosen me by returning, but she had yet to voice it, just as I had yet to reveal everything that thundered in my heart. I couldn't assume she would stay with me. I couldn't ask it of her after everything she'd been through.

The slow rise of her hand, extending toward me, spoke volumes. I took it, kissing her fingertips gently, one by one, leaving a trail from her hand up her arm until I pulled her close. She sighed, sliding that hand up my chest and curling it around my nape.

"Tell me you'll never leave me again," I said softly, not commanding it of her. "For I could not bear to be parted from you again. My heart cannot take it."

The smile on her lips would stay with me for the rest of my days, a surrender, a promise, all wrapped into one beguiling smile. It was the same smile I had seen the night I met her. Not false, but revealing. Only to my vision.

"I'll never leave you again," she whispered. "You've had my heart since . . . since you rescued me from being blackmailed. And for that, I can never repay you."

"I would never have let you marry him," I said fiercely, kissing her jaw as my hands slid over her delicate skin. "The only man you'll marry is me, if you'll have me. Because you, and only you, have my heart." I kissed her neck. "I love you." I kissed the hollow in her throat. "I love you."

I could feel her body singing beneath my lips and hands.

The sigh she released was light, fluttering away like her heart against my chest. "I love you, Grayson. You must have known."

"If I ever doubted you, I will never do so again." I lifted my head, catching her gaze. "Tell me you'll be my wife."

"I shall be your wife. Under one condition." I raised an eyebrow, waiting for her to continue. "That whether life be on the sea or land, you shall never leave me."

If she were any further away, I pulled her even closer with a growl and a vow. "No one shall keep us apart, Livie Blackwood.

Nothing and no one. Once you are my wife . . . no, not even then shall we be parted. I give you my vow on that."

Acknowledgements

There are so many people whom I would like to thank for making this book possible. To say the last 365 days have been crazy would be an understatement. So much has happened in my life, all good, that it took much longer than expected. But it has been well worth it.

We've uprooted our lives beginning last May and ending in September, which is a lot harder than you think it will be! Nevertheless, it has been an adventure I won't soon forget. But getting this book out sooner came at a price. The silver lining is that though this book may be about six months overdue for publication, the next three books are on the horizon. Bing, bang, boom! Let's go!

From my friends, family, and followers, to my beta readers and editor, to those with whom I can bounce ideas off, or just talk things through, I cannot possibly thank you all enough. This is my sixth book, and there aren't enough words to properly express my gratitude. I truly mean it when I say that I could not do this without you.

That you all put up with waiting for me or waiting on me is a testament that you actually like me. Humbled is what I am. Thank you from the bottom of my heart, for being there for me!

Find more books by Jodie Leigh Murray

by scanning the QR code below

Books are also available through:

Amazon

Barnesandnoble.com

Bookshop.org

Tertulia

Select Independent Bookstores